Kenzi's Grief

vs

The Ghosts of Esperance

JOSH VAN REYK

Kenzi's Grief vs The Ghosts of Esperance

© 2026 Josh van Reyk

ISBN: 978-1-7643131-1-7

To my amazing wife, Tracy-
This is just for you.

Prologue

Even as she said the words, "I don't want you to go," she knew they wouldn't change anything. This was going to happen. It had to.

"You know I have to, Mac. It's time."

Their words were true, but that didn't make it any easier.

"But what am I going to do now... without you?" It wasn't the first time she had been left behind, but that did not make it any easier. Not in the slightest.

"You do the same thing I'm doing, the same thing as everyone else...

...you move on."

Chapter 01

"I've already got my hands full with my stuff."

Kenzi stared blankly out of the car window, feeling like this move was just the latest disappointment in a long line of them. The glass was cool against her forehead, fogged slightly by her breath. Mountain after mountain seemed to slowly slide past, almost as if the car was stationary and the world was moving, which more or less summed up how she felt. The landscape outside was a patchwork of shadowed ridges and deep green forests, blurred by distance and disinterest. The car's upholstery itched at the back of her thighs, and the stale scent of long-haul travel clung to the air—fast food wrappers, old crayons, and the ever-present tang of baby wipes. Raindrops from earlier had dried into crusty outlines on the glass, leaving streaks like tear tracks on a dusty face. As usual, she was so caught up in feeling sorry for herself that she was unaware of what was happening around her and hadn't noticed her younger brother, Lucas, reaching over towards her.

She felt him latch onto her and start to pull at the leather band on her wrist. She jerked her hand away quickly. Her muscles tensed instinctively, as if preparing for battle. She looked sternly at Lucas. His mop of sandy hair stuck up in wild tufts, like he'd been rolling around on the backseat. His round cheeks flushed with effort as he tried to pry at her bracelet, lips pursed in determination. Even the smear of chocolate on his T-shirt seemed deliberately placed to annoy her. God, she hated him. He was her brother, and she knew that should mean something, but she couldn't help but feel that way. Everything he was, everything he represented, was an insult. Even his laugh grated on her nerves—too loud, too alive.

She held her wrist in her lap, safely out of the brat's reach. She caressed the band a little with her other hand and stared back out the window, drifting off into nothingness again.

As the car came to a stop, Kenzi snapped awake. Not that she was asleep, more that she had been staring out the window at nothing in particular for so long that she drifted into a daze in which time didn't seem to pass. It was like one moment she was in her bedroom, her haven. Then she was here, in Esperance—a small town in Western Australia, quiet, boring, where she knew nobody. A breeze stirred dry leaves in gentle waves across the cracked asphalt as the family car pulled into the driveway. The tyres crunched over gravel in a tired rhythm, and a soft whirr of the air conditioning died away, leaving behind an uncomfortable silence. Kenzi skulked out of the car- the breeze outside was dry and scratchy, the kind that carried dust instead of relief. Kenzi looked up at the massive old wooden house her parents had dragged her to. The house loomed like a forgotten relic, with flaking white paint, creaky wooden steps, and shuttered windows that blinked like tired eyes in the afternoon sun. The gutters sagged like frowns along the roofline, and vines crawled up one corner like they were trying to escape. This move truly felt more like a punishment than a 'fresh start.' How in the hell could this be what she needs right now? Like anyone, especially her parents, would know what she needs, SERIOUSLY!

"Hey, Kenz, can you get your bro-"

"I've already got my hands full with my stuff." Kenzi quickly grabbed as many of her bags from inside the car as she could, hoping her mother would leave at that. The bags were heavy, but she clung to them like armour, shielding herself from responsibility. Kenzi wasn't naive enough to believe that her parents hadn't noticed how she did whatever she could to avoid doing anything with her little brother Lucas- she just hoped it was easier for them to let her get away with it. Except for the move across the country, her parents had pretty much been staying off her back for a while, just because it was 'easier' than trying to make her deal with everything. As Kenzi dashed off towards the house, the weight of the bags shifted on her shoulders, pulling at her thin frame like the baggage of her own guilt. As Kenzi dashed off towards the house, her mother looked at her father as he started to unload the car. He was tall, with dark hair peppered by stress and a kind face that looked more tired than old. The bags under his eyes were as much emotional as they were physical. She shot him a 'she did it again' look, to which he replied, "I know, I know. Just a bit more time. Once we get settled in here, maybe she'll start to come `round."

"I hope so, Peter. I know you don't want to pressure her too much, especially with what happened, but sooner or later, we are going to have to deal with this."

Peter knew that his wife was right. Ever since the first day they met, he had been in awe of her strength and determination, and as he stood there looking at her, sharp-featured and graceful in a worn-out sort of way, her blonde hair twisted into a messy bun that barely held together, he knew she was right. He'd been the one tiptoeing around Kenzi's emotions, but how could he not? The last few years had been horrible for their family, and it was too much for a seventeen-year-old to handle. Was it not his duty as her father to protect her? Even from reality?

Kenzi swung open the heavy wooden door to their 'new' home and was immediately hit by what she could only describe as an "old people" smell. It wasn't just must or age—it was layers of time, stories pressed into the floorboards. The air was thick with the scent of mothballs, stale roses, and lemon oil polish. The house had belonged to her Grandmother, Sarah, who had apparently lived in it for a very, very long time. Kenzi didn't know her Grandmother very well and had actually never met her Grandfather, who had died before she was born. Kenzi had some very faint memories of playing in the backyard of this place when she was very young, but her father's work had taken them all the way across the other side of the country, making it hard for them to visit her, and the events of the last couple of years had made it nearly impossible.

Sarah had been getting sicker for a while now, and everyone, more or less, knew the end was coming soon. As her father was an only child, everything her Grandmother owned was left to him in the will, which included this musty old place. With the timing of the inheritance, her parents saw it as just the opportunity they needed to start over.

Although it had been like forever since Kenzi had been in this house, she seemed to remember the layout and made her way directly to the upstairs bedroom, which was now hers. As she walked towards the stairs, she looked around the living room. There was a lone recliner chair in the middle of the room, facing an older-model TV. It was hard to tell what colour the chair was, as it had faded a lot with age and use. The polished wooden floors reflected the light coming in from the windows, as did most of the other furniture, which was mostly wooden as well. This place was very different to her old house, which was definitely more modern.

She carried her bags up the stairs, with each step creaking under her weight. She had to steady herself from tipping over, but she was determined to keep going. Anything to get to her room, where she could be alone for a while. Although the trip had been relatively quiet, she needed some alone time. It was her preferred state lately.

As she walked down the hallway, she noticed a framed photo of a young woman. Kenzi looked at it for a moment. The woman was probably in her early twenties, sitting on the edge of a building roof, focused on a thick textbook. She was obviously studying, but she also looked really happy. Kenzi thought it must have been her Grandmother. She looked like a cliché- tight white shirt tucked into a pleated skirt, long enough to cover her knees. Her hair was light brown, pulled back in a ponytail, with a small fringe hanging over her glasses. Her Grandmother had always been a bit of a mystery to Kenzi, and this picture made her feel even more like a stranger.

She looked up from the frame and caught her reflection in the dusty hallway mirror. The glass was spotted and cloudy, as if trying to obscure the truth. Dark, tangled hair framed her face like ivy around a cracked window. Her eyes—so brown they were almost black—looked too old for seventeen. There was nothing special or unique about her clothes. Looking a certain way didn't matter anymore. The only thing that looked special was a leather bracelet on her left wrist, which was old and probably too tattered to still be worn, but Kenzi never took it off. She couldn't.

The smell in her room was no different from the rest of the house. It's not the place that was dusty or hadn't been cleaned; all the wood, of which there was a lot, was lovingly polished, but everything seemed to have its place, and it had not moved from it for a long time. Obviously, her Grandmother lived here and took good care of it, but it just didn't feel like there had been any 'life' here for a while. Even the air hung still, like it hadn't been disturbed in weeks. Kenzi dropped her bags on the floor, making a loud thud! The timber floors seemed to make everything louder, something that would take some getting used to. Kenzi walked over to her new bed and lay down, looking up at the ceiling. She looked at the cobwebs in the corner of the roof and thought that no one must have spent much time in this room for a while.

Strangely, this fact comforted Kenzi; it was something she could very much relate to, and she actually, just for a brief moment, felt as though this wasn't the worst thing that could have happened. Not that she was happy, no, that's not a word she uses anymore, but more that she wasn't totally and completely miserable.

She wasn't 'out of place' anymore.

Chapter 02

"Maybe extreme is exactly what we all need."

Over the next few days, Kenzi's family settled into their new house. Boxes were unpacked. Cupboards were filled. Their lives were quickly beginning anew. The sound of the scrape of furniture legs on hardwood echoed faintly through the halls. Dust floated in sunbeams that slanted through the windows, marking time like an hourglass. Cardboard flaps curled like tired petals, and the sound of packing tape being ripped echoed through the hallway like distant thunder. Each drawer closed with a heavy thud, as if the house was swallowing bits of their past whole. The rooms, once stale and silent, began to hold the weight of footsteps and voices again.

Olivia was in the kitchen, packing groceries away. Although she was in a new kitchen, she still knew where everything belonged, emptying the bags into the pantry and fridge with ease. She placed a packet of sugar onto a shelf in a high cupboard, next to various other baking supplies. As she closed the door, she caught a glimpse of her husband's reflection in the glass cupboard door as he entered the room from the living area. The scent of cardboard and cleaning spray lingered in the air. For a brief moment, she was taken back to an almost forgotten moment in her old kitchen a few years back—a moment filled with laughter and flour on noses—, and a small tear ran down her cheek. God, they looked similar.

"Hey, you," said Peter as he entered the room. The sound of drawers slamming and cupboard doors squeaking open quieted, as if the room were preparing for a conversation. He walked in with his usual slightly-too-long stride, rubbing the back of his neck, eyes scanning the half-filled pantry. "Oh, ah. Hey, yourself," replied Olivia, quickly wiping away the tear as she turned around. "Well, it's official. The last box is unpacked; we 'live' here, now." Peter made those little quotation marks with his hand as he spoke, with a big smile. He did that a lot, even when it wasn't necessary, which he knew, but he kept doing it. It was his thing.

Olivia looked at her husband. He was kind of scruffy-looking today, a stark contrast to the semi-formal clothes he usually wore. The faded band shirt he was wearing had noticeable holes and should have been thrown away a long time ago. Peter always held on to his clothes until the very last moment. Olivia wasn't sure if it was nostalgia or a childhood of financial struggles that drove his inability to just throw things out. His dark hair seemed to have more greys shimmering through than normal, but that could just be a bit of dust. Looking at

Peter usually seemed to calm whatever was stressing her, but recently Olivia had been having more trouble than usual.

"That's great, baby." Olivia paused for a moment, her hand lingering on a can of tomatoes. The way she stood there, one hip resting against the bench, gave away more exhaustion than ease.

"...Peter?"

"Yeah, Olive?" Peter was the only person who called her Olive. Neither of them remembered when or why that became his nickname for her, but he always called her Olive, and that always made her feel special. There was something grounding about it. Something that reminded her she wasn't just someone's mother—she was still her own person, too.

"We did the right thing, didn't we? Moving here, I mean. It was the right thing to do?" Olivia's voice was starting to weaken a little as she spoke. Although she followed her husband's plan and believed it was best for her family, she still had doubts. Even with everything they went through, Brisbane was their home; they had raised their family there, they had built a life there, it was a safe place, and this house wasn't theirs. It echoed with the memories of someone else's life. So, how on Earth could they expect to rebuild their family here? The kitchen light buzzed faintly above them as if adding its own uncertainty.

"Absolutely," replied Peter, exuberating enthusiasm as always. He reached out and held Olivia's hand. His touch was soft and gentle, and his fingers were rough in places from the recent physical work of moving homes. Olivia looked at her husband, his face smiling, but his shoulders stooped, bearing the weight of everything.

"Look, I know that picking up our lives and moving them clear across the country may seem a bit extreme, but maybe extreme is exactly what we all need. A fresh start. A chance to move on." Peter put his arms around his wife, trying to comfort and reassure her. She leaned into him with the weariness of someone clinging to a raft in open water.

"I hope so, I really do. There's got to be some way to snap Kenzi out of the dark hole she's in," as she fell slowly into Peter's arms. She looked up at the ceiling and towards the noise coming from her daughter's room.

Kenzi's room had been unpacked on the same day she arrived in Esperance. It had taken about twenty minutes for Kenzi to unpack all her belongings. Now, they may seem an impressive task, but there wasn't really all that much to unpack. Since she had gotten home a few months ago, Kenzi just didn't see the point in 'things' anymore, and if she couldn't put it on herself or her phone, it didn't mean a thing to her. The only exceptions, of course, were a few small photos, one of which she was currently holding in her hand. She sat on her bed, just looking at the picture, and then around her new room.

The curtains were sun-faded, casting dusty stripes across the bed. A spiderweb clung stubbornly to the corner of the ceiling, undisturbed. Her backpack slumped beside the bed like it had collapsed under the weight of her resistance.

She turned her body slightly round, her eyes shifting from the chest of drawers to the shelf above the window and then over to her bedside table. Kenzi gently placed the photo on the bedside table, turned it slightly, and then cracked what could only be described as a happy frown. It really was a lovely picture of her brother. That may be surprising, but really, it isn't. In the stillness of the room, the silence wrapped around her like a soft but smothering blanket. The floor creaked faintly under her shifting weight, as if remembering someone else's steps long ago.

Kenzi lay there, thinking about tomorrow. The past few days had been spent at home, which was still a word that didn't quite feel right. The removal van had arrived not long after her family, so most of the time was spent unpacking and setting everything up anew. But that was all over, and the focus was now shifting forward, to their new life. A new life, which included a new school. Kenzi hadn't been at school for a few months now, and even before the move, the idea of school hadn't bothered her too much. She had always done well at school, so it had never been a source of frustration or angst for her. But, going back to her old school after being away for so long, hadn't been a concept she really wanted to experience, and the idea of starting fresh in a new school where, theoretically, no one knew anything about her, did hold some hope for Kenzi.

She wasn't ready to even think about the concept of moving forward just yet. But the idea of not going backward was a good one. Kenzi was pretty confident she could slip into an uneventful routine at school. While that wouldn't make things better, it shouldn't make them worse, and that was good enough for now. That would be good enough for the rest of the school year. Then she could move away to college, and maybe that could be the fresh start she needed.

Kenzi closed her eyes and listened to the sounds of the new house. Everything was louder here. Although Lucas was downstairs, she could still hear his little squeaks echoing off all the wood. She could hear the murmur of her parents in the kitchen below. She couldn't make out what they were talking about, but she assumed it was probably her. It usually was. She rolled over onto her side and looked out her window. She could see a small red bird in the large tree outside her room. It darted around a nest that looked like it was precariously resting on a branch that seemed to be too small to safely carry its weight. The bird's movements, although they were very quick, were calming for Kenzi. She closed her eyes and drifted off.

Chapter 03

"You're not special. You know that, right?"

The days quickly turned into weeks, and life in Esperance for Kenzi's family moved along as expected. Peter started his new job and was off to work each day. Olivia set about rearranging all the furniture in the house, which slowly transformed into a blend of old and new, making it seem like their old place but with a really old twist. The walls began to carry echoes of familiar rhythms—Peter's coffee spoon tapping in the morning, Olivia's soft footsteps in the hallway, Lucas's occasional delighted shrieks. Lucas, who was now quite adept at walking, at least as well as a toddler could, was finding all the places he shouldn't get into and causing trouble for his Mum. Cabinets clattered, drawers slammed, and Olivia seemed to exist in a constant state of swoop-and-rescue.

Kenzi had been enrolled at school and thrown back into the joys of senior year. She had never had any trouble with schoolwork; it always came easily to her, which is probably why it wasn't such a big deal that she was forced to change schools halfway through her last year. Everyone knew that, above all else, it would not be a problem and that she would continue to do well. Even after everything that had happened, she had never let her grades slip. She may have given up on friends and fun, but she made a promise to herself to keep up her studying; it was always special for them. For the most part, it was just as before. Kenzi went to school, paid attention in class, ate her lunch alone, and then went home. Her path was a well-worn groove. There was one exception to the routine she had gotten herself into: she had a weekly appointment with the school's student advisor to talk about...her feelings.

Kenzi slouched in her chair, eyes drifting from one cringe-worthy inspirational poster to the next. A bright yellow cat smiled above the words 'Believe in Yourself,' while a mountain shouted something about perseverance. The hum of fluorescent lights could be heard over the sounds of other students talking in the hallway. The air conditioner clicked to life, pushing a cold draft across her legs. Kenzi looked around the room and scoffed. The walls were too bright, the chairs too soft, the fake plants too green. It all screamed: 'I'm trying too hard.'

She looked at the woman sitting across from her. The term 'woman' didn't really seem right to Kenzi. Mrs Fox barely looked older than the seniors she counselled-her jumper was obviously too large for her, and her side part betrayed her attempts to look professional. A pair of scuffed ballet flats peeked out from beneath her trousers, one heel flattened as though she never quite took the time to fix it. She perched on the chair too carefully, like a guest in her own office. A small notepad rested on her lap, its corner dog-eared from nervous fingers. Kenzi thought about the effort she must have put into the whole setup, trying to make it feel like a safe space for kids to open up. It wasn't working. If Kenzi didn't feel she could talk to her parents about it, what would make anyone believe she could speak to a stranger?

Kenzi had had three meetings with Mrs Fox since starting at her new school. They all went the same way. Standard questions about how Kenzi was adjusting to the new school, how she was handling the workload, how her homelife was, and if she was feeling sad or depressed. Nothing of any real substance. Nothing that Kenzi couldn't fob off with a 'fine' or 'ok.' The meeting often had long, awkward silences as well. Pretty much, how most of Kenzi's interactions with adults, which was a term she used loosely here, would go.

"Kenzi," said Mrs Fox, in a very forced, non-assertive way. "I know that you are only required to attend these sessions to continue attending school here and that we can't 'force' you to talk, but I believe it would help."

"Hmmph" was all Kenzi was prepared to muster. She crossed her arms and sank deeper into the too-cushy chair. Kenzi was not interested in talking about anything, especially not with a stranger.

"Ok then, how about you just listen?" Mrs Fox waited for a response, some reaction on Kenzi's behalf, but there was none, so she decided to keep talking.

"You're not special. You know that, right?

Kenzi looked at Mrs Fox in the eyes, which was a first. It wasn't the response that Mrs Fox had hoped for, but at this point, she would take what she could get and run with it. There was a flicker there—annoyance or curiosity, she couldn't be sure.

"I know you're not stupid. Your grades are amazing, so I know that you're smart enough to know that tens of thousands of other teenagers have been in the exact same position you're in now, and guess what? Most of them probably felt exactly the same way you do now. They all thought their problems were so much worse than anyone else could imagine. But they were wrong."

She was a lot rougher than she usually would be, rougher than she was supposed to be. Still, she could tell it was the only chance she had of ever getting through to Kenzi and maybe helping her, even if just a little bit.

The silence in the room shifted, less dismissive now—more charged.

Kenzi was surprised, but she wasn't going to give Mrs Fox the satisfaction of showing it. She kept staring at her blankly.

"I hope you're not expecting to get a rise out of me."

"Well, it's not what I really want, but I'm just trying to get something, anything out of you."

"What? You want me to talk about what happened? Is that it?" Kenzi was starting to get a little snarky now, which she didn't really like to do. Maybe it was the thought of another pre-manufactured therapy session, or perhaps she was just over it. She just couldn't be bothered enough to stop herself.

"That'd be nice, Kenzi."

"Nice," thought Kenzi to herself. Nothing about this is "Nice." This woman really has no idea what she is doing. If she wanted Kenzi to talk, she better be prepared for what Kenzi was going to say.

"Ok. Fine. Did I try to kill myself? Yeah. Will I try again? I don't know. Is that what you want to hear?"

As Kenzi said the words aloud, she felt a small weight leave her chest and fire across the room at Mrs Fox. She hated talking about what had happened, what she had done. She had done it enough to see the discomfort it usually brought on anyone around who heard her story, and she was hopeful that the same would happen here. Maybe it would upset Mrs Fox enough that should would drop the matter, and not bring it up again.

"It's a good place to start." Mrs Fox leaned forward in her chair, hoping to prompt Kenzi to keep going.

Kenzi could tell what Mrs Fox was trying to do, but she really didn't want to give her any satisfaction.

"But I'd much rather hear you tell me why."

Kenzi was starting to get angry now. She really did not want to be here and REALLY did not want to talk to this person about something so personal. And besides, if this woman had done any sort of research into Kenzi, surely she would know why she did what she did. ANYONE could figure it out, and ANYONE would understand.

"You're kidding, right!?"

Mrs Fox wasn't kidding. She knew the answer to her question, but that wasn't what was really important here. She wanted Kenzi to say it out loud, own it, and accept what had happened. She knew that unless Kenzi was able to deal with what had caused this whole mess, there was no way she was ever going to get past it and no way to make sure she didn't try to hurt herself again. Mrs Fox gently placed her hand on the file on her desk, which was obviously about Kenzi. The folder was thick, creased from handling, and the edges were just slightly frayed.

"Look, I think I know why you did it, but I really want you to say it."

Kenzi was ready to let loose. If there was one thing she hated talking to people about more than what she did, it was why she did it. That hurt WAY more. She could feel tears starting to form in the corner of her eyes, and she really didn't want to cry in front of this woman.

She took a breath, trying to calm herself, but before she could respond, the school bell rang across the campus, signalling that their meeting was over and that it was time for Kenzi to go home. THANK GOD. Kenzi quickly got up and headed for the door. The chair squeaked back against the floor, and her footsteps echoed louder than usual on the polished linoleum.

"You did well today, Kenzi. But there's still plenty more to talk about next time."

Kenzi pretended not to hear Mrs Fox as she rushed out the door. She didn't think anything good had happened today and dreaded having to talk about it again next time. As she walked down the hallway, squeezing past all the other kids rushing to their next class, she wiped away the tears with the end of her sleeve. The hallway was busy and loud, and Kenzi kept to herself as she walked towards her locker. She opened it and shuffled through her books, getting ready for her next class. Before she closed it, she looked at the photo that she had stuck to the back wall of her locker, and she felt calm again. Looking at him always made her feel better.

Chapter 04

"At least you'd be damned well living some sort of normal life a teenager should be."

Kenzi walked through the front door to her home, and just like every other day, her Mum and little brother were playing on the floor in the lounge room. There were toys everywhere. The kind of chaos that only Lucas could create. As much as she would like to avoid it, she would have to walk through the lounge room to get to the kitchen to get a drink before retreating to her bedroom. Kenzi was pretty sure her Mum knew this, which is why she was always in the lounge room when she got home. Waiting. Ready to ambush her. Olivia sat on the floor with Lucas, but she wasn't hunched over; she always had good posture, even when playing.

Plastic dinosaurs lay toppled like fallen statues beside a crayon-scribbled colouring book. A rubber ball rolled lazily under the couch, bumped by Lucas's earlier chaos. The sunlight filtering through the lounge room window gave the scattered toys a golden glow, as if trying to make the disorder feel homely.

Kenzi tried to walk past without engaging too much. Olivia looked up from her spot on the ground. Although her hair was tied back, there were large strands of it hanging down around her face, fallout from a day spent on the ground with a toddler. Kenzi would feel sorry for her, but it was all of her own making. She chose to have another kid so she could deal with it. Actually, Lucas was a good distraction for Kenzi. Her Mum had been so focused on him, even after Kenzi got home from the hospital, that she had pretty much left Kenzi alone. Which was how Kenzi liked it.

But Kenzi knew that right now, she and her Mother would have to go through the afternoon routine. She would play her part and then go to her room until dinner time.

"Hey, Kenzi. How was school today?"

"Fine."

"And Mrs Fox?"

"Fine."

"Dinner's at seven. We're having chicken."

"Fine."

The conversation was almost word-for-word, exactly the same as the afternoon before and the afternoon before that. It was clear that Olivia was desperate to have some meaningful interaction with her daughter, but just didn't know how to get it back on track. And Kenzi, well, she couldn't really commit to too much more than she was giving out. She knew her Mum was only trying to help, but she just couldn't find the energy to meet her halfway. With the well-practised routine of afternoon chit-chat out of the way, Kenzi made her way to the kitchen, grabbed a drink out of the fridge, and then headed up to her room.

After Olivia watched Kenzi walk up the stairs, she was screaming to herself in her mind, "Is that it?! Is that the best you can do? Get up there and talk to your damned daughter!" But she didn't. Instead, she focused on her son, Lucas, the one child who actually wanted something to do with her. She knew it was only because he didn't really know any better at this age, but she didn't care. She would take any form of affection from any of her kids that she could get.

It was strange. Growing up, Olivia had never really pictured herself as becoming a mum. She knew it would eventually happen, but she never thought about what it would actually mean or how it would change her. But as soon as her first child was born, she couldn't believe how much love she could have for someone else, and how much joy she got from just being close to them. That's what had made the last few years so hard. She loved her kids so much, and it killed her that she hadn't been able to see what Kenzi was going through. She knew it was tough, of course it was tough, but she never dreamed it was that bad. And since Kenzi had tried to kill herself, Olivia was desperate to make it all better, but she couldn't. She didn't know how to. And it felt like Kenzi didn't want her to. Like she had lost any chance she had of getting back what she once had. She knew things could never be what they were before, but she couldn't stand the thought of things staying the way they are now.

Olivia looked down at Lucas, so small and innocent. He was playing with some toy dinosaurs, making cute little roaring sounds as he smashed them together. His curls bounced as he threw himself into the battle, baby-fat hands gripping the plastic T. rex like it was alive. A streak of green marker ran down his forearm, evidence of an earlier art project gone rogue. The image conjured up memories of Kenzi from that age, and she smiled a little. She looked around the room at the chaos that Lucas had left in his wake. She hadn't realised that the mail had been knocked off the counter during their adventures throughout the day. She crawled over on all fours to the pile of letters on the ground. She picked them up, shuffled them around in her hands to make a neat pile, and placed them back on the tray on the stand near the front door. She noticed the pile of brochures from various universities on the bench. She became acutely aware that Kenzi was in her senior year and that she was most definitely going to move away for university. She knew that if things didn't change before Kenzi moved away, they would stay broken forever. She had to do something, but she had no idea what.

Olivia looked over at Lucas, who was still entertaining himself. She took it as an opportunity to sneak away and start making dinner. She may be failing at talking to her daughter right now, but she would make sure her daughter was fed. It would have to do for now.

About an hour later, Peter returned home from work. Because the garage isn't actually connected to the house, it generally means that no one inside can hear his car pull up, so, from time to time, he can sneak in the back door, and today, he used this as an opportunity to catch Olivia unaware in the kitchen. She was busy working on dinner and didn't hear him creeping up behind her.

"Hey, Sexy!" he whispered in her ear as he appeared right behind her, close up against her, firmly grabbing her but. He did this often. Not the sneaking-up part, but the but-grabbing part. It was never in a derogatory manner, just a way that he'd frequently shown her affection and let her know that he was still attracted to her, which he was, in a big way.

"Ah!" screamed Olivia, completely caught off guard. The scream was simply an impulse, and as soon as she made the sound, she realised exactly what was going on; she was not afraid, just surprised, pleasantly. Olivia quickly turned around to see her husband, hoping to grab him back, but he backed away quickly, fearing he might get hit with whatever utensil she was holding, which she wasn't going to do.

"Hey, yourself."

"Dinner smells great, Olive."

"S'just chicken."

"Well, it's great-smelling chicken. Where're the kids?" Peter had started emptying the contents of his pockets into a bowl on the counter as Olivia turned back to her cooking.

"Lucas is having a sleep-"

"Nice"

"I know, right? And Kenzi is in her room."

"Been there since she got home?"

"Yup."

"Enough's enough?"

"Yup."

"Kay. Wish me luck."

As Peter headed up the stairs, he was running over in his mind what to say. He and Olivia had talked a lot about Kenzi for apparent reasons. They had debated for a long time exactly how long they could let her keep acting the way she had. It wasn't healthy. She couldn't spend all her time in her room. She had to get out and back into the world.

As Peter approached the door to Kenzi's room, he could hear the sound of some angsty band's attempt at music coming from it. The cliché was not lost on him. He was hesitant to see what was inside as he turned the doorknob and slowly opened the door. Ever since he found her lying on the floor in her room, eyes wide open, small bits of vomit dripping out of her mouth, he was always afraid of going into her room; even if it was a new room, he was still so frightened to see her like that again. But he didn't. At least not this time. She was just sitting at her desk, working on her homework. Although it was quite a relief, it made it all the harder to have the conversation he had been putting off for too long. Here she was, not doing anything wrong as such. In fact, she was doing her homework, something he or Olivia never had to push her to do, and he was going to get mad at her. Being a Dad is crappy some (most of) the time.

"Kenz? You got a minute?"

"Sure." The enthusiasm just oozed out of her, not.

Peter walked into his daughter's room and looked around at the lack of personality. It felt as empty as he feared Kenzi had become. He tried to look casual and leaned against the dresser, which shifted from his weight, and he nearly fell. He quickly steadied himself.

The air in the room was cooler than the rest of the house, like the space held its breath. A single poster peeled slightly at one corner on the wall, and her desk lamp cast a sharp cone of light onto her homework. There were no decorations, no clutter—just order, silence, and effort. It was the room of someone who was doing everything to survive unnoticed.

"Listen, Kenz, ah, you can't just sit in your room every afternoon. You've, ah, you really need to get outside and do something."

"Do something? Like drinking? Or smoking? Or god-knows-what all the other kids at school are doing while I'm here, doing my homework. Is that what you mean?"

Kenzi was being a smart-arse again, probably because of the frustrating meeting she had with Mrs Fox earlier in the day. She didn't mean it.

"You know that's not what I mean, I. No. Wait. That's exactly what I mean."

Kenzi was a little caught off guard by that.

"At least you'd be damned well living some sort of normal life a teenager should be." Peter's voice was starting to get a bit sterner than it had in a very long time, and he was walking around the room, his footsteps heavy on the wooden floor.

"Christ. I'd much rather be worried about you getting drunk with other kids than having to worry about you being alone in her, maybe ki-"

"Dad!" Kenzi quickly cut off her Dad. No matter how bad things were, how bad she'd let them get, she still felt really horrible that he was the one who found her, and she knew that it was the worst thing that could have happened to him. She hated that he had to go through it, and hated it even more that he had to talk to her about it.

Peter took the pause as a good time to compose himself again.

"Listen. All I'm saying is that we'd be a lot happier if we knew there was something else you did with your time aside from school. I know that making friends is probably a stretch."

Kenzi breathed a little sigh and relaxed back into her chair. This was an easier conversation to have.

"Probably?"

"But surely there's something else you could be doing. Maybe going to the mall and actually buying something that you can't download. Heck, maybe you could even get a job and make some money for yourself."

"A job?" thought Kenzi to herself. This was the first time her Dad had ever mentioned to Kenzi that she was getting a job. He had always earned really good money, so she had always gotten a reasonable allowance, so there had never been any talk about her getting a job.

"Is money a problem? I mean, I know that your new job isn't as good as your old one, but you guys are doing ok, right?"

"What? No, don't be silly. We're doing fine. In fact, after selling our old house, we're doing pretty damned well. I just thought a job might be good for you. Give you somewhere to go, something to do." Peter really wasn't sure what he was doing right now, and was making it up as he went. He thought about leaning on the dresser again, but remembered what happened, so he kind of just stood there, probably looking as uncomfortable as he was feeling.

"I, ah..."Kenzi could always tell when her Dad was lying to her to make her feel better; he'd been doing it a lot lately, but this wasn't one of those times. She could tell that the only reason he wanted her to get a job was so she would be out in the world, talking to people, which she really did not want to do. She could also tell that it was tough for her Dad to ask her to do it. She knew that he and her Mum had been putting off having a conversation like this for a long time, and she felt bad that he had to have it. And so, even though she really didn't want to, Kenzi decided to do something for someone else.

"... ok, Dad."

"Ok?" Peter was shocked. It was NOT meant to be this easy. Was this a sign that things might be starting to head in the right direction? Were they finally going to get on track? No, it's too soon to start thinking like that. Just take it as a start for now.

"That's great! I, ah, we could go to the mall tomorrow and see if anybody is looking for-" he could feel himself bouncing a little, showing his excitement.

"No!" Kenzi was a bit louder than she wanted to be. She could see her Dad was getting excited, and she didn't want it to get too out of control.

"I mean, I can go by myself after school."

Peter could tell he had gotten all he was going to get and that there was no point in pushing it any further.

"Oh, of course, right. Ah, anyways, dinner will be ready soon, so I'd better check if your Mum needs any help settin' the table. See you down there soon?"

"Yeah, Dad."

Peter headed for the door. He desperately wanted to grab his daughter and give her a big hug, but he didn't.

It had been a long time since she had wanted to be touched by anyone. He was excited, but he knew it still wasn't time for anything major. So he just left, pulling the door gently behind him.

His hand hovered for a second over the doorknob, reluctant to let go of the moment, before he turned it and pulled the door closed with the softest click he could manage. He let out a big sigh and headed back downstairs.

"Booyah-ow!" As Peter entered the dining room, he tried to punch the air but misjudged and hit the door frame.

"Wha-, you right?" asked Olivia as she turned to see what her husband was up to. Peter was shaking his hand, trying to make the pain go away as he replied, "Yeah, yeah, fine."

"So? How'd it go?"

"Good. Real good! Well, I think it did. She, ah, she's going to start looking for a job." Peter could feel himself starting to bounce with excitement again. He was keenly aware that he was often too enthusiastic about things and that his body usually showed this. He didn't mind it most of the time, but this was a serious thing, so he tried to calm himself.

Olivia put the pile of plates she was holding down on the table, a little in shock.

"A Job? Why does she need a job?"

"Well, 'cause, ah, I'm not really sure. I started talking about Kenzi going out more, and then we started talking about my new job, and somehow we decided it would be a good idea for her to get a job, to, you know, give her a reason to go out more." Peter paused a little, starting to think that maybe his talk didn't go as well as his wife would have liked.

"S'that ok?"

Olivia knew that whatever conversation Peter had just had with Kenzi would have been hard. Of the two parents, it was always going to be easier for Peter, as they were closer, but it would still be hard. The fact that it hadn't ended in shouting and doors slamming was probably a miracle, so she knew that her husband must have some sort of success, and no matter what it was, she was going to support him.

"Um, yeah, I guess. No, it's great, Peter, really great. I mean, ideally, she should be going out because she wants to, but if having a job is the thing that forces her to start going out, then that's good."

Peter snuck closer to his wife. Well, not snuck, but kind of pretended he was sneaking. "So, I did good?"

Olivia could see a mile away what Peter was up to. But she was still ok with it.

"Yes. You did good."

"So, maybe I get some sort of reward?" Peter was right up against Olivia now, his hands gently touching her side, forcing a cheeky smile across his face.

Olivia started to blush a little. Even after nineteen years of marriage, Peter could still make her feel special.

"If you play your cards right...you never know."

"Sweet!" Peter did a little victory dance as he left the room. It was a good day.

As he shuffled his feet in exaggerated celebration, the overhead light swayed gently above the dining table, flickering once, as if it too approved of his small success.

"It's a start", thought Olivia to herself. She was relieved to know that even if she couldn't have a proper conversation with her daughter, at least her husband could, and he was definitely the sort of person who could keep that momentum going. Maybe it wasn't too late.

Chapter 05
"Now, back to that nonsense of you trying to kill yourself."

The next day at school seemed to drag by just that little bit slower than usual.

The classroom clock ticked audibly, each second stretching out like gum under a desk. The scent of whiteboard markers clung to the air, mixing with the faint must of worn textbooks. Outside, a lone magpie warbled in the courtyard, a sound somehow both peaceful and mocking.

Kenzi was not looking forward to the afternoon. Not one bit. Kenzi knew that now that her Dad had gotten started on this whole 'get a job' thing, he was not going to stop buggin' her about it until he had one. He could be a real pain in the ass like that, but strangely, it was also one of the things that she actually liked about him; he never seemed to give up. The more she thought about it, the more it actually felt nice inside. Thinking about something like that, like an actual nice thing about someone else, wasn't something that she had done for a while. It caught her off guard. As she walked through the hallway to her next class, she actually smiled - a genuine smile. She quickly looked up to make sure nobody was looking at her. Safe. Kenzi knew that she didn't have to get a job today. She still had a good couple of weeks of her Dad reminding her about it, so there was no real need to put too much effort into it just yet. But still, she did have to go out after school and at least pretend as though she was looking, so that's what she was going to do.

School was over for the day, and Kenzi was walking through the business part of the town, as much as one could call it that. The town of Esperance was a series of short streets and crooked sidewalks. Old brick buildings leaned into one another like aging relatives. There were cafes with peeling signs, shops with dusty window displays, and people who moved slowly enough to notice. Rusted signs leaned into crooked fences, and every porch sagged with history. Although there was quite a large mall in Esperance, there wasn't much else around. Kenzi knew that if she were going to get any sort of job, it would probably have to be there, so she stayed away today.

Kenzi was walking down what could probably be called one of the main streets of the town, feigning interest in the various businesses she passed. She'd decided she would give it at least half an hour of pretending to look for a job before heading home, and she was very relieved when she checked her phone, and time was pretty much up. Kenzi walked with her hands shoved deep in her pockets, the breeze tugging at her sleeves. She passed a butcher, a chemist, and a boutique full of beige dresses no one under sixty would wear. A few locals nodded politely as she walked by, their smiles small and cautious, like they knew who she was. Maybe they did. The late afternoon sun angled low between the buildings, casting long shadows that made the streets feel quieter than they were. A breeze tugged at loose flyers taped to light poles, setting them fluttering like anxious thoughts. The sidewalk was uneven, patches of it cracked and chipped, and her boots scuffed lightly with each step as she drifted past tired shopfronts.

Kenzi turned down a street to make her way home, but before she could go further, she walked straight into a lady, and the two of them nearly fell over.

"Ooph. Sorry." Kenzi stayed upright easily, but the lady had a bit of trouble and had to let go of the sign she was moving to keep from falling.

"That's ok, dear, no harm do-" the lady stopped talking. Kenzi looked at the lady, who was quite old, older than she had first thought, and her mind started racing.

The lady was probably as old as her Grandmother was when she died, but she was pretty thin, almost athletic-looking. Her grey curls were piled messily on her head, and her glasses sat low on her nose. Her eyes, though ringed with fine lines, were sharp and mischievous, the kind that seemed to catalogue a whole person in a glance. The corners of her mouth twitched upward, like smiling was her default setting, even mid-shock. The lady stood there, almost frozen. Like she had seen a ghost.

"Oh god, she's having a heart attack," she thought. "I've killed her."

Kenzi slowly reached out towards the lady.

"Are you ok, ma'am?"

There was no reply. The woman was just kept staring at Kenzi, really staring at her.

"Ma'am?"

"Oh, ah, sorry. Yes, I'm, I'm fine, thank you." She was still staring at Kenzi. It was starting to creep her out a bit.

"It's just that, my god, you look just like her. I'd seen pictures, but wow, you are a dead ringer."

The lady was starting to smile now, which only creeped Kenzi out even more. Who was this old lady, and just who did Kenzi look 'just like'?

"Just like...who?" Kenzi's voice actually cracked a little bit, showing that she was pretty uncomfortable with what was going on.

"Why, your Grandmother, of course. You are the spitting image of Mac."

Kenzi felt a bit relieved, but not completely. It was good to know that the woman wasn't hurt, but she still didn't know who she was.

"You knew my grandmother?"

"Knew her? We were best friends from the day we could talk. Oh, where are my manners? My name is

Josephina Walters, but everybody calls me Jo." Jo put her hand out. "And it is very nice to meet you, Kenzi."

Kenzi shook Jo's hand, though she was still not really sure what was happening.

"Hi, ah, Jo."

"Well, don't just stand there, kiddo. Give me a hand with this thing."

Jo grabbed hold of the sign she had knocked over. It read 'Jo's Books' and had a big 'open' written on it. Jo grabbed the sign and started dragging it back inside the shop, much quicker than Kenzi had expected, so she quickly jumped forward to help.

"Oh, um, ok." Kenzi picked up one side, and Jo got the other. The sign was heavy, heavier than Kenzi had expected, and she was pretty surprised that Jo didn't seem to have any trouble lifting it. Kenzi tried to make it look like she wasn't having trouble, but she didn't really pull it off. They carried the sign just inside the shop and placed it against the wall.

It wasn't a big shop. There were probably only about five rows of shelves, all full of books, most of which looked almost as old as Jo did. It wasn't very well-lit, and there was that really old-book smell in the air. Sunlight filtered through lace curtains, making the book spines glow like relics. It was kind of creepy, but for some reason, it didn't creep Kenzi out. In fact, she almost felt comfortable there, kind of like she'd been there before.

"So, how are you settling in? It's such a lovely house, your Grandmother's. I know she'd be happy you were all there now. 'Course, she'd obviously have liked it if she were around to be there too, but what are ya gonna do?" Jo was tidying up as she talked, preparing to close the shop. It was strange hearing her talk about her Grandmother. Kenzi was expecting Jo to get a bit choked up, maybe even cry a little. They were best friends, after all. But she didn't. In fact, she was starting to smile even more now. Weird.

"It's nice, I guess. Could be a lot worse." Kenzi didn't really know what to say.

She didn't like the house, or the town, or anything, but she didn't want to say anything to hurt Jo's feelings, which, like a lot of things today, surprised her. Why did she care about this stranger's feelings? Jo was still busy moving all over the shop, moving this, packing that. She was a lot more spry than she looked.

"I'll have to pop over soon and see you all. It's been so long since I last saw your father. I had hoped that he could make it back here for Mac's funeral, but ah, well, you know why that wasn't possible."

Kenzi knew exactly why they hadn't come for her Grandmother's funeral...her. She didn't know what to say. She was taken aback by how much Jo knew about her, which apparently was everything. Did her Grandmother tell her? That seemed odd cause she didn't really have that much to do with her at all. Fortunately, Jo didn't give her much time to respond.

"Oh, ah, speaking of which. Are you ok now?" Jo was right next to Kenzi, gently touching her on the shoulder. Her hand was light but steady, the kind of touch that felt like an anchor instead of a question. "I mean, ah, physically. Everything's fine, right?"

Great. This woman knows exactly what Kenzi did to herself. How she swallowed a whole bottle of sleeping pills, and how the doctors had to pump her whole stomach just to keep her from dying. This was the most uncomfortable conversation Kenzi had had in a long time, but strangely, she didn't want it to stop.

"Yeah, yeah. The doctors said I might have trouble eating some bad foods, but that's not really a problem. And helps keep the weight off." Kenzi was no longer in control of her mouth. There was no thinking about what to say first, which was how she had been operating since she woke up in the hospital. She was finally speaking her mind.

"What weight? You're a bloody twig, just like Mac was." It seemed like Jo was speaking her mind, too, which was nice. Every adult seemed to have some sort of agenda or plan when talking to Kenzi since she tried to kill herself. All were afraid they'd say the wrong thing. But not Jo.

"Mac?" Kenzi had never heard anyone call her Grandmother Mac, and Jo had done it every chance she got.

Jo was standing behind the front counter now, hastily picking up papers and books and shoving them into a large tote bag. Kenzi was still standing just inside the door, not sure of what to do or where to go.

"That's what I used to call your Grandmother. Everybody did. Her maiden name was Mackenzie, which is obviously where your name comes from, and somewhere along the line, people just started calling her Mac. Well, everyone except for your Grandfather. He was the only one who would call her Sarah. Was part of what made them so good together."

Kenzi knew that her Grandmother's maiden name was Mackenzie, but she had never really put two and two together regarding where her name came from. Her Grandmother was never really a big part of her life, and she had just assumed it was because she and her Dad weren't really that close, but if she was named after her, that couldn't be right.

Kenzi thought about her Grandmother, the picture she had seen when she first arrived in Esperance, and how strange it was for such a girly-looking girl to be called such a masculine name as Mac. She wondered if it would make more sense if she actually knew anything real about her grandmother. Thinking about it even made the idea that a little old lady would be called Jo, too.

Another name that she had always thought of as masculine.

"So...Mac and Jo?"

"Exactly. Probably why we started being friends in the first place." Jo went back to cleaning. Kenzi wondered if Jo was always so casual with everyone, or was it just cause of her Grandmother.

"Now, back to that nonsense of you trying to kill yourself," Jo was yelling from behind one of the shelves. Kenzi was shocked again. Surely Jo knew that Kenzi wouldn't want to talk about it, but she obviously didn't care. Kenzi was getting weary of exactly where this conversation was going.

"Now, I know that you and M-"

"I should probably get going." Kenzi quickly interrupted Jo before she could finish. That was more than Kenzi felt comfortable talking about right now. She had finally reached the limit.

"Oh, ah, of course." Jo realised she was pushing things too far. She realised that, even though she was missing her friend, and this girl, who was the closest thing she had to her, was here now, she probably needed to stop before she said something too inappropriate. The last thing she wanted to do was scare Kenzi away.

"Well, I'm all done here, so I'll walk you out and lock the shop up."

"Ok." Kenzi was relieved. She didn't think that Jo was going to stop talking, but thankfully, she must have realised that she didn't want to talk about it anymore. She just couldn't.

Kenzi walked out first, back into the street, and strangely, it felt like she was back in reality. Jo stepped out and locked the door behind her. The two just stood there for a moment, looking at each other, not really sure what to say. Jo went first.

"You tell your father I said hi and that I'll be over to see everyone real soon." Jo knew it was best just to brush over the suicide talk and give Kenzi a chance just to end it cleanly.

"I will." Kenzi started to walk away. "It was nice to meet you, Jo. See you later."

"You betcha." Jo stood there and watched Kenzi walk away. God, she reminded her of Mac so much.

As Kenzi walked down the sidewalk, she turned back to see Jo still there, smiling. The wind blew past Kenzi, messing her hair a bit, and she felt a shiver run down her spine. She got this eerie feeling that someone was standing right next to her. But there was no one there. It must have just been the wind. So she continued home.

Later that night, Kenzi was sitting at her desk, working on her homework while listening to some music. As she was writing, she couldn't help but think about Jo, possibly the most forward person she had met. Thinking about her made her think about her Grandmother, 'Mac,' and how little she knew about her. She thought about what Jo had said, that they looked so alike, a dead ringer, she said. She pictured the photo of her Grandmother on the hall outside, and how that woman in it looked so full of life, which didn't seem to match how Kenzi thought she herself looked. What else did they have in common? Would her Grandmother have reacted the same way that Kenzi did? Would she have been stronger? It's strange. She never wanted to know anything about her Grandmother, but now that she'll never see her again, she found herself wanting to learn more. She finally wants to interact with another person again, and they're dead.

Yup, that's about right.

Chapter 06
"Why, my dear, when have you ever known me to 'go easy' on anyone?"

The next day, after school, Kenzi headed straight home. She had spent the previous afternoon 'looking' for a job, and that was enough to buy her a few days' grace with her father, so she didn't feel the need to pretend again today. The weight of her backpack shifted as she walked, but for once it didn't feel too heavy. A thin layer of clouds dulled the afternoon light, casting the street in a grey, calm atmosphere. She kicked a small rock along the footpath absentmindedly, counting the seconds until she could collapse onto her bed.

As she approached her house, she could see an unfamiliar car parked out front. Immediately, she tensed up. The car was a glossy maroon sedan—clean, polished. It gleamed like it didn't belong. Kenzi's stomach dropped with the kind of dread you get when a teacher calls your name unexpectedly. Her hand twitched at her side as she contemplated turning around and going out to pretend to look for a job again. She probably would have done it before the move. But a small change was starting to form inside Kenzi, especially after meeting Jo yesterday. That whole thing could have been a terrible experience, but it wasn't. It was kind of nice. Perhaps this could be the same.

Kenzi put her hand on the doorknob, took a deep breath, and turned the knob, walking inside. As soon as she was inside, she could see her parents sitting in the lounge room, talking to whoever was over. She couldn't see the other people; they were sitting with their backs to the front door. Before Kenzi could sneak into the kitchen to muster up some more courage, her mother spotted her- damn.

"Oh, Kenzi, you're home. Good. Come on and say hi to-" before Olivia could finish, one of the mysterious guests turned round and interrupted her.

"Howya doin', Kenz?" It was Jo. Kenzi's mood changed immediately. She was almost excited. Kenzi dropped her bag and headed into the lounge.

"Hey, Jo. I'm good, thanks." Kenzi was struggling to hide her excitement.

"You didn't tell me you met Aunt Jo," said Peter. Kenzi was caught out. She had forgotten that she hadn't told her father about what happened yesterday. She still wasn't sure why she had kept the meeting a secret. Maybe it felt like something too delicate to explain. Something private. Something hers. Her mind quickly started to race, coming up with some sort of reason or excuse, but before she could get anything out, Jo stepped in.

"I asked her not to say anything. I wanted this visit to be a surprise." Peter could tell that Jo was covering for Kenzi. He had seen her do it, what seemed like a million times, with his mother growing up. He knew better than to call her on it, and if he knew Jo, he knew she was already up to something important.

"Oh, ah, mission accomplished then," he replied.

"Kenzi, this handsome gentleman sitting next to me is my husband, Quinn," Jo said, motioning towards the other guest. Kenzi hadn't taken any notice of him or the large dish of some sort of food he was holding. She knew he was there, but she was fixated on Jo. She stepped closer to him as he stood up to shake her hand. He was obviously quite old, much like Jo, but he was rounder, in the belly. Not fat, just comfy. She couldn't help but snicker at his suspenders and bow tie. She didn't think people actually still dressed like that. His cheeks dimpled when he grinned, and his eyes crinkled into crescents that made him look more like a cheerful grandfather from a picture book than a dinner guest. The bow tie might have been ridiculous, but on him it seemed oddly fitting.

"Pleased to meet you, ah, Mister? Asked Kenzi as she shook his hand, which was a lot softer than she thought.

"Quinn is fine," he replied as he sat back down. Kenzi noticed how he looked at Jo as he did. In fact, he didn't really look anywhere else but at Jo. Some people might think it was out of some kind of obedience, as if he were waiting for her to tell him what to do, but Kenzi knew better. She'd seen that look before. It was the same look her Dad had most of the time. The kind of look that tells you they are truly and completely in love with the person they're looking at. It kind of made her sick and happy at the same time.

Kenzi's thoughts drifted back to her Grandmother. She wondered if she and her Grandfather were that close, too. Her Grandfather had died when her Dad was pretty young, so she knew almost nothing about him. She'd never really given it any thought, but her Grandmother must have raised her Dad pretty much on her own. She was starting to think that they must have been close, a lot closer than she had ever realised. It must have been really hard for her Dad, not being able to be here with her at the end. She started to feel quite sad, almost selfish. She knew that what she had done had a real impact on her parents, but she had never thought it cost her father something so...important. A small tear began to run down her cheek. She quickly wiped it away, hoping that no one saw, which they didn't.

There was silence. Everyone was seated, all looking at Kenzi, who was just standing there, staring off into nothing. Kenzi realised and tried to come up with something to say, but before she could, Jo, in what seemed to be a habit for her, broke the silence.

"Well, this lasagne isn't going to serve itself." Jo stood up as Quinn handed the dish to her. "Kenzi, help me set the table." God, she was forward. What was strange was that no one seemed surprised. Her Mum, who was always the first person to offer to do something, especially in her own home, didn't even budge. In fact, she even smiled, taking pleasure in the fact that Jo was going to make Kenzi help. It seemed like Jo had an effect on everyone. She quickly followed Jo into the kitchen.

"Cutlery's here, and the plates should be over there' said Jo as she led Kenzi into the kitchen. Again, Kenzi was taken aback by how bossy Jo was. This was her house, after all. If Kenzi wasn't in such awe of her, she was pretty sure she would hate Jo. But she didn't. So she did as Jo asked. As Kenzi started getting the plates out of the cupboard, Jo jumped up and sat on the bench in the kitchen, making herself at home. Kenzi wondered how many times Jo had done the exact same thing – probably a lot.

"So, Kenz," she started, "how's school goin'?"

"Er, um, good, I guess' replied Kenzi, somewhat relieved the conversation was about something as simple as school and not any of the other more stressful topics she would have expected Jo to dive into.

"You be able to catch up for the time you had off after your accident?" Kenzi normally didn't like it when people called it an 'accident.' There was nothing accidental about it.

"Yeah, no problems at all."

"That's good. And you have plans for after senior year?"

"Probably college. Curtin University has some good programs."

"My grandson, Bobby, is in his first year at Curtin. He loves it there."

"Oh, ok."

Jo could tell that Kenzi wasn't too interested in talking about college, so she decided to change the subject.

"You know, your Grandma was smart, too. Well, 'book' smart at least. Was the first in her family to go to college."

"Yeah? That's cool." Kenzi couldn't stop the smile beaming across her face. She tried to turn her face away from Jo as she walked out of the kitchen with her pile of plates, knives and forks headed for the dining room. Jo didn't need to see Kenzi's face, though. She could hear the joy in her voice, which in turn made her smile. Jo could tell that hearing about her Grandma was something that Kenzi wanted and probably needed right now, and she knew that if there was something she could do for the girl who reminded her so much of her best friend, then she had to do it.

"You know," started Jo as she followed Kenzi out, carrying the lasagne, "I could tell you more 'bout her. If you wanted."

Kenzi was about to blurt out a 'Hell yeah,' but was able to restrain herself and simply replied, "Sure."

Jo just smiled back at her. They both knew it was a big deal but were happy to play it down a little.

"Come an' get it!" yelled Jo.

Everybody made their way into the dining room, squeezing into the open spots around the over-crowded table. Kenzi made sure she got a place next to Jo. Everybody was enjoying the dinner, and most of the discussions were pretty uneventful, mostly just 'catch-up' between Jo and Peter, so Kenzi wasn't really paying attention. It wasn't until the meal was almost finished that Kenzi actually had to participate.

"I forgot to ask, Kenzi", started her father, 'How did the job-hunting go today?"

Kenzi didn't really know what to say and could only let out a "Um.." before Jo jumped in.

"Job-hunting?"

"Yeah, uh, that's what I was doing when I bumped into you yesterday."

"Well then, it must have been destiny. I was just thinking about hiring someone to help out a little at the store. Give me some free time to spend at home with this hunk," said Jo, gently grabbing Quinn's arm and giving it a little squeeze. He just goofily smiled back.

Jo continued, "The job's yours if ya want it."

"Yeah!" replied Kenzi, but Peter was quick to interject.

"No!" His voice was loud and clear. He had wanted Kenzi to get a job so she could meet new people, people her own age, not so she could spend her spare time in a dusty old bookstore. But Peter quickly got control of his emotions, realising that Kenzi seemed a bit excited by Jo's idea. If it was the only way he was going to get her out of the house, he should take it.

"I mean, ah, are you sure you can afford that, Jo? We wouldn't want Kenzi to be any sort of burden to you guys." Peter knew that he wasn't fooling Jo, but hoped that Kenzi wouldn't realise what he really felt.

"S'no burden at all. I need help. Kenzi needs a job. Win-win. B'sides, it'll give us girls a chance to get to know each other better, which I'm sure your mother would have liked." Jo played the dead-mother card well on Peter, knowing that would finalise the discussion right away.

"All right then, Jo," said Olivia, "But don't you go easy on Kenzi, you make sure she does her job right."

"Why, my dear, when have you ever known me to 'go easy' on anyone?" replied Jo with a very cheeky smile on her face. Everyone chuckled a little and went back to eating and talking about stuff that didn't really mean anything to Kenzi. Kenzi didn't say much else for the rest of the night. Her mind was racing with all the things she wanted to ask Jo about her Grandmother, but she knew they would have to wait for now.

Chapter 07
"Surely there's got to be something good going on in your life at the moment."

Another uneventful day at school quickly led to Kenzi's appointment with Mrs Fox. Kenzi sat in the chair in the middle of the room, directly opposite Mrs Fox's and stared blankly at her. God, Kenzi hated being there. She looked at the woman. That didn't feel like an appropriate term to describe her, seeing how she couldn't have been much older than twenty-five. She couldn't have been out of college long at all and really didn't look like she'd had any sort of 'trouble' in her life that made her qualified to help others deal with theirs, especially someone like Kenzi.

Kenzi didn't like being here at the best of times, but after the last session, Kenzi was feeling especially frustrated. Kenzi hated talking about when she tried to kill herself, with anyone, especially strangers. But the one thing she hated to talk about more was why she did it. She couldn't do that. Not with a stranger. Not Jo. Not anyone. Not even her parents.

Before she had tried to kill herself, she had tried to talk about it all with her parents, but that never really worked. No one really knew how to talk about it. How could they? It was just so bad. So she didn't. And then it got worse.

And that's how she got here. In this room. With this stranger. Talking about all the things that were too hard to talk about.

Kenzi slouched further into the chair, and the cushion hissed slightly beneath her as she leaned back, arms folded tightly across her chest. She thought how great it would be if she could just slouch entirely into the chair and not have to talk to Mrs Fox again.

The office always felt too still, as if it had been staged rather than lived in. The blinds were tilted half-shut, slats of sunlight striping the beige carpet like prison bars. A faint hum from the old fluorescent tubes pressed against the quiet, interrupted only by the occasional click of the air conditioner sputtering to life. A dusty plant sat in the corner, its leaves glossy in the way that made Kenzi certain it was fake. Everything about the room seemed designed to feel safe, but instead it reminded her of a waiting room for something worse. Fluorescent lights buzzed overhead with a quiet insistence, and the walls—too beige, too bare—seemed to shrink in closer with each second.

"I've given our last talk a lot of thought, Kenzi," she stared, "and I want to apologise for how tough I was on you. I know you're dealing with a lot, and I want to try to be more sensitive about how you're feeling."

Kenzi was caught a little off-guard. She had expected this session to be as frustrating as the last. She still wasn't ready to engage too much.

"Um, it's ok, I'm over it already." Kenzi wasn't really over it, but she was going to take the opportunity to move on. Mrs Fox didn't buy what Kenzi was saying for a second, but wasn't going to push the issue any further.

"That's good to hear. Now, while it would be good for you to talk about what...happened before your accident," Mrs Fox was choosing her words very carefully, "I think I'd much rather find out what you would like to talk about."

Kenzi was surprised again. And maybe a little intrigued. Anytime someone had spoken to her about all the...stuff that happened, they tended to ask annoying and probing questions, trying to uncover some sort of buried truth that, once spoken aloud, would make everything better. It had been a long time since anyone asked Kenzi what she wanted to talk about.

"Um, what ah, what do you mean?"

Mrs Fox got up from her chair, slowly walked around to the front of her desk. Her movements were careful, deliberate, designed to disarm. Her shoes clicked softly on the floor, a muted rhythm that filled the space left by silence. Her cardigan slipped from one shoulder as she leaned, revealing a thin wrist and chipped nail polish, the kind of details that made her look less like a professional and more like an ordinary young woman fumbling her way through adulthood. Kenzi's eyes drifted to the desk in front of her. A neat stack of files sat at one corner, edges lined up too carefully, as if order could mask the chaos inside them. A mug of peppermint tea steamed faintly beside them, its aroma almost soothing. The details struck her as ordinary, but not unpleasant, the kind of ordinary you could live with if you had to. When she got around the front of the desk, right in front of Kenzi, she leaned back onto it, just sitting on the edge. It seemed like a move she had rehearsed and used to make the students feel more comfortable. It annoyed Kenzi. But what annoyed Kenzi more was that it actually worked.

"Well, let's not talk about the negative today; let's try to talk about something positive. I know that you're not really happy about moving here, but surely there's got to be something good going on in your life at the moment. Even if it's something really small or insignificant, I want to hear about it." Mrs Fox could immediately see a change in Kenzi - the frown that had been plastered across her face since the day they met was now more of a non-expression. Perhaps her 'idea' could work.

Those words, "I want to hear about it," hit harder than Kenzi expected. Nobody ever asked her that, not her parents, not teachers, not even Jo yet. Usually, the grown-ups came armed with their shovels, digging for reasons, explanations, apologies. But this was... different. She felt a flicker of suspicion, like maybe it was a trick.

Still, the tiniest part of her — the part she didn't admit existed — leaned toward the idea that perhaps she could actually choose what mattered. The thought startled her, like spotting a light on in a house you thought was empty.

Lately, it's been hard for Kenzi to think of anything good in her life. But not now. It was easy to pick.

"Oh, ok. Well, I got a job."

"A job?" Mrs Fox could barely hide her surprise. "That's great! Where?"

"Jo's Books."

As Kenzi spoke, she noticed the clouds outside shift slightly, revealing the sun behind them. Sunlight slipped through a gap in the blinds, laying a pale stripe across the floor between them. Dust motes hovered lazily in the light, suspended like they had nowhere urgent to be. For the first time since she walked in, Kenzi noticed the quiet as something softer than suffocating.

Mrs Fox's first reaction was shock. She had been to Jo's Books before, and it didn't really seem like the kind of place where a teenager would like to work. Still, she could just see the smile starting to appear on Kenzi's face, so she figured either Kenzi was really into reading or there was some other reason she wanted to work there.

"I know the place. I've bought a few books from Jo." Mrs Fox could see that this might be a topic Kenzi kept talking about, so she kept prodding.

"I didn't realise you were that into books?"

"I'm not, not really." Kenzi was starting to lose interest again. If Kenzi wasn't really into books, Mrs Fox decided there was another reason why she wanted to work there. The only other thing about that place was the lady who runs it, Jo.

"Ah, well," she paused a little, making sure to take particular notice of Kenzi's reaction to her next statement, "Jo's great, isn't she?"

"Yeah, she's really cool." Kenzi started to smile again, "Did you know she knew my Grandmother? They were best friends."

That was it. That was why Kenzi wanted to work there. Mrs Fox knew that Kenzi's Grandmother lived in Esperance, but didn't really know much else about her. If Jo was, in fact, best friends with Kenzi's Grandmother, and this was something that interested Kenzi, Mrs Fox knew it was something worth encouraging.

"Really? I didn't know. Were you two close? You and your Grandmother?"

"No, uh, I don't even remember her very much. We didn't really get a chance to visit her that much before she, ah, before she died."

Kenzi was sitting up straight in her chair, even leaning forward a bit.

"I'm sorry to hear that."

"Yeah. I think my Dad really misses her. I mean, he doesn't talk about her, but ah, but Jo said they were really close; it was just the two of them when he grew up.

Turns out I'm actually named after her, in a way, her maiden name was Mackenzie."

It was probably the longest sentence that Kenzi had said in any of her sessions with Mrs Fox. She had finally found something that Kenzi was willing to open up about.

"I look just like her, too. Jo says I'm a spitting image of Mac. That's what people used to call her."

Usually, Kenzi would go out of her way to look grumpy during these sessions, but she couldn't hide the smile she was starting to wear whenever she talked about her Grandmother or Jo.

"Wow, Kenzi, that's really cool. It sounds like talking to Jo about your Grandmother is helping you to feel more connected to her, which is great to see. Do you know anything else about her?"

"Nah. But Jo said she'd tell me about her. I think that's actually why she gave me the job. I think she misses her, too."

Kenzi's hand drifted to the leather band around her wrist, tracing the worn edges with her thumb. She tried to imagine Mac wearing something like it, but the image wouldn't come to mind. What she could picture, though, was the photo in the hallway at home, her grandmother perched on the rooftop with that stupidly big book, her smile wide and fearless. Kenzi felt a strange mixture of pride and hollowness. If Jo was right, and she was really the "spitting image," then why didn't she feel any of that same fire? The thought tightened her chest, equal parts comfort and accusation.

"That's great. I'm really happy for you, Kenzi. You'll have to tell me all about her next time we meet." Mrs Fox thought she might be reaching a bit too far. Yes, it was a good session today, the best they'd had, but she knew it could turn at any minute.

"Thanks. You bet." It didn't turn. The two just sort of sat there, looking at each other with somewhat goofy looks on their faces for a moment. Kenzi noticed the poster behind Mrs Fox's desk again. She'd rolled her eyes at it at the start, but now, the faded colours didn't look quite so ridiculous. The sunrise didn't feel like it was laughing at her anymore. If anything, it looked patient — like it could wait as long as it needed to. The hum of the lights was still there, but it blended into the background now, less a buzz in her skull and more a steady white noise she could almost rest against.

Luckily, before the moment could turn awkward, the bell rang.

"Well, I guess that's it for today. See you next time, Kenzi."

"Yeah, see ya," said Kenzi as she walked out the door. It was the first time she really said goodbye to Mrs Fox, a fact that she picked up on.

Chapter 08
"Nothing stays golden forever."

The bell above the door jingled as Kenzi stepped into the shop, her eyes adjusting to the dimmer, cozier lighting. The scent of old pages, lavender, and something faintly citrusy wrapped around her. Dust motes danced lazily in shafts of light from the front window, and the creaking floorboards underfoot added to the place's strange sense of stillness. It felt like stepping into a memory.

The whole space felt like it existed in its own pocket of time—dusty yet cared for, like someone had loved it in the quietest way for decades. A tapestry of mismatched rugs softened the wooden floor, and mismatched lamps cast little pools of amber light in the corners. It was the kind of place where you whispered without meaning to.

Jo sat behind the counter, feet up on an old fruit crate, flipping through a battered copy of something literary and long-winded. The sunlight caught in her short, grey curls, making them look almost silver. Stacks of books surrounded her like a fort, and a chipped mug of something that smelled faintly herbal steamed beside her.

The pages of the novel in her hand moved slowly, like she was rereading a part she already knew by heart.

"Look what the cat dragged in," Jo said without looking up.

Kenzi managed a smile. "You said I start today, right?"

"That I did. You're lucky, it's quiet. Gives me time to train you without actually training you."

Jo waved a hand toward the back. "Shelves are sorted by vibe more than logic. You'll figure it out. You alphabetise something too strictly, and the regulars get twitchy."

Kenzi raised an eyebrow. "What kind of bookstore is this?"

"The kind that knows books aren't the only things people are here to find."

There was something cryptic and comforting in Jo's tone, like she was talking about more than just the shop. Kenzi felt it settle in her chest like a puzzle piece she didn't know was missing. That made Kenzi pause, but she didn't respond.

Instead, she wandered through the narrow aisles. The bookshelves loomed high, some crammed with novels stacked two rows deep, others displaying handwritten notes about customer favourites. There were throw blankets tucked in corners, mismatched chairs for reading, and the occasional teacup perched on a shelf like a forgotten relic. She ran a hand along the spines—some cracked and brittle, others slick with laminated covers from decades past. Her fingers lingered on a copy of To Kill a Mockingbird that looked like it had survived a hundred readings. There was comfort in that. A quietness. This wasn't a regular job, and Jo definitely wasn't a normal boss. But something about the place felt grounding. She couldn't explain it, like the walls hummed softly with memory.

"Mac used to get that look," Jo said, suddenly beside her.

Kenzi jumped. "Sorry?"

"Your Gran. Mac. Especially when you're focused like that. Same set to the mouth, same fire in the eyes." Kenzi blinked. She didn't know how to feel about that. She hadn't been called fiery in a long time.

"I don't really remember her that much. I guess when we moved to Brisbane, it got hard for us to visit as much, so I didn't get to know her, and now, I never will."

Jo smiled fondly. "Well, that's why you're here now, ain't it? I can tell you anything you want to know about, Mac." It was so strange for Kenzi to hear someone call her Grandmother "Mac." She was always just "Gran." She couldn't help but smile, which Jo took as a sign to keep talking.

"She was my person, back in the day. We were inseparable. She was the clever one, I was the loud one. I got us into trouble, and Mac talked her way out of it. She made everything feel possible."

She chuckled and sat down on a different crate. Kenzi would have thought it was strange to have so many crates randomly placed around a bookstore. Somehow, it seemed to match Jo's personality perfectly. Jo gestured for Kenzi to sit, too. Kenzi hesitated, looked around for a nearby crate, but they were all out of reach, so she just lowered herself to the floor, back against the bookshelf. The wood was cool through her hoodie. She rested her hands on the floor, palm down, to steady herself a little, and could feel the dust on the ground. It didn't seem dirty, just aged, which was a little comforting.

Kenzi couldn't think of the last time she just sat on the ground, especially in public. It seemed so childish. Like something Lucas would do: get dirty, then whinge about it, and then their Mother would have to comfort him. So annoying. But, like a lot of things lately, it didn't feel that way, not here, not with Jo. She seemed to have this infectious energy about herself. Like, it wouldn't really matter what she asked of Kenzi; she would probably just do it. It sounded like it might have been that way for her Grandmother, too. From what she had heard about her Grandmother, she was brilliant, and that certainly matched the picture of her in the hallway at home. Kenzi could see how Jo might have gotten them into trouble, which actually sounded fun.

"You want to hear something funny? We were a bit of a gang, really. Me, Mac, Tom, Quinn, who you met the other night, and Trevor, your grandad. Esperance felt too small for all that energy. Mac was the dreamer, quiet, but sharp as hell. She wanted to be an engineer, a physicist, or something, some kind of brainiac. Tom was charming, cheeky as anything. Always had grease under his nails from working at Trevor's Dad's garage. His dark hair had a permanent cowlick, and he never seemed to own a shirt without a smear of oil across the chest. He was the type of boy who grinned too easily, like he knew every secret but refused to keep any. Trevor, your Grandad, was solid. Loyal. The kind of guy who didn't say much, but when he did, you listened. And Quinn, Quinn was the one who made us all laugh. He had this way of making the hardest things feel like they weren't so bad."

Jo wasn't looking at Kenzi anymore; she was staring out the window, as if she was watching her memories play on an old-school projector. Kenzi glanced out the window, too. The sunlight had faded to a softer gold, and the shop felt even more removed from the outside world. She imagined the five of them—Mac with her notebooks, Jo with her grin, Tom with his dirty hands, Quinn with his jokes, Trevor steady beside them. Ghosts of youth echoed in the same air she breathed.

It made Kenzi think of her life before it all went wrong. How nice it was to just be around people you cared about. It was bittersweet.

"We were kids, but we thought we had it all figured out. Used to sit on the roof of the garage with a couple of stolen beers, talking about the future like it was a movie we were about to walk into. Mac always talked about getting out, going to college, and changing the world. We all had our own dreams, but out of everyone, I also thought that Mac would make 'em come true."

Kenzi's gaze switched back from the window to Jo, wholly caught up in the story.

"She just had this way about her. Like, when she said she was going to do somethin', you just knew she would. Mind you, it wasn't always for the best; she messed up just as much as the rest of us. But she always owned it. Learned from it. Never stopped going forward."

Kenzi tried to picture her Grandmother at that age, but all her memories of her were from when she was younger. She didn't remember much, but her Grandmother always just seemed like a regular old lady, nothing really remarkable or driven about her at all. But she had raised Kenzi's father pretty much all by herself, so she must have been pretty capable. She would have had to have been.

Kenzi couldn't help but think of her father now. How it was so similar to the way that Jo described Mac. When he got his mind on something, he saw it through. Kenzi had never really been that way herself. Not that she was flaky or unreliable, just not as driven, even with her school work. She always did her best and did well, but it didn't feel the same. She'd never really felt that drive. Definitely not in the last few years, that's for sure.

Kenzi's attention was pulled back as Jo continued.

"It was such a wonderful time when we were all young. Before life had really thrown anything bad at us. We were so naive. I never thought those times would end, ya know?"

Jo looked away from the window for a moment, blinking a little too fast.

"Of course, it did end. Nothing stays golden forever. But those days—they still shine, even if the edges are a bit worn."

It had been a while since anyone had shared such a genuine sentiment with Kenzi. Everyone's well-wishes and pleasantries had felt so forced and insincere. But this moment here, it was real. It was so comforting to hear about her Grandmother, it made her feel close to her, a feeling Kenzi hadn't realised she had missed so much. If she had any doubts about agreeing to work with Jo, they were all gone now. This was where she needed to be now.

Kenzi nodded slowly. "You really loved her."

Jo smiled, eyes misty but steady. "Still do."

Kenzi crossed her arms in a kind of self-hug. She could feel the roughness of her leather band pressing against her arm, reminding her it was there.

Jo reached out towards Kenzi and gently placed a hand on her knee. Kenzi didn't generally like being touched by others, but this was nice. She looked up at Jo and smiled.

"I'm really glad you're here, Kenzi." Her words seemed to float across the room and wrap around Kenzi, warming her even more. Kenzi closed her eyes briefly, basking in the feeling. She opened them and smiled at Jo.

'Thanks, Jo. I'm really glad I'm here, too."

The two sat there in the moment, both basking in the warmth of better times.

The rest of the day passed in a dreamlike rhythm. Customers trickled in, and Jo floated between sales and storytelling. Kenzi learned to wrap books in brown paper, ring up the ancient till, and stack new arrivals without toppling a leaning tower of cookbooks. The weight on her chest didn't lift, not entirely, but for the first time in a while, she didn't feel crushed by it either. And then, just as she was shelving a stack of worn-out paperbacks in the quiet of the far aisle, she felt it.

A chill.

Subtle but sharp.

Like someone had walked over her grave. Just like when she first met Jo. Again, she felt as though someone was right next to her. She turned. No one was there. But for a second, the air had smelled different, like engine grease and bonfire smoke. Kenzi rubbed her arms through the sleeves of her hoodie, trying to trap some warmth against her skin. As she released herself, she held her leather band tight in her hand, rubbing its rough texture. She felt her heart steady. Touching the band always seemed to calm her.

"You ok?" Jo called from behind the counter.

Kenzi nodded slowly. "Yeah. Thought I heard something."

Jo didn't respond, but she watched her a little longer than necessary. Then she returned to her book. Kenzi turned back to the shelf—but her eyes kept flicking toward the back room. Toward the scent that was gone now. As if it had never been there at all.

Chapter 09
"She smiled."

Kenzi kicked off her shoes by the door, shrugged off her hoodie, and hung it on the stand in the entrance hall. The overhead light flickered a little, casting warm shadows across the polished wooden floor. Kenzi lingered for a moment in the living room, alone. She could see the rest of her family in the dining room. It looked a little chaotic, but that was always the case with Lucas.

She knew that she had stayed later at Jo's than she had planned, but she hadn't realised how late it had gotten. It must have been dinner time, as the house smelled like roasted vegetables and something vaguely burnt. The warmth from the oven had filled the rest of the house, and it wrapped around Kenzi like an unwelcome hug. Kenzi knew she would have to head straight into the dining room to join the rest of her family for dinner. Normally, she would have plenty of time alone after school before having to play family, but not today.

Kenzi took a deep breath and headed towards the dining room. Even though she had taken her shoes off, her footsteps were still heavy and loud on the wooden floor. Although they had been there for over a month now, Kenzi still hadn't gotten used to how different the house was. It reminded Kenzi that although some things were starting to feel better now that she was here in Esperance, it still wasn't home.

As Kenzi got closer to the dining room, she could hear her Mum and Dad talking. Hearing her Dad's voice without seeing him played tricks on Kenzi, reminding her of a time long passed. Kenzi felt sad and happy at the same time. She pushed on to join them all.

The table was cluttered with crayons, a stack of folded laundry, and a mostly empty cup of apple juice with a toddler-sized bite mark on the rim. It was a large table, not surprisingly, made out of wood. Even with all the stuff that shouldn't really be on a dinner table on it, there was still plenty of room for the four of them to eat without it feeling cramped.

Olivia sat at the table with Lucas in her lap, helping him maneuver a bright green spoon into his mouth half-successfully. A few peas lay scattered across the floor like confetti. His bib hung crooked, half-soaked with juice, and his spoon made more contact with the table than the plate. Each victory bite left a smear of potato across his chin, which he wore proudly like war paint. Kenzi could see her Dad in the kitchen through the open doorway that connected the two rooms. He stood at the stove, poking at something in a frying pan with intense focus. Steam curled above the baking dish like smoke signals, and the scent of thyme clung to the walls as if trying to make itself at home. The kitchen window was fogged with condensation, glowing golden under the overhead light.

Even though her Dad worked full-time, it wasn't unusual for him to cook dinner. He and Kenzi's mother had always shared most of the household chores. Kenzi had never really given it much thought; it had just always been that way. She knew that it was probably a bit strange that he did so much; a lot of her former friends' dads never really seemed to help out as much. Having a greater understanding of her dad's childhood, Kenzi wondered if being raised by a single mother had instilled those habits in her father. She pictured him as a teenager, having to help out around the house more than his friends did, since both parents were there. She was starting to gain a bigger appreciation for how much her parents were probably shaped by their childhood, and wondered how the last few years had shaped her.

Olivia looked up from the plate of food that she was struggling to get Lucas to eat to see her daughter entering the room. She was keen to find out how her first day working with Jo went, but didn't want to be too pushy.

"You're home late," Olivia said without looking up.

Kenzi shrugged as she pulled her chair out to sit down. "I stayed after to help Jo shelve some stuff."

Olivia smiled faintly, passing a napkin to Lucas. "She always manages to rope people into that."

"She's kinda cool," Kenzi said, sliding into the chair across from her Mum. She knew she would have to give her parents a rundown about her first day, but she wasn't really ready to share too much with them. They no longer had that kind of relationship.

"Old, but not annoying-old. She was telling me a bit about Gran." Kenzi was trying hard not to give out too much, just enough to move the conversation forward.

Peter looked over his shoulder and gave a nod. "Yeah, those two were thick as thieves. Jo's good people."

Kenzi paused, then added, "It's weird in there. Cozy. Smells like paper and dust and lemon or something. And Jo talks a lot, but it's not annoying. It's kinda nice."

Peter came over with a plate and set it in front of her before sitting down. The food was a bit uneven, some charred carrots, a generous helping of mashed potatoes, and a piece of chicken that had seen better days, but Kenzi didn't mind.

Olivia reached across the table and gave Kenzi's hand a slight squeeze. Her fingers were warm, calloused at the tips.

"It's good to see you settling in a bit," she said softly.

Kenzi pulled her hand away and shrugged off her Mother's attempt at familiarity. She still wasn't ready for any of that sort of thing. She was still too mad. Lucas banged his spoon against the table, delighted, which caused enough of a distraction for everyone to move on.

Peter cleared his throat. "Well. Since you've got yourself a job now,... I figured it might be time."

He stood and left the room. A second later, Kenzi heard the jangle of keys. When he came back, he held them out to her. They were old-looking. Stained and worn from what looked like a lifetime of use.

"What's this?"

"Your grandfather's truck," Peter said. "It's old. Needs work. You'll need to put in some time—and probably money—to get it reliable. But I figured, with a bit of love, it could be yours."

Kenzi stared at the keys. Although Kenzi had gotten her licence over a year ago, there had never been any talk with her parents about her getting a car, especially after what happened.

"You're giving me a truck?"

Peter grinned. "I'm giving you a project."

Olivia chuckled softly. "Your Dad's being sentimental. That thing's ancient."

Kenzi took the keys slowly, the cool metal settling into her palm. Something about it felt weighty. Real. Like a piece of the past had been handed to her—not the broken kind she usually tried to avoid, but something worth holding on to. Kenzi wasn't sure if this was some sort of attempt on her parents' behalf to curry favour with her, or if it was more of her Dad's efforts to get her out of the house, but it didn't matter.

Kenzi knew that the end of senior year was in sight, and then it would be time for college, which brought with it a whole bunch of things that had to be planned, her own car being one of them. This was a good first step. This was maybe a starting point for something new.

Lucas burbled something incomprehensible and clapped his hands. Olivia smiled and kissed his head, but her eyes drifted back to Kenzi. They were soft. Hopeful, even. For the first time in a long time, dinner didn't feel like an endurance test. It felt almost normal.

Later that night, the house had quieted. The dishes were done, Lucas was asleep, and the living room lights had dimmed to a soft glow. Kenzi had gone upstairs after dinner with a mumble about homework and shut her door. Olivia curled up in the corner of the couch, legs tucked under her. Peter joined her, his arm draped casually over the back of the couch.

"She talked about Jo," Olivia said quietly, as if saying it too loudly might undo the moment.

Peter nodded. "I noticed."

"She seemed... lighter," Olivia added. "Like there's room in her for something else now. Even just a little."

Peter didn't say anything right away. He stared across the room at the darkened hallway. "It's the first time she's said more than ten words at the dinner table in months."

"She smiled," Olivia said, voice cracking slightly.

"I know."

They sat in silence for a long moment. Not because they had nothing to say, but because the quiet felt full for once.

Peter leaned forward, rubbing his hands together. "I really hope she can keep this up, even if it's just small steps. Jo... Jo's good for her."

"She's helping," Olivia whispered. "And that truck... that might give her something to pour herself into."

Peter nodded. "That's the plan."

Peter turned back to look at his wife, her face dimly lit by the buzzing fluorescents above. Her hair was out, and there was a bit of food, no doubt from Lucas, stuck in it. Peter didn't mention it-it was cute.

"We've all been in a spin for so long, and it has cost us all so much. I don't want to jinx it, but it's starting to finally feel like things might be getting back to normal."

Olivia could tell everything was weighing on her husband. Even though he had an enthusiastic tone, she could feel the sadness and doubt. He had been the one who got them through all the mess, she knew that. They had always been able to lean on each other for strength throughout their relationship. The last few years had

been too much for Olivia to handle, and she was all too
aware that Peter had carried the large majority of the load
for them both. His strength had only made her love him
more, but she knew what he had given up.

Olivia took Peter's hand in hers, gently caressing
it.

"You got us here, Peter."

"*We* got us here, Olive."

Olivia disagreed with her husband, but the
sentiment still felt good. She leaned forward and kissed
him softly on his lips. She slowly pulled away, stood up,
still holding his hand in hers, and led him up the stairs.

Kenzi was in her room, lying on her bed. She
heard her parents' footsteps as they made their way down
the hallway to their room. The whole house seemed to go
to sleep around her now, but she wasn't ready yet. She
held the keys in her hand, dangling them above her head.
As they slowly turned, they reflected the moonlight that
snuck in through her curtains.

Although her Dad had referred to the truck as
belonging to her Grandad, Kenzi thought that her Gran
probably drove it more than anyone. Kenzi found herself
wanting to be closer to her Gran, and although hearing Jo
talk about her was great, having this real, tangible thing
felt good. It was a connection to her past, and maybe a
link to her future. She gently placed the keys on her
bedside table, next to the photo of her brother. She

looked at them both until her eyelids grew too heavy, and she drifted off to sleep.

Chapter 10
"It might not feel that way right now…"

Another week had passed. Kenzi had been spending most afternoons with Jo, listening to stories about her Grandmother, and she was starting to feel closer to her than she ever had. She had heard about the time Mac had tried to jump a small creek on her pushbike but ended up totally soaked and lost the bike. And how Mac had made her own prom dress from scratch, and how proud she was walking into the dance hall, twirling around in front of everyone. And she remembered the stray dog she had adopted in middle school, and how she would sneak it into school in her backpack, and how, even though it was old and matted, she loved it so much.

The stories were nice. Calming. Inspiring. Breathing a little bit of life back into Kenzi. It was starting to make everything just a little easier. In fact, it was the first time she had made it to her appointment with Mrs Fox on time.

The school office was too bright. The kind of fluorescent lighting that made everything look a little sickly. Kenzi sat in the overstuffed chair opposite Mrs Fox's desk, chewing on the inside of her cheek. Her backpack was slung at her feet, her hoodie sleeves pushed over her knuckles. The windows rattled faintly whenever a door slammed somewhere down the hall, the kind of vibration that reminded her the building was older than it looked. A wilted fern drooped in the corner, its leaves coated in a faint layer of dust, as if it had given up years ago. Kenzi thought it looked how she usually felt—still alive, but only just.

The fluorescent lights buzzed overhead like impatient bees, and the plastic chairs along the wall stuck slightly to the backs of students' thighs. The scent of dry ink and disinfectant hovered thickly in the air, making it feel more sterile than safe. A dusty stack of forms sat untouched on the counter, and the faint smell of hand sanitiser lingered in the air. Somewhere down the corridor, a locker slammed, and muffled laughter echoed briefly before disappearing again.

Mrs Fox, in her usual knit cardigan and flower-print blouse, tapped a few keys on her computer and then turned, giving Kenzi her full attention. The cardigan was the same mustard-yellow one from last week, its elbows gently worn and its sleeves pilled. Her glasses sat low on her nose as if she'd been reading for too long. The faint smudge of ink on her thumb betrayed the nervous habit of fiddling with pens, and her hair, though neatly pinned, kept slipping strands forward, softening what might have been a too-serious face. A ceramic mug with a chip in the rim steamed beside the keyboard, smelling faintly of

peppermint tea. She looked up at Kenzi, her smile small
but steady.

Although it had been easier for Kenzi to make it to
the appointment, she was still apprehensive about how it
would go. Yes, it wasn't horrible last time. It had been
nice to talk about Jo with Mrs Fox. It was probably easier
to talk to her than to her parents about it. No, not easier,
just less pressure. Kenzi's parents had been so worried
about her that every conversation since moving to
Esperance felt like a sort of test to prove that things were
ok, so she had purposely not given them too much
information, just in case she said the wrong thing, and
they felt the need to get more involved in her life. She was
content with the space that was between them now. Still,
sometimes the space felt less like breathing room and
more like an ocean she'd been left floating in alone. Jo's
stories were like little buoys scattered across it, things she
could grab hold of for a while before the water threatened
to pull her under again. Talking to Mrs Fox about it,
hadn't carried that same weight.

All that aside, Kenzi still expected this session to
go differently and for Mrs Fox to ask the same sort of
probing, uncomfortable questions she had in the past.
She could tell that Mrs Fox was about to start talking, and
she gripped the end of the armrest tightly in anticipation.

"So, how's it been going at the bookshop?" she
said, tone light. Kenzi released her grip slightly.

Kenzi nodded. "Yeah, ok. Just shelving books and stuff."

"That's great. Jo's a good woman. She was very close to your Grandmother, right?"

Kenzi's eyes didn't lift from the corner of the desk, but her shoulders weren't as tense. It seemed like she was safe from the uncomfortable talk, at least for now.

"Yeah, she was really close with her. I think that's why she gave me the job; I remind her so much of her. She's been telling me stories about when they were younger."

Mrs Fox smiled. "Sometimes people who knew our loved ones differently can help us see them differently, too. It's important to remember. And it's important to find new ways to connect, even with what's gone."

Kenzi nodded slowly. She didn't speak, but her fingers picked absently at a loose thread on the cuff of her jumper. Her shoulders were hunched slightly, as though bracing against a cold breeze only she could feel. For once, she didn't feel like leaving immediately.

That was new.

Kenzi looked up at Mrs Fox, who was looking back at her. Not staring, but just looking. Waiting. Kenzi expected her to ask another question, but she didn't. She just sat there, looking, but not in a judging way, just in a patient way. As if she were giving Kenzi permission to say more if she wanted to. Kenzi had heard many stories about Mac from Jo over the past week, and they had all made her grandmother come to life. More alive than Kenzi ever thought of her. As she leaned more, she felt closer, especially as Jo regularly commented on how much Kenzi reminded her of Mac. Kenzi still didn't believe it too much. Mac seemed so full of life. Like she really lived it to the fullest. That seemed the furthest thing from Kenzi right now.

Kenzi's thoughts drifted with the hum of the overhead lights, each memory of Jo's stories flickering like old film reels. She could almost smell the grease of that creek water, the starch of the handmade prom dress, the damp fur of the dog. The images weren't hers, but they played in her mind with startling clarity, like she'd borrowed Mac's memories for just a moment. One story in particular came to mind for Kenzi, and she couldn't help but share it.

"She got arrested once, Mac, er, my Gran." It was still a bit weird saying 'Mac' out loud, at least to people other than Jo. Mrs Fox leaned forward, looking intrigued by Kenzi's statement.

"Yeah?"

"Yeah, it was at one of the protests back in the 70s, for women's rights." Kenzi could feel herself sitting up straight in the chair, much less tense. "Jo had a cutout from the newspaper at the time. She and Gran, and a bunch of other women, were all chained up outside the town hall. She said that Gran had organised the whole thing. The police broke it up pretty quickly, and they all spent the night in jail, but there weren't any real charges."

"Wow," was all that Mrs Fox responded. Kenzi noticed that she wasn't saying much, but it was nice, like she was actually listening to her story. Kenzi waited for the usual follow-up question, the one that would prod at her until she shut down again. But it never came. Instead, Mrs Fox just looked at her like the story itself mattered. Kenzi realised, with a slight jolt, that maybe not every adult was waiting to dissect her; perhaps some just wanted to hear her.

"Jo said they did that kind of stuff a fair bit. That Gran really fought hard for that stuff, like she really believed in making things better."

"We all owe women like that a lot. They really made a difference for all of us. It's quite inspiring." Mrs Fox looked away from Kenzi, kind of over her shoulder, looking off into nothing, and took a sip of her tea. Kenzi had thought the same about the story, and it was nice to have someone share that feeling. It caught Kenzi a little off-guard.

"Jo said that she sees the same kind of fire in me, but I don't really believe that." The words stung a little, not because Jo had been wrong, but because Kenzi wanted to believe her. She tried to think there was still something burning inside, not just a pile of ash she kept sifting through. But wanting and believing were different things, and she wasn't ready to close that gap yet. Kenzi adjusted in the chair and tucked her hair behind her ear, looking down away from Mrs Fox, whose gaze had returned to fix on Kenzi.

"Oh, I think she's right, Kenzi. It might not feel that way right now, but I'm sure you'll find something that you believe in."

Kenzi didn't look up; she just kept looking down at her hands in her lap. She didn't believe it. There was nothing she cared about that much. Well, she cared about learning more about Mac, and she had the car to work on, but those were personal things, just for her. She really couldn't see herself being passionate about something bigger than that anytime soon. A breeze slipped through the open window, rattling the blinds and carrying in the faint scent of cut grass from the oval outside. It clashed with the sterile smell of disinfectant inside, two worlds pressing against each other. For a second, Kenzi let herself imagine choosing the fresher one, the one that felt alive.

"Either way, thank you for sharing that story with me, Kenzi."

Kenzi looked up at Mrs Fox, who was smiling at her. It felt genuine.

Before she could respond, the bell rang. Kenzi glanced at the clock, surprised at how much time had passed. Usually, every second in this room dragged, heavy as wet clothes. Today, it had slipped through her fingers. That was new, too—and she wasn't sure if she was ready to admit she didn't hate it. Usually, the bell sounded like a starting horn, a signal to flee the room as fast as possible. But today, it was different. It reminded her of the sound a soda makes when it opens: a slight hiss of pressure escaping, a little release.

Kenzi didn't say anything. She just smiled, picked up her bag, and slung it over her shoulder as she walked out the door.

It felt lighter.

Just a little.

Chapter 11
"There's only so much loss someone can take."

Later that afternoon, Kenzi stepped into the bookstore, the bell above the door jangling its usual offbeat chime. The door gave its familiar groan on the hinge, and the warm scent of paper and cinnamon met her like a welcome back hug. Dust motes danced lazily in the light slicing through the high front windows. Jo was perched on her usual crate behind the counter, reading glasses sliding down her nose.

"There she is," Jo said, not looking up. "The shelves missed you."

Kenzi rolled her eyes but smiled. "Long day. Your books better behave."

Jo waved a hand. "Books are easier than people. Even the messy ones."

Jo adjusted her glasses with the back of her hand, smudging a faint dust streak on her cheek. Her cardigan, stretched and faded at the elbows, hung loosely around her frame, but there was nothing frail about her. She perched on that crate like it was a throne, eyes glinting with the kind of sharpness that missed nothing.

The shop was quiet, the kind of quiet that felt full rather than empty. Kenzi slipped into her routine—stacking returns, sorting through a new box of paperbacks, straightening displays. Each creak of the floorboards seemed to say, 'You're home.' The whirr of a tiny desk fan hummed in the background, and the occasional rustle of pages broke the silence in all the right ways. Jo didn't interrupt much, letting the silence stretch out between them like an old blanket.

Jo was happy that Kenzi was spending time in the shop, while she was just sitting alone in her room all afternoon. Still, Jo had only offered the job as an excuse to talk to Kenzi about...everything. She had seen Kenzi starting to light up a bit over the last week or so, especially when she shared stories about Mac, but Jo had done most of the talking, and she really wanted Kenzi to start opening up about herself. Before Mac had passed, she and Jo shared everything, always had, so she knew pretty much everything about what Peter's family had been through over the last few years. Jo had a pretty good idea about why Kenzi had tried to hurt herself, but could still see the weight of everything hanging hard over Kenzi and that she still needed to deal with it all.

Jo felt a responsibility towards Kenzi. Mac had always been there for Jo, and now, this young woman who reminded her so much of her friend was here and clearly needed help, so she was going to do what she could.

"I haven't told you much about Tom, have I?" said Jo, breaking the silence in the shop.

Kenzi blinked, startled. "Uh. No, not really. He was one of you and Mac's friends when you were younger, right?" She had gotten more comfortable referring to her Grandmother as Mac since learning more about her. She had always been a bit of a mystery to Kenzi, and she never really paid much thought to her, but now she was becoming this *real* person, someone she wanted to know more about.

"Yeah, he was. Actually, he was more than just a friend to me. We were in love," replied Jo, who was leaning back in her chair, smiling as she looked off into nowhere.

"Wait? But I thought you and Quinn had been together forever?"

"Ha! Feels like that sometimes. That man is the love of my life, but in the beginning, he was just Quinn, and at that time, Tom and I were it. He had grease on his hands and stars in his eyes. Worked at the garage with Trevor, but always dreamed bigger. He made everything feel like it had a purpose, even the boring stuff."

Jo's voice softened. "We were gonna leave Esperance. Make something of ourselves. Then, one night, he was just... gone. Car accident. One of those blink and it's over things. No warning. No goodbye."

Kenzi didn't move. Her hands rested on a half-shelved book, her chest suddenly tight.

"I thought I'd break," Jo said. "But Quinn pulled me through. He'd been Tom's best friend. Somehow, in helping each other with our grief, we found each other, and we've been together ever since."

Kenzi swallowed hard. Her eyes burned, but she blinked fast. She didn't want to cry. Not here. Jo could see that she was starting to get to Kenzi. She just had to push a bit further.

"But that loss of someone who meant so much never really goes away," Jo said, her voice almost a whisper now. "You just learn how to carry it."

Kenzi couldn't speak. The air in the shop felt thinner somehow. Her throat ached with something old and sharp. Jo didn't press her. She watched for a moment, then said quietly, "It's the sudden ones that cut deepest, I think. The ones you never see coming. Leaves you with all the words you didn't get to say."

That cracked something open.

Kenzi touched her leather band, hoping to draw some strength from it. Kenzi pressed her lips together hard. "My brother," she said, barely louder than a breath. "My *older* brother, Mark. He... he died in a car accident too, just like that. One day, he was there. The next, he wasn't."

It was always hard for Kenzi to talk about Mark. He was her older brother, but they were so close, more like best friends than siblings. He had been gone for over three years now, but it still hurt so much. There was almost nothing left of him in Kenzi's home, especially since they moved to Esperance. She held the leather band tighter now. It was Mark's, and she hadn't taken it off since putting it on when her parents had brought his things home from the morgue.

Jo's face softened even more, and she gave a reassuring nod. Of course, Jo knew about Mark, but she could tell it was hard for Kenzi to talk about him – it was hard for all of them to talk about him.

"I remember him from when you both were much younger. He was so full of life, so much that it filled every room he was in, making everyone happier." Jo could see some tears starting to form in the corner of Kenzi's eyes, but kept going. She knew Kenzi had to talk about it, to feel it. "He loved you so much. That was obvious; he was always talking about how great you were, even at such a young age. I can't imagine what it would have been like for you when you lost him."

Jo's eyes were fixated on Kenzi, watching her every move. She could see that her breath had slowed, like she was trying so hard to keep everything from spilling out.

" I know it broke Mac. She'd already had so much loss, Tom, Trevor, and then to see your Dad go through that with Mark. She was one of the strongest people I knew, but there's only so much loss someone can take, you know?"

Kenzi didn't answer right away. Her throat burned and her eyes blurred, but she held it in. All of it. Just nodded, turned back to the shelf, and tried to remember how to breathe.

Jo could tell that she had gotten everything out of Kenzi that she could right now. But that was ok. She could tell it was hard for Kenzi to even say Mark's name. Jo had spent a lot of time with Kenzi over the last few weeks, and she had never even mentioned Mark, not even hinted that he existed, as if it was too hard to think about. Even when she had visited their home, neither Peter nor Olivia mentioned him, and there were no pictures of him anywhere. It's like the whole family had to pretend that it never happened. It was all they could do to survive.

So, she knew that getting Kenzi to talk about him, even just briefly, was huge. She didn't want to push her any further. She had pried the door open a little; it was up to Kenzi to decide when to open it more.

Jo knew she probably shouldn't say anything else for a while, but she still wanted to be there for Kenzi. She got up from the crate and started to walk over to her, deciding if a hug or just a hand on the shoulder would be enough. As she walked over, she noticed the clock on the wall and remembered she was supposed to be at Kelly's house to watch the kids for the night.

She didn't want to leave Kenzi, not right now, not like this. She was so raw, and Jo wasn't sure if she should be alone right now. But maybe that's what Kenzi needed.

Kenzi's sadness had driven her to hurt herself, and Jo was worried that talking about Mark might bring up similar thoughts. But then she thought about the change she had seen in Kenzi. Hearing about Mac seemed to build her up a bit. She was strong, just like Mac.

She can handle this.

"Oh, look at the time!" Jo's words seemed to snap Kenzi back to reality. "I'm sorry to leave you like this, but I've got to leave early. You ok to lock the place up?"

"Ah, yeah, of course," Kenzi was still reeling a bit from the talk about Mark. She didn't want to talk about it anymore, but that didn't mean she wanted to be alone. Jo wouldn't be leaving now, unless she really had to. That wasn't the kind of person Jo was. She had been so good to her; she didn't want to let Jo down.

"Great, thanks, kid!" Jo said over her shoulder as she darted out the door. Even though she was pretty old, she still moved so quickly that she surprised Kenzi.

As Kenzi went back to work, she couldn't help but think about Mark. She missed him so much, but it was always painful to think about him, so she tried to avoid it. Hearing Jo talk about Tom kind of unlocked a door to the special place in her heart where she kept Mark. It hurt to think about him, but it was a good hurt. Kenzi was lost in her thoughts in the quiet. As she stood there alone, she felt the chill again and then something more.

A whisper. Not words, not exactly. More like the sensation of someone standing right behind Kenzi. A warmth, a breath, the faintest echo of an engine's idle. The hair on her arms stood, and little goosebumps were forming. She thought maybe Jo had come back, but she hadn't heard the bell chime, and she knew no one else was in the store. But she knew she wasn't alone.

"Hey, Mac!" came a voice from behind her.

<h1 style="text-align:center">Chapter 12</h1>

<h2 style="text-align:center">"What the hell just happened?"</h2>

Kenzi spun around fast, heart hammering in her chest. A guy stood near the back of the aisle. Not there a second ago. Young—maybe early twenties—with dark jeans, a tucked-in white T-shirt smudged with oil, and a leather belt worn smooth at the edges. His boots looked like they'd walked through a different decade. His jet black hair was slicked back, but not in a try-hard way. More... classic. Like James Dean stepping out of a black-and-white photo. He looked as startled as she felt. His hands hovered awkwardly near his sides, fingers flexing like he wasn't sure if he should shove them in his pockets or reach for something that wasn't there. For all his James Dean looks, there was a boyish uncertainty to him, a crack in the calm exterior. A jolt shot through her spine like she'd been dropped into ice water. The overhead bulb buzzed softly above, suddenly too loud in the silence. The scent of old paper and wood polish felt denser now, as if the room were closing in around her.

Kenzi stared. Her throat tightened. "Where did you come from?" Kenzi's heart was starting to race. She thought she was all alone in the bookstore, and now some stranger was there. He tilted his head slightly, studying her. "You really do look just like her. The eyes, mostly. But you're younger. And the voice—different."

She took a shaky step back. Her heel scraped against the worn timber floor with a rough squeak. Her hand gripped the edge of a nearby shelf, anchoring herself to something. Her heart was racing now.

"Listen, I'm not sure who you are, or who you think I am, but you need to leave," she said, trying to keep her voice even. "We're closed." The man blinked, then looked around, as if seeing the bookstore for the first time. His expression flickered between recognition and confusion.

"I, I didn't mean to scare you," he said. "It's just... I come here sometimes. Not always on purpose."

His actions didn't make Kenzi feel any better. A minute ago, he was calm and collected, but now he seems a bit unsure and even a little confused. She could tell that he wasn't just going to leave because she asked. There was no point yelling- there was no one around. Kenzi reached for the phone in her pocket without looking away from him. "Ok, that's it. I'm calling the—"

"Tom," he interrupted quickly, raising his hands in surrender. "My name's Tom. I'm not going to hurt you, I promise."

Kenzi paused. She didn't call anyone, but she didn't put her phone away. She just stood there, frozen. There was something about this man. Something strange, yet familiar. There was a weird stillness in the air. The hum of the overhead lights seemed louder than it should be. The smell of grease and smoke that had lingered earlier suddenly returned, stronger now. Not unpleasant. Just... familiar in a way that made her stomach twist. He seemed calm again. Perhaps she could resolve this without calling the police.

"Listen, Mac..." Tom paused for a moment, "Kenzi. I need you to take a breath for me, ok?"

Hearing this stranger use her name should have freaked Kenzi out, but strangely, it didn't. It actually made her feel calm. She relaxed her shoulders and let her hands drop down alongside her body. She still held her phone, but not as tightly. She felt her heart start to slow. This wouldn't be the first strange meeting she had had since moving to Esperance. When she first met Jo, it was almost as weird. Maybe this was just another person she had forgotten.

"Good, now, I have to tell you something, and it's gonna sound weird, but I just need you to keep an open mind, ok?

Kenzi was unsure what was happening, but she no longer felt scared.

"Ok..." she responded.

"I'm Tom. As in *Jo's* Tom."

Kenzi's stomach started to turn again. What did he mean he was Jo's Tom? As in Tom, who Jo used to date when she was younger? That can't be right. Jo's Tom died years ago.

Kenzi wasn't calm anymore. Her heart was pounding in her chest. This was not just some other person she had forgotten. This man was crazy.

"This is a joke, right? Like, you know, I'm the new girl in town, so you thought you'd have a little fun. Dress up in this clichéd '60s get-up, wait for the right moment, and then what? Pretend to be the ghost of the crazy book lady's former boyfriend?"

Tom looked down at his clothes, then back at Kenzi. "Hey! There is nothing cliché about these clothes."

"Whatever!" snapped Kenzi. "Look, you've had your fun, but now you really need to lea-" Kenzi tried to push past Tom, but her hand moved straight through him, and the lack of resistance caused her to trip forward, falling right through him onto the floor. She lay there on the floor for a second, trying to process what had happened. She quickly flipped over, steadying herself with her hands.

"What? What the hell just happened?" Her voice was cracking slightly as her pulse started to race again. Tom crouched slowly, keeping a respectful distance.

"That's what I'm trying to tell you, Mac. I'm a ghost."

His words hung in the air for a moment. A ghost? "Ghosts aren't real," thought Kenzi to herself. There had to be another explanation for what had just happened.

Kenzi quickly jumped up, almost knocking over a shelf as she used it to get leverage. She took a few steps back from Tom.

Kenzi was shaking all over now, like every part of her was desperate to move. To get away. Before Kenzi hurt herself, when she was at her lowest and struggling with her thoughts of depression and suicide, she never felt like she was going crazy. Everything she was feeling at that time made sense to her. She missed her brother so much and couldn't bear the thought of a world without him. So much so that she felt there was no other option for her. But through it all, she always felt in control.

This. What was happening now. Kenzi did not feel in control. She had no idea what was happening to her, and it scared her. Her mind scrambled to make sense of the situation.

"Nope! No way. You're not a ghost. You're...you're a hallucination. Yeah, that's it. I was just talking about Mark, and it was hard, and this is just, just my grief. Yeah, that's it!"

Although she was saying the words out loud, they were more for her benefit. She was trying to convince herself. That made sense. Even after everything that she did when Mark died, and even after that, she must not have dealt with it properly, so that's what must be happening now. This must just be her, her subconscious mind processing everything, albeit in a strange way. That certainly made more sense than a ghost.

Kenzi turned and headed for the door. She wasn't sure she believed what she was saying, but she definitely did not want to be there anymore.

"Mac! Wait!"

She didn't respond or look back as she locked the door and rushed away from the store. It must have just been the grief. Talking about Mark for the first time in a long time must have just triggered something, and Jo had just mentioned Tom, so that must have been why she hallucinated him. He wasn't a ghost. He was just her messed-up mind trying to process. Kenzi walked quickly through the streets, trying not to look too far ahead or at anyone she passed. She just wanted to get home and have a shower.

That would sort her out.

Chapter 13
"Maybe... a friend."

An hour or so had passed since Kenzi left the store. She had made it all the way home, had a shower, and grabbed a snack without any other 'hallucinations.' Luckily, her interactions with her family had been small. No one had picked up on any change in her behaviour or mood, so she must be doing a good job of pretending that her experience in the bookstore didn't happen. That was the easiest thing to do.

She was in a better place recently. Her time spent with Jo, learning about her Grandmother, had been good for Kenzi, and she was starting to feel inspired about life again. Heck, even her meetings with Mrs Fox had been good, which was very hard for Kenzi to admit. Everything must have been going better, she thought, for her to have said Mark's name out loud. She had felt safe at the bookstore with Jo. And Jo obviously already knew about Mark, so that made it easier for Kenzi to talk about him. It was hard to do, but Kenzi felt it was the right time, and it felt good, if only for a moment. Like, somehow, by saying his name, new life had been breathed into his memory, which had definitely faded from the family as of late.

But then that whole thing with Tom happened, and now Kenzi wasn't sure she was really ready to talk about Mark. It was going to be hard to fully deal with it all, she knew that, but hallucinations were way too much for Kenzi to deal with. Maybe if Jo hadn't left, she would have spoken more with her, and that would have been better. Surely she wouldn't hallucinate with other people around. She's messed up, for sure, but not *that* messed up. That was it. That was what Kenzi had to do. Put today behind her, not think about Mark again until she was around other people, like Jo. That should be ok. In fact, she actually wanted to do that with Jo. She had a way of bringing her Grandmother to life with her stories; maybe she could do the same for Mark.

Feeling a bit more sure of herself, Kenzi decided to have a look at the car her Dad had given her. Even though she would be alone in the garage, she would be focused on the truck, and that should be enough. She knew it was old, and her Dad had mentioned it needed some work, but she really had no idea what to expect. She opened the side door to the garage and walked inside. The air inside was heavy with dust and the scent of oil and rusted metal. Shafts of sunlight pierced through the slats of the garage door, highlighting swirling motes in the air like floating secrets. The whole area was quite messy, full of various tools and containers. It was clear that this room hadn't been used for much of anything for many years. In the middle was the car, her car. It looked old- real old. It had been her Grandfather's car, so it had to be at least 50 years old, and it certainly looked that way. As she walked around to the driver's side, she ran her hand along the chassis, leaving a trail in the dust. She opened the door and sat behind the wheel, dust leaping off the bench seat as she sat down. She slid the key into the ignition and tightly closed her eyes as she tried to start it. It made a deep whirring sound as it struggled to turn over.

"Sounds like a problem with the alternator", came a voice from beside Kenzi.

It startled her! She turned to see who was there. It was Tom again.

'I told Trevor that he needed to buy a new one, not use an old, refurbished one."

Kenzi jumped up out of the car and slammed the door. "Nope. Not gonna do this again. You were gone. You were just my brain's weird way of dealing with the stress of talking about Mark, but I'm over that now. I'm good. You can go now." Kenzi waved her hands at Tom, like she was trying to shoo away some birds or critters. It didn't work.

Tom got out of the car and leaned against it, opposite Kenzi. The way he leaned there—boots crossed at the ankle, shoulders relaxed—was unfairly casual. Like he belonged in that garage, like the shadows themselves bent around him. Yet his eyes, when they flicked toward her, carried a softness that unsettled her more than any ghost-story fright could.

"Don't know what to tell you, Mac. I'm no hallucination," Tom said with a wry smile.

"What? You really expect me to believe that you're what? A ghost?"

"Well, yeah. Crazy as it sounds."

"And what? I'm the only one who can see you? Like, like we've got some sort of special connection that means we can talk? Sure, right. That's crazy! I'm crazy! I've finally lost my mind." Kenzi spun around and fell back against the car.

Tom was standing next to her now. "You're not crazy, Mac, and I'm not a hallucination."

Kenzi turned her face to look at Tom. "Isn't that exactly what a hallucination would say?"

"You got me there, Mac." Tom walked away from Kenzi, towards a tool bench against the wall. It seemed like he was looking around for something, but not really sure what. Like he was trying to find some way to make Kenzi believe him.

"Look, all I know is that normally, no one can see or hear me, but I can see and hear them all. I can't normally touch anyone, or anything; I just kind of flow through it all. S'been that way since I died, more or less."

Tom turned around to face Kenzi. There was something about his eyes that started to put Kenzi at ease. They were kind and calming. If he was just a hallucination, he certainly wasn't a scary one, at least not now. Kenzi leaned back farther in the car, her body naturally relaxing to match the shift in her mood.

"But that's changed now," continued Tom. "Something about the way you spoke about your brother, ah, Mark, I could feel a change in me. It's hard to explain, like a shift. Not fully, just a little."

Tom leaned back against the bench, resting his elbows on the top and placing the tips of his fingers into the front pockets of his jeans. Kenzi was taken aback by how effortlessly cool he looked doing it.

"I think that's why you can hear and see me. And why I can touch, well, things now. Somethin' 'bout what you're goin' through has opened you up to, well, er, this kinda stuff."

It made sense, kind of, what Tom was saying. If he was a hallucination, he was doing a good job of convincing her he wasn't. But that still wasn't enough. If Kenzi was going to let go of rational thought and just fully go with the whole ghost thing, she would need more proof.

"Ok, that all sounds, er, ah, reasonable, I guess, but it still doesn't prove anything. A hallucination would be able to do all those things too."

Tom looked like he was going to say something, but suddenly stopped, and looked at the door, as if he had heard someone else there. Kenzi hadn't heard anything, but turned to see if there was anything there. It was Lucas. He was just standing there in the doorway, looking at Kenzi. Kenzi glared at him. She didn't like him being around at the best of times, and she really didn't want him anywhere near her right now.

"What?!" she barked at him.

"Mum said dinner soon."

The one thing that Kenzi hated doing more than looking at Lucas was talking to him. It was nothing like when she would speak with Mark. Talking with Lucas always felt cheap and fake. She always kept their interactions short.

"K. Bye!"

"Bye, Kenzi. Bye, Mister!" Lucas turned and tottered away.

Tom stood up straighter and pointed to the doorway. "See! Lucas just saw me, too. I can't be a hallucination if you both can see me. Right?"

Kenzi was in shock. Tom was right. Lucas had seen him, too. Which means he wasn't just in her head. He was really there, well, kind of. She took a few steps away from Tom, just to put a little distance between the two of them. Not because she was scared, she needed a bit of space to think.

She wanted proof, and there it was, kind of. Up until that point, it had just been her and Tom, so it was easy to chalk it up to a hallucination. But now, Lucas had been there too, and he had seen Tom. So, either Lucas was a hallucination too, which seemed unlikely, or Tom was really a ghost, which was doubtful as well. She didn't really know which option to go with.

"Ok. Let's just say for a second that I might, I *might* believe that you're a ghost. I'm not really sure that's any better than me just being crazy."

"It's much better than that. Look, I've been stuck here forever, and you're the first person that I can talk to, and you clearly need someone to talk to, so maybe that's why this is happening."

"What? Like you're some sort of cosmic therapist? No thanks, already have one of those, and that's more than enough."

"No, not a therapist, maybe, maybe a *friend*."

Kenzi looked uneasy at Tom's use of the word friend. Tom could tell he might be reaching a bit far.

"I'm just saying, there's obviously a reason why you can see me. And maybe, maybe, that's not so bad."

"What about Lucas, huh? Why can he see you, too?"

"Dunno. Maybe he needs someone to talk to as well."

"Pfft," scoffed Kenzi. That kid is doted on by their mother; he didn't need anything from anyone else.

Tom didn't respond. The inner workings of her family were probably too much for him to get into right now. He just stood there, looking at her, kind of like he was waiting for a starting gun to go off at a race. He was waiting for Kenzi to accept it, but Kenzi didn't know what to think. On one hand, she was relieved that she wasn't going crazy. On the other hand, she was talking to the ghost of her Grandmother's best friend's dead boyfriend. Kenzi had kind of been stuck living with the ghost of Mark's memories for a long time, so maybe it makes sense that she gets to live with a literal ghost now.

It actually felt a little special to talk to a ghost, like something just for her. Like maybe all that pain she had gone through, perhaps this was a bit of payback, a reward even, this experience.

"Ok, fine. But, but there have to be some rules to this, this thing,' said Kenzi as she just gestured to Tom and herself. "I can't really live my life with a ghost hanging around all the time. I may not be crazy, but people will definitely start thinking I am if they see me talking to myself."

The relief was written all over Tom's face. He relaxed again.

"That's fair. What'd you have in mind?"

"Um, well, you can't be around me all the time, like I still need my own space. Like, we can talk, but, ah, it can only be here, in the garage, just the two of us."

"Deal!" Tom was quick to agree to anything, as long as he could still talk to Kenzi. He had been alone for so long that he wasn't going to do anything to jeopardise this chance.

This seemed like a smart approach to it all. Kenzi still wasn't completely sold on the idea, but this little agreement made it easier. But that was enough for now. Agreeing to talk to a ghost is a big deal, and that was all that Kenzi was ready to commit to today.

"Ok, good. Well, I have to go inside for dinner now. You just, stay here, or go wherever you go, just don't follow me, ok?"

"Ok. 'night. I'll ah, I guess we talk tomorrow?"

"Sure," said Kenzi over her shoulder as she left the garage.

Kenzi had been through a lot over the last few years, but none of that had prepared her for the idea of ghosts being real. Or that she would actually talk to one of them. It was too much to think about now. For now, she just wanted to have dinner and go to bed.

Chapter 14
"That Girl Has Been in a Rush Every Day of Her Life."

Kenzi had made it through the rest of the night without any more trouble. Conversation at the table had been their usual, with her parents asking just enough about her day to seem like they cared without being too intrusive to upset her, which was perfect, given what had happened earlier. Kenzi went to sleep almost right after dinner. Both because she didn't want to risk seeing Tom again, and also because she was drained. The afternoon had really taken it out of her.

The same applied to school. There was no appointment with Mrs Fox today, so Kenzi managed to get through the day with minimal interaction with anyone. It was senior year, so all of the other students were well and truly occupied in their own groups, and for the most part, everyone left Kenzi alone. She wasn't sure whether it was just a case of 'strange new kid' vibes, or whether her early rebuffing of engagement from some of the others had been taken seriously. Still, either way, she was happy with her place at school. Alone.

Kenzi was on her way to the bookstore now. She was walking slower than usual. She was still reeling from the events that followed the last time she was there. Even though Lucas had also seen Tom, she still wasn't one hundred per cent convinced that he was real. How could he be? That was crazy! It had all started at the bookstore, so she was apprehensive about going back there, even with the 'deal' she had made with Tom. As she approached the store, she was relieved to see another lady with Jo in the shop. Kenzi thought that maybe, somehow, by someone else being there, Tom wouldn't be there either. If he wasn't a hallucination, that is. Which he totally still could be. Her steps dragged slightly, scuffing the sidewalk. A low, unsettled hum buzzed beneath her skin. The world felt too quiet—like something was holding its breath.

Kenzi opened the door and walked into the bookstore; the smell of lavender and old books always hit her strongly. It was the same scent every time— comforting, grounding, but now edged with a strange tension, like a favourite song playing just off-key. The shop was dimmer than usual. Outside, the overcast sky pressed grey light through the front windows, leaving the corners in shadow. Dust clung to the glass in faint streaks, softening the outlines of the shelves. A brass lamp on the counter flickered now, and then, its glow wavering like it couldn't quite decide whether to stay or fade. Kenzi caught herself slowing down, as though the room were heavier today, pulling at her steps. Even the familiar lavender scent seemed to have a bitter note beneath it, sharp as old smoke she couldn't place.

The other lady was standing close to Jo, and she could tell by their body language that they were pretty familiar with each other. This lady reminded Kenzi a bit of her mother; she thought they must be around the same age. She was wearing tight denim jeans with a loose top half-tucked into them. She was taller than Jo and had jet-black hair, very straight, with a large fringe that almost covered her eyes. Her eyeliner was smudged at the corners, not from neglect but from a day lived at full pace. The silver hoop in her ear glinted when she moved, and her grin carried a mischievous ease that made her seem younger than she was, like the world had never quite managed to slow her down. She was a bit dishevelled, not messy, maybe 'busy', Kenzi thought. There was something strangely familiar about this lady. Before Kenzi could give it any thought, both ladies realised she was there.

"Hey, Kenz. Long time no see," said the strange lady as she rushed over to hug Kenzi.

"Oh, ah-" before Kenzi could respond, she was already being embraced tightly by the lady. Although Kenzi had no idea who this lady was, her hug didn't feel awkward. Sure, it was tight, but it was nice, familiar. She hugged her back and leaned in, catching a face full of the lady's hair, smelling of tangerine or some other fruity-smelling hair product. She blinked, caught between reflexive discomfort and a nagging pull of something half-remembered.

The lady released Kenzi, stepped back, leaning on the front counter. She placed one hand in her jeans' front pocket, using her elbow to hold herself up against the counter, and let the other hang down beside her leg. Kenzi thought about how effortlessly cool this woman looked like someone out of an old pin-up magazine or something. Kenzi was staring, probably more than she should. She didn't know who this woman was, but she clearly recognised Kenzi. Kenzi couldn't help but think about what happened last night with Tom. She was starting to make a habit of strange meetings at this place. At least this was with a real person again.

"You have no idea who I am, do you?"

Kenzi looked down, tucked her hair behind her ear, and then looked back at the lady, who had a big smile on her face. She looked over to Jo, hoping to glean some sort of clue, but Jo had the same goofy smile on her face. She looked back at the woman, and a thin shaft of sunlight caught the edge of her hair, turning the straight black strands into a glossy curtain that nearly hid her expression. For a strange moment, Kenzi thought she looked like a figure from one of the shop's old paperbacks — stylish, untouchable, a little too sharp around the edges. The thought unsettled her, though she couldn't say why.

"Sorry, no."

"That hurts, that really hurts." The lady's expression went from a big smile to what looked like genuine sadness. The lady turned to Jo.

"Like, you change someone's nappy, you feed them, you take care of them, and they don't even have the decency to remember you. Kid these days."

Kenzi didn't know what to do. She genuinely had no idea who this lady was. She obviously thought they had some relationship, and Kenzi had hurt her feelings. She stepped closer to try to put her hand on the lady's arm.

"I'm so sorry. I, ah-"

"Don't sweat it, Kenz. I'm just messing with ya!" The lady's expression changed back to a big smile. Kenzi was reminded of her interactions with Tom the night before, and how he had similarly teased her. Was she really that naive?

"You were about four years old when your family moved to LA, so it's no surprise you don't remember me."

"Oh, ok. Thanks." Kenzi kind of just stood there. She really had no idea what was going on.

"I'm Kelly. Jo's daughter."

Kenzi look at Kelly, then at Jo, and then back to Kelly. She couldn't really see a family resemblance between the two. She must look like Quinn did when he was younger- that must be where the jet black hair comes from.

"Ah, yeah. Nice to see you again." Kenzi stepped back a little.

"Right! I'm off," Kelly kissed Jo on the cheek and then darted out the door. "Nice to see you again, Kenz!"

And just like that, she was gone. She was out the door and closed it so fast that it blew some papers off the front counter, like a whirlwind. The sudden emptiness made it feel like Kelly hadn't just walked out — she had been erased. Jo knelt down to pick up the papers, shaking her head.

"That girl has been in a rush every day of her life!" Jo stood up and placed the papers back on the counter. "Heck, she was even rushin' to come into the world. Born eight weeks early."

Kenzi moved closer to Jo and leaned against the counter. She knew enough about pregnancy and childbirth to know that a baby born that prematurely would probably have some sort of health issues for the first few weeks or months.

"Wow, that's early. Was she ok? I mean, when she was born. Were there any problems with her?"

"Ah, nope. Not at all." Jo quickly moved away from Kenzi and started walking around the counter to her usual sitting crate. "Everyone was surprised, but she was totally fine, a good size, too. Doctors said I was probably lucky she came early, cause if she had stayed in much longer, she might have gotten too big for a natural birth. Guess she was just ready to come."

Jo was sitting now and picked up a book to read, and gestured to the rest of the shop.

"Nuff about that. You got work ta do."

"Ah, yeah, on it."

Kenzi thought it was strange that Jo didn't want to talk about Kelly anymore. Usually, once she gets talking about something, it's hard to get her to stop. If she didn't want to talk about it, Kenzi wasn't going to push it, so she walked off to start sorting the returns for the day. The books felt heavier than usual as she shifted them into place, each one landing with a muted thud. Dust puffed up in tiny clouds, catching in her throat and eyes until she blinked them clear. Even surrounded by stories, she felt the silence settle thicker, like the walls were leaning closer to hear what she wouldn't say.

As Kenzi walked around the bookstore, she kept an eye out for any signs of Tom. There were none — no chill, no presence, no whisper of smoke or grease. The usual golden haze from the front windows was dimmed today, blunted by overcast skies. The lamps overhead flickered faintly, casting quiet shadows that seemed less magical and more tired. A paperback leaned awkwardly off the edge of a shelf, as if it had tried to escape. One of the reading chairs had a torn armrest, the padding beneath just barely peeking through. The silence wasn't silent either — a distant clock ticked, wood creaked underfoot, and somewhere behind her, a bookmark flapped against the side of a table with no breeze to stir it.

It was the same shop she'd come to rely on, but today it felt stiller. Like, even the walls were holding their breath. Either Tom wasn't there, or he really was a hallucination. Kenzi didn't want to think about it too much, as both options were equally unsettling.

If he was just her imagination, did that mean all the words he'd spoken were really hers? Her own mind trying to comfort itself? The thought left her unsettled. Because if Tom wasn't real, then so was the reassurance she felt last night, fake, fragile, a trick she'd pulled on herself. But if he was real… if ghosts really could linger, bound up in memories… then what about Mark? Could he be out there, too? Watching her. Waiting. The idea was both terrifying and tempting, and Kenzi hated herself for wanting it.

Kenzi toyed with the idea of talking to Jo about it. Of all the people in her life right now, Jo seemed like she would be the most open to the concept of ghosts, or at least the least likely to see it as some sort of cry for help from Kenzi. But how would that even go? *After you left yesterday, I saw the ghost of your dead boyfriend, oh, and again at home. We're gonna hang out and chat sometime.* Jo might be cool, and all that, but even she would struggle with a statement like that.

Also, there was something different about Jo right now. Kenzi couldn't put her finger on it, but she definitely got the vibe that Jo didn't want to talk too much now. Could it be Kelly? They seemed really close, so it was strange that her being here had somehow upset Jo. Maybe she should ask Jo if she was ok. But that also felt a bit weird. Jo had well and truly established herself as the one who takes care of the other in their relationship. Kenzi wasn't sure if she was ready to change things up between them. Especially right now, with her new normal. The events of last night notwithstanding, Kenzi had been looking forward to seeing Jo today. The idea of possibly talking to her more about Mark, although probably hard and painful, had been on Kenzi's mind all day and had carried her through the mundane school day. Something about the way Jo could make the past feel alive had given her hope that remembering Mark wouldn't hurt quite so much. But now, with Jo being weird and distant, the thought felt all wrong. She'd waited so long to say his name out loud, and now that she finally wanted to... she couldn't.

It hurt, not being able to talk about Mark more, which was strange. For the longest time, talking about him was too painful, and that's why she stopped. But now, here, it was the first time that it felt like the right thing to do, like it would be good, it would help. But she couldn't. Not today, not with Jo being the way she was today. Kenzi couldn't help but think about how she felt when she first met Jo, and how excited she was to hear more about her Grandmother- a connection that only appeared after she was gone. That felt so similar to now. She wanted to move forward, but it was so hard.

Kenzi resigned herself to tucking Mark back down for now. If Jo wanted to talk, she would. Kenzi was just going to stay quiet, do her job, and then go home. That was all for today, and that was okay. As she gathered the returns into a neat stack, Kenzi let her fingers linger on the spines a little longer than usual. Some covers were cracked, some faded, some stiff with newness — all of them holding lives she would never read. For a moment, she envied the characters inside: their stories already written, their endings already known. Hers felt like a book someone had torn in half, the middle missing, the rest unreadable. She rubbed at her leather band until the skin beneath it burned. Tomorrow she would try again — with Jo, with Tom, maybe even with herself. For now, she just had to make it through the day.

Chapter 15
"I Still Cry in the Shower Most Nights."

Kenzi's shift had continued without any other-worldly interactions. She hadn't talked to Jo much, and Jo hadn't talked to her, either, which was strange. Usually, Jo would talk Kenzi's ear off, but today, she was quiet, almost evasive. Kenzi couldn't help but think about why Jo was so different. Was it something she had done? Did it have something to do with Tom? Was it Kelly? It really didn't make any sense, but Kenzi hadn't pushed it.

As Kenzi opened the gate to her house, her eyes flicked over towards the garage, which was closed, and looked as quiet as it ever had. She half-expected to see Tom's face in the window, staring out like a dog waiting for their owner to come home, but there was no sign of him, at least from the outside. He must be inside, maybe in the car again, she thought. She would change and head out right away. Just to check. Just to see if he was there again. Not that it would confirm or disprove that he was a ghost. Just, just in case.

When she walked inside, she kicked off her shoes and let the door thud closed behind her. The house smelled like reheated vegetables and baby wipes. The living room was littered with blocks and abandoned picture books, and a sippy cup rolled lazily off the couch cushion as the door shut. A lullaby track played faintly from Lucas's toy piano in the corner, slightly off-key but relentless. Somewhere, Lucas was shrieking with glee.

The house felt tense, more so than usual. It wasn't that there was more mess than Lucas and her mother would create throughout the day; it was just different. Also, there was no sight of either of them. Usually, Kenzi's mother would be in the living room when she got home, in prime position to interrogate her about her day at school. But not today. First, Jo was *off* at the bookstore, and now this. Kenzi hadn't realised how much routine had formed around her since moving to Esperance, which was possibly why things were starting to feel, not better, but less bad. But today was different, like something the world had shifted, just slightly. Yesterday was a big day, no doubt, and maybe Kenzi was just experiencing its aftermath.

Kenzi realised she had been standing in the entrance hall for a few minutes, and decided that lingering any longer would give her mother the opportunity to return. Although the idea of a little return to routine was enticing, she was still feeling raw, both from the talk about Mark and the whole Tom of it all, so she decided to take advantage of the opportunity to avoid her Mother this afternoon. She made a beeline for the stairs, already halfway up when she heard it.

"Kenzi?"

She stopped. Her stomach tightened. "Yeah?" She turned half around to see her mother.

Olivia appeared at the bottom of the stairs, her shirt smeared with something orange and suspiciously crusty. Lucas was perched on her hip, both hands in her hair, holding them like reins. She looked exhausted. Her eyes were ringed with tiredness, her shirt blotched with the kind of mess that comes from both love and chaos. Strands of hair clung damply to her temples, her usually neat curls sticking out in wild directions thanks to Lucas's sticky grip. The faded blouse she wore was tugged off one shoulder, the buttons strained where little fingers had clearly played tug-of-war. Even exhausted, her posture carried a thread of grace, like someone used to being composed, caught in a rare moment of unravelling. Lucas babbled in her arms, fingers sticky with mashed banana, tugging her curls like reins on a worn-out horse. Usually, her mother always looked well put together, even after a whole day with Lucas. It wasn't that she worried that much about her appearance; it was just something that always came naturally to her, like a natural grace.

Not today, though. Today, she looked frazzled. Kenzi knew that Lucas was a handful. Not that she had really experienced it too much herself, but she had front row seats to the stress he put her mother and father through. He had been getting better at walking, which also meant he was getting good at running, and it looked like he had run their mother ragged today. As Kenzi stood there, looking at her mother, she actually felt a bit sorry for her. Just a bit.

"Can you watch him for fifteen minutes? I just need a quick shower. I'm—" Olivia gestured to herself, "—disgusting."

Kenzi didn't know what to do. She really wanted to get out to the garage, to see if Tom was there. But she could see that her mother was struggling, and felt like she should help. She tried to do the math in her head. She was almost ready to fully accept that Tom was actually a ghost, so seeing and talking to him was a big deal. Helping her Mum seemed like the right thing to do; that's what she should do. She was almost ready to agree, but something yanked at her, pulling her back to all the times she was struggling after Mark died, and how her Mother did nothing to help her. Why should she help her, especially with Lucas? She never wanted another brother; that was all her parents' choice. They can live with it.

Kenzi turned back to head up the stairs, letting out a sharp "I've got stuff to do," as she did.

"Please, Kenzi."

Kenzi could hear the desperation in her mother's voice. Another unusual occurrence for her. It pulled at Kenzi, but the force of the past pushed her on.

"I said I have stuff to do," snapped Kenzi as she continued up the stairs.

Something inside Olivia broke. "You always have stuff to do. Except none of it involves helping anyone in this house."

Kenzi stopped and sharply turned around. "Excuse me?"

"You heard me." Olivia's voice rose, brittle and sharp. "You do nothing but hide in your room or that dusty shop. You haven't lifted a finger for this family since we moved in. Since before we moved in. You don't do anything with your brother, and you can barely talk to me at all."

Kenzi's chest clenched. "My brother? You want to talk about my brother? Which one? The one whose name you can't even say anymore, or the one you replaced him with?" Kenzi was starting to yell now. She never liked to get mad or raise her voice, but she couldn't help it. She had been closed off and guarded for so long, so much so that any sort of comment like that would have just bounced off her. Talking about Mark, meeting Tom, Jo's behaviour, Kenzi hadn't fully realised how much it had affected her. She couldn't deal with it all. She was too open, and her Mum's comments had cut her deep, and everything was just flowing out now.

"Replaced him- is that *really* what you think?" Olivia's demeanour seemed to change in an instant. She didn't look angry anymore. She looked hurt. Like she had just been punched in the gut, and all the air was pushed out of her.

"What else am I supposed to think? I always felt you loved Mark more than you did me, and that, that was ok, I understood it, I loved Mark so much, too. Then he died, and you just shut down. Stopped talking about him completely, and every time I tried to talk about him, you would change the conversation or leave the room. So maybe you didn't really love him that much. And then, not even a year after he was gone, you get pregnant with, with him," Kenzi pointed accusingly at Lucas, who had stopped making noise or moving at all, and was just staring at Kenzi. "Then, after he was born, you took down all the pictures of Mark, like you wanted to completely erase him." Tears were running down Kenzi's face now. Letting out all her emotions had opened her whole body up, releasing a pressure that had been bubbling for what felt like forever.

Olivia's mouth opened, then closed. "You think I wanted to erase him?" she whispered. "Nothing could ever replace him. I know he meant the world to you, but he was my son, MY SON, and when he died, a piece of me died along with him." Olivia's voice was loud and stern now. It was so loud that Peter must have heard from the kitchen, and she could see him starting to enter the lounge room to see what was happening. She shot him a quick look, and he knew it meant to stay away, which he did. Olivia was upset, but she knew she had to get this out. She had been so desperate to repair things with her daughter for so long. She had hoped it would be through a positive experience, but maybe this was what they both needed. To get it all out.

"I know I wasn't there for you when Mark died. I couldn't be much of anything to anyone at that time, and I'm sorry, I'm so sorry, I will carry that guilt with me forever. But you have to know, your father and I never chose to have another child; it was the furthest thing from our minds, but somehow, in working through our grief together, a miracle happened, a wonderful new life to maybe help us heal." Olivia jostled Lucas a little and kissed him on the forehead, causing a little smile on his face. "And he has been an amazing gift, but there is no way he could ever replace Mark. I think about him every day, every single day! God, I still cry in the shower most nights. Every time I look at Lucas or your father, who both remind me SO MUCH of Mark, I have to hold back the tears." Tears had started to run down her face now, an irony that was not lost on her.

Kenzi had never seen her mother like this before, so raw, so honest. Where was this person years ago? It felt too late, too little, not enough, fake.

"Then where is he, Mum? Where are all his pictures?" Kenzi gestured around to the house.

Olive's face twisted. "Because," she paused, taking a breath. Her voice softened as she continued, "When Lucas started to crawl, he started to reach up and pull things down, and I was so scared that he might accidentally break something of Mark's, a picture of him, anything—and I couldn't bear that. I wasn't trying to forget. I was trying to keep him safe." Olivia wasn't yelling anymore; she didn't have the breath for that anymore, but she wasn't calm either, her voice crackling through the tears.

The room felt too quiet. Even Lucas had gone still, resting his cheek against Olive's shoulder.

For the longest time, Kenzi had focused on what Mark's death and how her parents dealt with it had done to her; she had never really thought that the way her parents acted may not have always reflected how they were feeling. She started to feel a little guilty about what she had said and more so about how she had acted.

"I ah, I didn't know that," Kenzi mumbled.

"Well, maybe if you talked to us instead of treating us like strangers…"

Kenzi looked away. Her throat ached, full of words she wasn't ready to say. They all stood there motionless for what felt like an eternity, and neither Olivia nor Kenzi was sure what to say next. They had both been keeping so much inside for so long, and now that it was out there, no one knew what to do next. Sharing so much raw emotion hadn't really helped the other person. If anything, both were feeling worse, learning how their actions, or lack thereof, had affected the other. Olivia so badly wanted to take Kenzi in her arms and hold her tight, squeezing all the pain out of her, but she could tell that Kenzi wasn't ready for that yet, so she just stood there. The silence and inaction lingered on.

Kenzi didn't know what to do now. She knew she couldn't just leave to go to the garage, but she didn't want to keep talking either. Kenzi looked at her mum, at the tear-streaked face and the toddler clinging to her, and something in her chest ached. It wasn't forgiveness. Not yet. But it was something close. She wanted this moment to end, so she did the simplest thing she could. She took Lucas gently from Olive's arms without another word. Olive looked like she might say something, then just nodded and disappeared upstairs. Kenzi dropped onto the couch. Lucas curled beside her and offered her a sticky piece of cereal. She didn't take it, but she didn't brush him away either.

As she sat there on the couch, holding Lucas but keeping him at arm's reach, she let out a big sigh and wiped the tears off her face with her hoodie's sleeve. She was stunned. She tried to process what had just happened, but it was all a blur of words and emotions. She wanted to take it all back, but she couldn't. It was out there, for better or worse. She had finally said words she didn't even know she had to say. But, she also heard things she didn't realise she needed to hear.

It was bad, but it was also good. She felt lighter, like the release had let something heavy out. But now she had new guilt to carry. Things hadn't been anywhere near good between her and her mother, and Kenzi had no idea if they were going to get better or worse. For now, she would just sit.

Chapter 16
"Pretty Smart for a Dead Guy."

The afternoon and dinner had passed by without any more talk, anymore anything really, almost as if Kenzi had just switched to autopilot, and now Kenzi found herself outside the garage. Although she had planned on going out there today, the events of the afternoon had kind of derailed her a bit. But now she was here. Standing outside, with her hand floating just above the door handle, not sure if she wanted to open it or not. Kenzi still wasn't sure what to think about Tom. Was he a ghost? Was he a hallucination? She wasn't sure which she wanted to believe, but maybe spending time with the dead was exactly what she needed now. God knows that time with the living was too hard tonight.

Kenzi stepped into the garage. The kind of quiet that settled in the garage wasn't empty—it was full of old echoes, lingering fumes, and unsaid things. Even the dust in the corners felt like it was holding its breath. The air inside was colder, still carrying that faint motor oil tang and a sense of history that hadn't faded. She closed the door behind her and just stood there for a moment. She looked around for signs of Tom, though she wasn't really sure what they would be. The garage smelled of oil or grease, which reminded Kenzi of Tom, but it could also just be the garage's smell.

She walked around the car, her eyes darting all around the room, but there was no one there. She thought about calling out to him, but that felt too strange to her. Like saying it out loud would make her look crazy, not that anyone was around, but it was too much all the same. She had already said so much today, probably too much, so gathering the strength to call out to someone was too hard.

As she got back around to the front of the car, she stopped. He wasn't there. What did that mean? Was he just a hallucination because of what she had said about Mark? If so, surely the fight would have brought him back out. But if he wasn't a hallucination, and he was a ghost, where was he? Although they had talked briefly about what being a ghost was like for Tom, there was still so much about the whole thing that she didn't know. Like, if it was Kenzi that brought him out, made him able to touch things and talk to her, what happened when she left him? It was all a bit much to think about now.

Kenzi walked to the driver's side and opened the door. It was stiff and heavy, and creaked loudly as she opened it. Kenzi looked around to see if the noise had attracted anyone. Nothing. She crawled in, sat on the old bench seat of the truck, and pulled the door shut, which was even louder than when she opened it. It was old and musty. So much so that she wound the window down, the handle tight as she turned it. She wiped the dust off the steering wheel and just sat there, holding onto it. She probably would have left out a big sigh, but there wasn't that much air inside her now. She was still feeling slightly lighter after her fight.

Kenzi closed her eyes and leaned back against the chair, just sitting quietly. Breathing in and out, listening to the lack of sounds in the garage. It was peaceful. Normally, she would spend her afternoons alone in her room, but she could always hear the noise of the rest of the house, gnawing at the edges of her peace. But here, she was far enough away from everyone to just be alone. But then...

"Ya know, I'm actually a bit surprised ya came back," came a voice from outside the car.

She jumped, then rolled her eyes. "Do you seriously have to do the whole 'ghost popping out of nowhere' thing?"

Tom was sitting on an overturned crate, arms resting on his knees. He drummed his fingertips absently against his thigh, the rhythm out of sync with anything tangible, like he was keeping time with some other place. His gaze flicked up to meet hers, steady and unhurried, as if he'd been expecting her all along. He looked as solid as ever, though the shadows didn't quite cling to him right. The edges of his form shimmered faintly, like heat rising off asphalt. His boots were scuffed, his presence unreal but grounded, like a dream with gravity.

"Ha! Sorry, this whole *talkin' to the living* thing is new to me," he said, with a slight smirk.

Kenzi opened the door, with another loud creak, and got out of the car. She closed the door and leaned back against the car. While the peace and quiet of being alone was nice, she was happy that Tom was there. She had feared that yesterday was just a once-off, a symbol of her grief cracking everything open, and not the type of supernatural encounter she had read about in many YA novels. But here he was again. A ghost. Right here. A Ghost that only she could see. It made her feel special, and she really needed that today.

"Heh, after what happened inside, you'd think it was me who was new to talking to people."

Kenzi was surprised by how at ease she felt with Tom, as if she could just say what she was thinking. What she was feeling. A pause stretched between them. Kenzi looked at Tom, who was looking back at her. She wasn't sure what she expected him to say in her response to her, and he didn't look like he was trying to figure her out. He was just sitting there, listening, waiting to hear her speak.

Kenzi cleared her throat.

"I had a huge fight with my mum today."

"Sounds rough."

"It was." She glanced at him. "I was just so angry with her, and I, I probably said some really mean things. But, I couldn't stop myself; it just all came out."

Tom leaned forward slightly, his arms open. "Must have needed to. Besides, she's your Mum, she'll forgive you."

Tom's words felt warm, genuine, and nice. She had had many, what she would call, fake conversations about things over the last few years; it was nice to feel this again.

"I don't know. I've never seen her like that. Not even when Mark, my brother, died." She paused for a second, becoming all too aware of how talking about her dead brother might make someone like Tom feel. Tom didn't react; he just sat there, quiet, listening.

"God, every time I start to think that maybe things are getting better, like maybe I'm getting better, something bad happens, and I feel like I'm right back where it started. Stuck in all this pain and misery," Kenzi stepped forward away from the car, kind of walking around the room, throwing her arms in the air.

"You really gonna complain to the ghost about being stuck?"

Kenzi stopped and quickly turned around to face Tom, afraid that she had offended him.

"No, I, ah, I mean-"

He smirked again. Tom enjoyed seeing Kenzi squirm; it reminded him of her Grandmother and how he could do the same to her. Tom stood up, slowly walked over to the car, and leaned back against it. He was closer to Kenzi now, but not too close to make her feel awkward.

"I'm just joshin' ya, Mac. She was the same, you know. Your Gran. So smart when it came to books and all that stuff, but gosh, it was easy for her to get one over."

Hearing Tom talk about her Grandmother immediately put Kenzi at ease.

"But seriously. That all just sounds like life, ya know. I'm kinda lucky, I never really lost anyone, back when I was alive, didn't really have anyone, aside from Jo and the others, so I don't really know what that's like. But I've certainly seen a lot of other people going through it," said Tom as he stood and walked to the window, looking out at nothing.

"You mean, since you've been, ah, dead?" Kenzi didn't really know how to phrase it without being too blunt or harsh. Talking to a ghost was obviously a new thing for Kenzi, and she really had no idea how to do it...right.

"Yeah. It's kinda hard to explain, but since my accident, I've kinda just been drifting in and out of, ah, here, I guess. Like, I'm not always awake, I guess, but I've still seen plenty of other people living their lives." Tom was still looking out the window. Not at anything, more like he was looking at a memory. Kenzi moved closer. She stood in front of the same bench, but at the opposite end. She didn't want to get too close.

Kenzi hadn't thought about what Tom must have gone through since he died. She purposely hadn't thought about it; it was all just too weird. But hearing him talk about his experience, Kenzi couldn't help but think about her experience since Mark had died, and how she had felt like she wasn't really there, too. It was the first time she felt as though someone else might understand her.

She moved a little closer to Tom.

"That sounds hard. Watching other people live their lives, while you're just *stuck*." Kenzi rubbed her leather band. "I can certainly relate to that."

Kenzi wanted to hear more, but she wasn't sure how to ask. She was talking to a literal ghost, and that concept was not lost on her. She wanted to know everything about it. The whole idea felt like a good escape for her. Like, there's this whole other world that only she has access to. Maybe she could learn more about it, and that would keep her distracted from the real world. Especially the world in her home right now. She and Tom had 'met' in the bookstore, and he was here in the garage. Did he go to other places?

"Can I ask, ah, when you're *here*," Kenzi gestured around, at nothing and everything, "I mean, when you're *awake*, is it only just here and the bookstore?"

Tom turned to face Kenzi.

"Nah, not just those places. Sometimes I'm at Jo and Quinn's place, sometimes it's their daughter Kelly's place. Heck, I've even been ta university with young

Bobby a few times. I don't have any control over when or where I am, just going along for the ride."

Tom turned around more and leaned back against the workbench, placing the tips of his hands into his jeans pockets. Somehow, he made leaning look effortlessly cool. Kenzi was absolutely captivated by what Tom was saying. It was all so unreal. She wanted to hear more.

"Like, I died, and any possible future I might have had died with me. And since I've been coming back, it's like I've been shown this whole life that I coulda had, with Jo, I mean. Like, if I hadn't died, maybe we woulda gotten hitched, and had kids, and grandkids. And that's what I'm seeing."

Kenzi felt a lump in her throat. Hearing his words stirred something inside her. She hadn't felt genuinely sorry for someone else in a long time. Suddenly, the whole ghost thing was too real.

"Oh, Tom…"

"Hey, I'm not complaining or nothin'. I've never thought of it as some sort of punishment or anythin' like that. God knows I wasn't the best person when I was alive, but I certainly wasn't a bad person. I'm not sure if there's a better place out there, waiting for me, but if I have to stay here and watch tha people I cared most about livin' happy lives, that ain't so bad."

Kenzi didn't know what to say. So many people had tried to make her feel better since Mark died, but none of their words had ever helped. So, the last thing she wanted to do was say something meaningless now. So she didn't. She just stood there.

"Look, I don't know everything about you, or what ya family have been through, but if I've learned anything in my time, it's that things always get better. Those kinds of fights, all that bad stuff, it only hurts so much because of how much the good means to you. That's what you gotta focus on, the good."

Kenzi still didn't respond. The silence between them felt different this time—not awkward, but... tentative. A truce. She wanted things to get better, but she couldn't allow herself to be happy, as if it would dishonour what Mark had meant to her. But something in Tom's words started to change her perspective.

"You know, you're pretty smart for a dead guy."

Tom adjusted his collar and slicked his hair back with his hand. "Shhh, you don't want to ruin my cool guy image."

Kenzi couldn't help but let out a little laugh. A sound she hadn't heard for a while. She felt better. About the fight. Tom's words had helped her see things from a different perspective. She wasn't fully over it, and definitely not ready to talk to her mother just yet, but it didn't feel as daunting anymore.

She wanted to stay and talk to Tom more, but it was also starting to feel a bit too much. She was willing to accept that Tom was a ghost, that he was real. It was really happening, and that was incredible. But she didn't want to push it too far just yet. She had confirmed she wasn't going crazy, and that was enough for now.

"Well, I, uh, better get back inside, but, I'll come back tomorrow. Promise."

"Sounds like a plan, Mac."

Kenzi wasn't sure why, but whenever Tom called her Mac, she felt different, like more confident. It was nice. She could definitely do with more of that feeling. She headed towards the door and opened it, but she didn't leave. She stopped in the doorway and turned to look back at Tom.

"Hey, ah," She felt like she needed to thank Tom for listening. It had helped, probably more than she expected. But the whole thing still felt strange. She didn't say thanks. She just smiled. He smiled back. She turned, gently closed the door behind her, and just stood outside. The night was quiet and cold, but it still felt nice. The buzzing light above the door shone down on her, casting a small shadow on the ground.

Kenzi took a deep breath in and let it out slowly. For the first time in a long time, she didn't feel completely alone.

Chapter 17
"Nothing Is Ever Truly Gone"

The bookshop smelled like musty paper and lavender furniture polish, and Kenzi found herself breathing it in like comfort food. There was a stillness here she couldn't explain—quiet, but not empty. Like the place had its own heartbeat, slow and steady. Sunlight filtered through the dusty windows, casting soft rectangles across the worn floorboards. The air felt heavier than usual, like the shop itself could feel her sorrow and had slowed its breath in solidarity.

She wiped down the front counter, trying to ignore the guilt still lodged like a rock behind her ribs. Kenzi couldn't help but think about her fight the night before, and how she had been so wrong about how her Mum had been dealing with Mark's loss. She had been so sure about her Mum, and Lucas, and it had hurt her so much that everyone just seemed to move on and forget about Mark. That's why it hurt so much when his photos all disappeared. That's why she did what she did. She couldn't bear to live in a world without Mark in it, but somehow, having his things, his pictures still around, helped keep him close, and then when they were gone, it felt like he had never been there at all. Finding out that her mother had removed the photos to protect them, to protect Mark, was hard. Good, but hard. She had been so angry at her mother for so long that she didn't know how to move past that now.

Tom was still on her mind, too. She was entirely on board with the "ghosts are real, and she can talk to one" thing now. She had only spent a small amount of time with him last night, but it had been nice. Somehow, the perspective of a dead guy who had spent the last fifty years or so floating in and out of other people's lives carried some weight. His thoughts on the fight, and how things would work themselves out, had helped. She wanted to see him again, if only just to have someone completely removed from everything and everyone else to talk to. Not just because he was a ghost, which was starting to feel more and more like a really cool thing to experience, but mostly cause he was easy to talk to, and Kenzi was finding those kinds of relationships helpful again. She and Mark had always been close, and they could talk about anything, and Kenzi hadn't had that since he left.

She wasn't ready to admit it out loud yet, but moving to Esperance had been good for her.

Kenzi was still wiping the counter. Her cloth moved in slow, concentric circles, barely lifting the thin layer of dust. The movement was mechanical—something to keep her hands busy while her thoughts played over and over in her head. She glanced over to Jo, who was in her usual spot, sitting on the old wooden crate, head buried in an old war-torn paperback, no doubt some weird literary cult-classic. They had spoken much since Kenzi had started her shift for the day. Kenzi was preoccupied with thoughts of her Mother and Tom and had all but forgotten how different Jo had been yesterday. Kenzi wanted to talk to Jo about so many things today. Mark. Her Mother. Mac. But she still didn't know how to get things back to how they were. Not that they were broken, but just out of alignment. She finished cleaning the counter and walked over to the bookshelves to start cleaning them. As she walked across the room, the floor creaked beneath her feet, the sounds almost deafening in the silence.

Jo glanced up from her novel at Kenzi. Jo could see that something was weighing heavily on her. Ever since she came to Esperance, Jo could tell there was a lot of pain and grief pulling at Kenzi. Still, she had thought she had seen some signs of light shining through over the last week or so, but today, she actually looked worse. It was as if everything was right back at the surface, like a raw wound. Jo watched from across the room, her mug cooling in her hands. She didn't press—didn't hover. Just stayed close, grounded and still, like an anchor waiting to be held. She had tried to Kenzi the space to open up, but that hadn't worked, so she decided to give her a push.

Jo adjusted her posture to lean a little closer, elbows resting on the counter like she had nowhere else to be. Her eyes stayed on Kenzi—not prying, just open.

"You alright, chicken?" Her tone was casual, but her eyes weren't. The light caught the streaks of silver in her hair, softening the edges of her sharp jawline. Her hands, lined and freckled, rested easily on the cover of her book—hands that looked just as comfortable hauling crates of novels as they did smoothing tears off a young girl's cheek.

Kenzi hesitated, the cloth still in her hand. "Huh? Oh, um, yeah, I'm..." She had spent so long fobbing off questions about her feelings that it had become an automatic response, and the words were out of her mouth before she could even think. But that was the old Kenzi, the one who was obviously wrong about so many things, and she wanted to do better.

'Actually, no. Not really."

Jo put the novel down, dog-earing her spot before closing it completely. She could see that Kenzi wanted to get something off her chest, but she also knew how guarded this girl was, so she didn't want to force it too much.

"Well, we can talk 'bout it, if you like. Or, we can just stay quiet. Whatever you need."

Kenzi was a bit surprised by Jo's approach. Since the first day they had met, Jo had been this sort of *force,* pushing and pulling everyone around to her whim. She was rough, but the good kind. Kenzi actually liked it. It was a good change from how the other adults in her life had acted around her. But today, she was softer. She wasn't sure if it was a residual effect from yesterday's weirdness or if she could sense that something was weighing on Kenzi.

The silence stretched between them, warm but weighted.

Kenzi wanted to talk, but she didn't know what about or how to start. She thought about what her Mother said, about how Mark's death had affected her. She thought about what Tom had said about focusing on the good stuff. Everyone had their own thoughts about it all, and she didn't know what to think. Then she thought about her Grandmother. She wondered how she had lost Tom when she was young, and if she had dealt with it differently from how Kenzi had dealt with losing Mark.

Kenzi set the cloth aside and leaned against the bookshelf, softly so as not to tip it over.

"Can, can I ask you something about my Grandmother?"

Jo was a bit surprised. She had agreed to tell Kenzi more about Mac when she started working in the shop, but she thought that what was bothering Kenzi was something new, something fresh. She feared Kenzi might have been deliberately talking about something other than what was really on her mind, but she was going to go along with it. As long as it kept Kenzi talking, it would be good.

"Of course, you can, love. After my kid and grandkids, she's my favourite topic of conversation."

Ok, this felt like Jo again. It instantly put Kenzi at ease. She let out a little sigh and took a deep breath in through her nose. The scent of lavender and books put her more at ease. There was so much she wanted to say, but she had to really control herself. She wanted to talk about Mac and how she handled losing her friend, but she had to be careful about how she spoke about Tom. She didn't want to slip up and say something that would get Jo suspicious. Kenzi looked down at her hands and rubbed her leather band.

"How did Mac handle it? When, ah, when Tom died."

That was good. That should be safe.

Jo leaned back against the shelf, arms folded, gaze unfixed. "She didn't fall apart. That always surprised me. Everyone thought she would. Sure, she was strong-willed and pretty outspoken, but there was still a delicateness to her. Her small stature always made her seem innocent, I guess. It was somethin' that she used to her advantage on more than a few occasions."

Jo chuckled a little at herself. Kenzi laughed, too, just a little, and the smile lingered on her face. She wasn't that tall herself and had often been judged by strangers for her size. It had always bothered her, and she had never thought about using that to her advantage before. Damn, Mac sounded cool.

"So, Mac didn't have any brothers or sisters of her own, so we all kind of filled that space for her. Tom was older than both of us, and he was kind of a big brother figure for Mac. Inasmuch as he liked to tease her, never in a mean way, in a playful way. Smart as she was, he could always get one over her, which he, of course, liked to do a lot, and although it made her mad, I know she liked it, too."

Kenzi thought about her exchanges with Tom. He definitely seemed to enjoy teasing her, too. Mark would do that sometimes, too, so it was actually kind of nice to have that again.

"So, when it happened, it hit her hard. Pretty sure it was the first time she had lost someone close. She cried, of course. But she never hid it, or shied away from talking about it, which I always thought was really strong, you know? Me? I could barely even say his name for the longest time, but not Mac. It was like she wanted to live it, to experience it, the bad just as much as the good."

Jo paused, looked out the window, and up towards the sky, lost in her story. Kenzi moved closer to Jo, almost as if she didn't want anything to come between her and the stories of her grandmother. Hearing about her strength gave Kenzi hope. A feeling she hadn't had for a while.

"I remember, when I was at my lowest, so mad at the world for taking him away. We were all together, the four of us, trying to drink away the pain. Mac said something that I've never forgotten. She said, 'Nothing is ever truly gone. Matter can't be created or destroyed; it can only be transformed. Tom's not gone; he's just something new. Even if he isn't physically here anymore, his effect on all of us still exists, and that's how we know he's still here- nothing can change that. It's like a magnetic field. You can't see it, but you can see the effect it has, and that's how you know it's real.'"

Jo blinked her eyes a few times as if she was switching off the memory and returning to the present.

"We all just kind of sat there in silence for hours. She was right. As long as we kept Tom in our hearts, he was never truly gone. He could never be. And that kind of made it a bit easier, letting him go."

Kenzi breathed a big sigh. She hadn't realised she had been holding her breath through Jo's story. She rubbed her leather band. Mark would always be there, with her, and nothing could change that. It didn't matter if there weren't pictures of him around the house, or if they were in a completely new home; he was still there, because of what he had meant to her.

A few tears started to slide down Kenzi's face. Jo walked over and gently wiped them away with her hand. Although it was a bit worn and wrinkled, it was still soft, and Kenzi closed her eyes and leaned into Jo's hand.

"I see so much of her in you, Kenz. You've clearly got her brains; anyone can see that. But I can see you've got her heart, too. And when you're ready to open it up again, you're gonna see there is so much in this world to enjoy."

Kenzi just stood there. It was nice, peaceful. Just what she needed. She hadn't handled Mark's death anything like what Mac had when Tom died. She wished she had been stronger, but she couldn't change that now. She could just focus on what she had learned. Mark was gone, and she would never see him again. But that didn't mean he wouldn't still be with her. She rubbed her band again. His pictures may not be up anymore, but nothing can change the time they had together. He would live on, as long as she wanted him to. And that was forever.

Kenzi went back to cleaning, starting on the front windows. As always, Jo's story had helped. She was feeling better. About a lot of things. About Mark. About her fight with her Mother. Even about herself. As she wiped the window, the clean surface reflected a little, and she saw herself in it. She looked different. A bit lighter, and a little more colour in her face. She pictured the photo of her Grandmother on the wall in the hallway. It was the first time that she started to see the resemblance. A warmth swelled in her belly and spread to the rest of her body. It felt good.

Chapter 18
"We're Gonna Figure This Out"

Kenzi's shift at the bookstore had finished. Dinner with the family was quiet. She and her Mother weren't talking, but it wasn't out of spite or anger, at least not on Kenzi's behalf. After talking to Tom, and Jo, Kenzi was seeing her Mother's side of the whole thing a lot clearer, and she wasn't as mad at her anymore. But she didn't know how to move past it. She wasn't sure how to apologise to her Mother, or even if she wanted to, and she didn't want to say the wrong thing and possibly start another fight. She just went back to saying very little and speaking only when spoken to. It didn't feel nice. Not anymore. Kenzi had found herself enjoying talking to others a lot more recently. Jo, obviously. And now Tom. Even her last talk with Mrs Fox wasn't horrible. She had missed the kinds of family dinners that they had when Mark was alive. They were always so full of talk and love. Kenzi wondered if things could ever be like that again.

That's what had led Kenzi outside, to the garage. That desire for contact. Conversation. Connection. Even though there was no guarantee that Tom would be there. He was a ghost after all, and he had said himself that he didn't really have any control over where he goes, so maybe this would be one of those times that he was at Jo's. Or even Kelly's, which seemed a bit strange. Regardless, she was going in. If Tom was there, great. If not, it was still easier than being inside.

The garage was cooler than outside, filled with shadows and the smell of dust, motor oil, and metal. Kenzi stepped inside, her boots echoing softly on the concrete. She'd never noticed how the old place seemed to hum with stillness, like it was waiting for someone to wake it up. A single shaft of dusty sunlight filtered in through a high window, lighting up the particles in the air like a slow, silent snowfall. The silence wasn't empty—it pressed in, like a thick blanket of thought and memory layered into the walls.

Kenzi didn't have to look around this time. Tom was there, leaning against the workbench as if it were part of him. He didn't startle her this time—but her chest still gave a little jump. His form was sharper today, like he'd been drawn in bold pencil lines. There was a softness in the way he watched her, not protective, but present, like someone willing to be still until you were ready.

"You're early," he said, voice mild, hands shoved in his back pockets.

Kenzi crossed to the truck. "Yeah. Had to get out of there."

He gave her a lopsided smile. "Easier to talk to a dead guy than your Mum?"

"Something like that."

Kenzi was now standing in front of the tool bench, randomly picking up and putting down various tools. Her fingers came away smudged with a fine black grit, leaving faint shadows on her palms. She rubbed them together without thinking, watching the dust smear, half-hoping Tom would comment and break the silence the way only he seemed able to. She had no idea what any of them did, but it just seemed like the thing to do. Each tool was cold and unfamiliar in her hands—alien objects with stories she didn't know. She let them clink softly as she moved them, filling the silence with sound that didn't demand anything. Tom hadn't moved, still leaning against the bench, facing away from Kenzi. Not *not* looking at her, but just in his own space.

"Jo was telling me about when you, ah, when you died today."

"Yeah..."

"Yeah. She told me it was my Grandmother who kind of got them all through it. Something about energy never goes away, or something like that." Her voice drifted as her eyes scanned the dusty outlines of the room, as if seeking the echo of her grandmother in the oil stains and spiderwebs. The space held more than just tools—it held pauses, unfinished things, ghosts in the shape of memories.

"Sounds like somethin' Mac woulda said."

"It got me thinking about all…" Kenzi gestured to the room, "…this. Like, why you're still here and not, I don't know, somewhere else, like heaven or whatever? Like, if Jo is still holding on to the memories of you, is that what's keeping you here? And if that's the case, is Mark stuck somewhere, too? Like, am I keeping him from moving on?"

Kenzi hadn't had that thought about Mark until she voiced her thoughts about Tom out loud. She had been feeling better about Mark today, like keeping him in her heart and her thoughts kept him alive, but now, here, standing with an actual ghost, trapped between life and death, her thoughts about her brother changed. Now she wasn't sure if she had to completely let him go.

It was strange for Tom to see Kenzi like this. She looked so much like Mac that it was hard to think of them as two completely different people. Mac was always so sure of herself, but Kenzi was clearly having some doubts.

"Nah, I don't think it's like that. It's kinda hard to explain, but I know it's not other people keeping me here. It's me. I don't really know what exactly it is, but I know it's my choice."

Tom turned to face Kenzi, still leaning against the bench. She had turned to face him now.

"I don't know the rulebook with all this ghost stuff. Ain't never met another one. But I gotta believe we can all move on if we're ready. I'm sure Mark's in a better place now."

Tom's words comforted Kenzi. More than she thought they would. So many people have said that Mark was in a better place since he died, but the sentiment has never held any weight before. Maybe because it was coming from a dead person. Maybe because of what Jo said. Heck, maybe even because of what her Mum had said. But Kenzi was starting to believe it.

"Yeah, I think you're right."

There was a silence for a while. Both of them just basking in the pleasantness of a better place.

Kenzi's thought shifted from Mark to Tom. She became unnervingly aware that he must have been stuck here, all alone, for close to sixty years. All because something was holding him here, stopping him from moving on. She felt an ache in her chest, similar to how she felt when Mark first died. She imagined what it must feel like—to watch life go on without you, with no one to talk to. It was the same feeling she'd had after Mark. Frozen while the world kept spinning. It was too much for her to accept.

"Ok. That's what we're gonna do," Kenzi said with a strong and confident determination she hadn't had for a while.

"What?"

"We're gonna figure out what's keeping you here, so we can, uh, resolve it, and you can finally move on." Kenzi wasn't playing with the tools anymore. Her hands were firmly pressing down on the table as she looked out the dust-covered window of the garage.

"You tryna' get rid of me already?"

'No, it's ah, it's just-"

Tom was making Kenzi squirm again. He really did enjoy it.

"I know, Mac. I get it."

Tom stood up and walked towards the car. Kenzi turned to watch him.

"Ok. I'll make ya a deal. You help me to figure out what's keeping me here, and I'll help you get this junker runnin' again."

Kenzi was a bit surprised. Not that Tom was okay with her trying to help him, but that he offered to do something for her in return, without her asking. She kind of expected him to just be happy to get Kenzi's help, without giving anything back in return. She obviously needed help with the car, so it was nice that he offered. He must have been a decent person while alive. No wonder his friends missed him. It made Kenzi want to help him more.

"Deal!" Said Kenzi as she moved closer to Tom, who was leaning back against the car. She put her hand out to shake on the agreement. Tom just looked at her for a second and smiled. Kenzi quickly realised what she was doing and pulled her hand back, rubbing the back of her neck in embarrassment. It was surprisingly hard to think of Tom as a ghost rather than just a regular person.

"Ah, er, right. Well, I probably just can't ask Jo too much about you, without, ah, seeming strange." Kenzi walked over to lean against the car next to Tom. They were probably closer than they had been since they first met. Up to that point, Kenzi had been keeping space between them. A little out of fear, he was a ghost after all, and a little out of habit. She had been keeping everyone at arm's length for years now. But recently, she had let a few people in, and she felt comfortable enough with Tom to do that for him.

Tom turned his head to look at Kenzi. From this position, it was clear how much taller than her he was, as Kenzi had to tilt her head back to look him in the eyes.

"That's a good point, Mac."

"But Jo's been telling me more and more stories about my Grandmother, when she was younger, so I'm sure you will come up again."

"Yeah, that girl does love ta talk. Her daughter, Kelly, is tha same."

Kenzi thought back to when she met Kelly at the bookstore. Although she didn't really look anything like Jo, they definitely had similar vibes. It was kind of the first time that Kenzi had really experienced that kind of thing. Both she and Mark never seemed too much like their parents, which probably made it harder when he died. Kenzi wondered if her father was like her Grandad. The stories that Jo had told her about her grandmother didn't really seem to match what she thought about her father. Not in a bad way, they just seemed pretty different. Kenzi had been finding herself thinking more and more about that type of thing lately. She had to remind herself to focus back on what she was doing right now.

"Right. So, do you have any ideas on what might be keeping you here? Like, any kind of, ah-" Kenzi tried to think about books and movies about ghosts, as if they were some sort of real guide on how it all works, "-unfinished business, I guess."

Tom looked away from Kenzi, kind of off into nothing, like he was trying to remember his life before he died.

"Ya know, I've thought about that a lot over the years. And there's nothin' I can really think of. I mean, sure, there were things that I kinda wanted to do, like drive cross the country, stuff like that. But nothin' really major. And me an' Jo were in a great place. I was actually thinkin' bout askin' her ta marry me, but I guess life had other plans."

Tom looked back down at Kenzi, who was equally sad and frustrated.

"I ain't even mad 'bout her and Quinn. He's a stand-up guy. Taken good care of Jo. I'm sorry, Mac. That's not really helpful, is it?"

"No, but that's ok. I'll ah, I'll keep talking to Jo about my Gran, and, ah, anything she says about you, I'll let you know. Maybe hearing something will jog your memory a bit.”

Kenzi really wasn’t sure what to say. She had decided to help Tom on the spur of the moment. She hadn’t really thought it would be an easy thing to do, but now, it seemed like a very hard endeavour. But that wasn’t going to stop her. She had resigned herself to it. She had a purpose now. Tom had helped her, and now she was going to help him. Maybe through helping him move on, maybe she could, too.

“Sounds good, Mac. Thanks.”

They both stood there for a moment, in silence, both looking forward, not really at anything. It was getting late, and normally, the night air would be getting a chill, but here, with Tom, Kenzi felt warm. The quiet was nice and calming.

“Say,” said Tom, breaking the silence, “Has Jo told you the story of your Gran’s first time driving Trevor’s car?” Tom chuckled a little as he spoke, and he had a big grin on his face. Kenzi’s ears pricked up, and her focus was immediately drawn to what Tom was saying.

“No! What happened?”

“Well…”

As Tom started to tell his tale, Kenzi closed her eyes, picturing all the events in her mind. The more she heard about her Grandmother, the closer they felt. The closer they felt, the better she wanted to be.

Chapter 19
"A Little Is Enough for Now"

Peter tiptoed carefully out of Lucas' room. He had just put him down for the night and was being very careful not to make a sound that might wake him. The nightlight glowed faintly blue behind him, casting a soft halo over the cot. The hush in the hallway was thick and velvety, like the house was collectively holding its breath with him. He slowly pulled the door closed, gently releasing the handle. He stood there in silence for a second, listening intently. Nothing. He was clear.

He walked down the hallway towards his daughter's room, making sure he missed the floorboards that had creaked since he first lived in the house. Each step was precise, avoiding known creakers with the grace of a practised routine. The faded runner rug muffled his movement, but the familiar scent of eucalyptus and old floor polish rose faintly as he moved. It was strange. The way the house hadn't changed, even with all the changes that had happened within the home, gave him a sense of comfort. There had always been so much love in the house, even though it was just him and his Mother for the most part, and the little things always reminded him of that love.

Kenzi's door was shut, like it was most nights, but Peter could see the glow of her light seeping out under the door. He knew she had been out in the garage earlier, but she was back inside now. He was happy that she had been out to the garage a few times now. He had hoped that fixing his Dad's old truck would be a good little project for her. Kenzi had been spending a lot of time at Jo's lately, which was good for her, but Peter really wanted her out in the world, not just at a musty old bookstore, so seeing her out with the car gave him hope.

Peter and Kenzi were reasonably close before Mark died, definitely closer than Olivia was with her, but that had been so fractured the last few years. Peter had tried hard to keep everything together, but he was spread thin, and his connection with his daughter had slipped. She knew she was struggling and had tried to help, but he had no idea how bad it had gotten till it was almost too late. Since they brought Kenzi home from the hospital after her accident, he had been trying so hard to find ways to help her, but she was keeping him at a distance. It felt like punishment. But lately, he had seen signs of his laughter coming back through, giving him hope again.

Peter had been giving Kenzi a wide berth since her fight with Olivia, but he thought it would be time for a little 'check-in' with her. He gently knocked on her door. "Kenz? Ok if I come in?"

"Uh, yeah, sure."

Kenzi's response seemed less cranky than he had expected, which gave him a little hope. He opened the door, but he didn't walk into Kenzi's room- he just stood in the doorway, leaning against the frame. Kenzi was sitting at her desk, a couple of open books in front of her. Her desk lamp cast a pool of amber light over the books, throwing soft shadows on the pages. A pencil twirled slowly between her fingers, and a forgotten hoodie was draped over the back of her chair like a second skin. It gave Peter a little comfort to know that, even with everything that had happened and was still happening, he never had to ride Kenzi about schoolwork. Kenzi turned in her chair to face him. She seemed a little apprehensive about what he might say. He didn't want to make it too intense. He knew it probably wasn't a good idea to ask about the fight directly, so he chose just to have a casual conversation, an easy way to do a quick 'temperature check.'

"I've seen you out in a garage a few times. Checking out your new car?"

Kenzi seemed to relax a little.

"Oh, um, yeah. It, ah, it doesn't start."

Peter was definitely not an expert on cars, but when he was younger, he had been shown enough about older engines that he was pretty sure he could get it running again. He thought this might be a chance to rebuild his relationship with his daughter a bit more. If he could help her with the car, maybe that would make up, just a little, for how much he had let her down.

"You know, I could, I could help you work on it. If you like."

"No!" The word flew out of her mouth before she could stop it. Peter blinked. Kenzi's heart jumped into her throat. She had to fix this—fast. She was still coming to terms with the whole 'Tom the ghost' thing herself, and there was no way she was going to talk to ANYONE else about it. They'd think she was crazy. She still wasn't 100% convinced that she wasn't. She felt a little more okay with the whole idea because it was contained in the garage, which made it easier for her to keep it a secret. Even if Tom hadn't offered to help her fix the car, she needed to do what she could to keep everyone out of there.

She looked at her dad, who was obviously a little shocked and possibly hurt by her response. She had to think fast.

"I mean. No thanks. I've ah, I've found a few good YouTube channels on how to fix older engines. I kinda wanted to give it a try myself, you know."

Kenzi didn't notice any change in her Dad's expression.

"It's just that I thought that if I could do this thing, this one thing by myself, and actually do it right. Then, that would be something I succeeded at."

Peter thought for a second. Ever since Kenzi's suicide attempt, he knew that she was struggling, but he had never really felt that she was 'failing' at anything; she certainly never let on. This was kind of the first time in a long time that he had gotten a little insight into how his daughter was feeling. It was his first chance in a while to actually support her.

"Ok, that makes sense. Just know that if you ever need help, ah, with the truck, I'm here, if you need."

He had bought it. Kenzi was safe, for now. She let out a little sigh of relief.

"Yeah, I know. Thanks."

Peter turned to leave, paused, and just turned his head back towards his daughter. She was doing better than he had expected, given the big fight she had had with her Mother, and that was good, but hearing her talking about 'failing' was rough. She wouldn't let him help with the car, and that was okay, but he was still going to take every opportunity to help her that he could.

"You know, you're not *failing*, Kenz. And ah, even if you were, that would be ok, you know. You've been through a lot, so ah, remember to cut yourself some slack."

Before everything that had happened, Kenzi had always been close to her Dad. Not as close as she was with Mark, but definitely more than she was with her Mum. He had always had a way of making her feel as though she was 'enough.' It was nice to have that now. Have that again.

Kenzi smiled and gave a little nod. Peter stood there for a moment, nodded, and then left. Peter lingered in the hallway for a moment after the door clicked shut. It wasn't much—but it felt like something. A crack of light under a door that had been closed too long.

As Peter walked down the hallway to his and Olivia's bedroom, he could see his wife sitting quietly on the bed, holding something in her hands. He couldn't see what it was, but he could tell from his wife's demeanour that it was something important, and also, something sad. He had always been able to read her. He slowed his walk a little, making sure not to startle her.

Her hair was pulled back in a hasty knot, but loose strands fell around her face, catching the lamplight like copper threads. The weariness etched beneath her eyes didn't dim her beauty; if anything, it sharpened the tenderness in her features, the quiet proof of years spent giving more of herself than she had to spare. Olivia sat with her knees bent, her lower legs tucked up under her thighs, Mark's school jacket bunched tightly in her lap. Her fingers traced the worn stitching along the collar, the patches she'd sewn back when he was still small enough to need help with everything.

She brought the jacket to her face and inhaled.

It smelled like linen. Maybe the cedar from the wardrobe.

But not him.

Not anymore.

She pressed the fabric to her face and closed her eyes, and for a while, she didn't move.

Peter stood in the doorway, unsure if he should speak. He knew that Olivia had kept Mark's jacket safe, sealed away in a special vacuum bag, to preserve it. It had been a while since he had seen her take it out. He knew that she did it from time to time, but she didn't like to do it too much, so as not to damage it. He knew that the fight with Kenzi had brought some things about Mark to the surface for Olivia. He never liked seeing his family fight, but he could tell that both Kenzi and Olive needed to get some of their grief out in the open. It was the only way that he thought that the two of them could start to move on, and maybe start to build some sort of semblance of a relationship again.

He looked at his wife. This amazing woman, who was always so full of strength, now looked vulnerable. He wanted to rush over and hold her, to make her feel better, but he could tell that wasn't the right move. This was about what she wanted. What she needed. So he would take his direction from her lead.

"Olive?"

She didn't respond.

He slowly walked over and sat beside her, shoulder to shoulder, and looked down at the jacket.

"I can't smell him anymore." She said, tears starting to form in the corner of her eyes, and her voice cracked.

Peter said nothing. He didn't really know what to say. They both sat there in that moment- truly alone.

Olivia sniffled before talking again.

"Is Kenzi right? Have I replaced Mark with Lucas?"

Peter was taken aback. There was such a feeling of doubt in his wife's voice, which was unusual. She was always so confident. It was one of the qualities that he had always admired about her, that had drawn him to her, that he had leaned on.

Peter took Olivia's hand in his. He could tell his wife needed some reassurance right now, and he was ready to give it.

"No way. I know how much Mark meant to you- still means to you, means to us both. I love Lucas so much, probably even more than I thought I could. But that doesn't mean I love Mark any less."

Peter squeezed Olivia's hand. Not too tight, just enough to show intent.

"And I KNOW it's the same for you. Enjoying Lucas and missing Mark aren't mutually exclusive. You have more than enough love inside you for them both, for us all."

Olivia turned and looked up at Peter. She could feel the sentiment behind his words, but they weren't helping.

"But she's right. I wasn't there for her. When Mark died, I just fell apart. I was so broken. But then when we got pregnant, I was just so happy. And when Lucas was born, I just threw myself into him."

Olivia's throat bobbed. She looked off into nothing.

"It was easier, you know. If I focused on Lucas, I didn't have to think about Mark as much. But I focused too much. I didn't realise what I was doing to Kenzi, and we almost lost her, too."

Olivia's tears were flowing freely now. Peter wiped them away with his hand, still holding her hand with his other.

"But we didn't. She's still here. We're all still here."

Peter paused for a moment. He so wanted to help his wife feel better.

"Look, losing Mark was horrible. The worst thing ever. And could we have handled it better? Help Kenzi more? Yeah, probably. But we probably could have done it a lot worse, too. I know you did the best you could- that you're still doing the best you can, and that's what matters."

Peter gently put his hand on Mark's jacket. Olivia held tightly onto his other hand.

"Mark's gone, but he will never be forgotten, you'll never forget him, and you'll certainly never *replace* him. Kenzi can see that now, and maybe that's a start. Maybe that's enough for now. I know the two of you will find your way back to each other."

Olivia leaned into Peter's chest. The movement of his breaths soothed her.

"I hope so, Peter. I hope so."

He rested his chin on her head, and they sat that way for a long time, the jacket folded between them like a shared memory.

Being there for his wife and his daughter made Peter feel better. His family was so important to him, and he always felt better when he could help. He hadn't done much tonight, not really, but he had done a little, and sometimes, that was enough.

Chapter 20
"All my favourite people in one place."

Kenzi's shift in the bookstore was almost over. Although she and Jo had talked today, she hadn't thought of a way to learn something, anything, that could help Tom figure out what was keeping him there. It was strange. Since everything that had happened with Mark and her, she hadn't felt like she had a purpose. Sure, she had still been completing assignments for school, but nothing had really felt like an important task for her. But now, helping Tom move on, she found purpose. It gave her drive. For the first time in a long time, Kenzi *needed* to do something to help someone else, and it felt good. Outside, the light had turned syrupy gold, stretching soft shadows across the wooden floor. The smell of book glue and lavender polish still lingered in the air, mingling with the subtle creak of old shelves settling into the evening.

Kenzi was putting some returns back on shelves, and placed the last book in place with a loud thud! Her new purpose also brought her new frustration, and it had started to spill over into her actions. The sound echoed louder than expected in the quiet shop, as if the books themselves had flinched. Kenzi clenched her jaw and stole a glance toward the counter, her heart tapping too hard in her chest. She paused, tentatively waiting to see if Jo had noticed and reacted. Nothing. She looked up at the clock, which had just struck five-thirty, closing time. Kenzi walked around the bookshelf and found Jo standing at the door, a large box of books in her hands. Kenzi thought to herself that the box must be pretty heavy, as Jo actually looked like she was struggling a bit with it, which surprised her.

"You ready to go, love?"

"Yeah...sure." Kenzi was frustrated with herself. She hadn't spoken about Tom at all today. She hadn't wanted to directly talk about him with Jo, as she thought that might seem a bit strange to be asking about a dead guy again, especially one that really didn't mean anything to her, well, not in any way that other people would understand. So, she had been trying to think of a way to steer the conversation in that direction, but with no success. She didn't think that Tom would be upset or annoyed with her if she had nothing new to tell him; he definitely gave off a more 'chill' and 'easy-going' vibe than that. But she knew she would be upset with herself if she hadn't succeeded, at least a little bit. She didn't feel the shift had been a waste, as she had learned more about her grandmother and even a bit more about her dad when he was young, which was nice, but it still felt like a failure. She didn't like that feeling. It was all too familiar to her, and she was really trying hard to overcome it. Then it hit her. Kenzi remembered that Tom sometimes appeared near Jo, like at her house, so maybe there would be something there that could help.

The thought knotted in her chest. She chewed at the inside of her cheek, feeling the pressure build behind her eyes. Every second that passed without saying something felt like watching a door close.

"Did you want some help taking those books home, Jo?"

Before Kenzi could pat herself on the back for her brilliant idea, Jo had already tossed the box of books at her. Kenzi caught it, and it sent her reeling back a bit-it WAS heavy. She steadied herself and smiled at Jo.

"That'd be great. Thanks, kiddo," said Jo over her shoulder as she started out the door.

Kenzi quickly followed her out. She realised she had never been to Jo's house before. That filled her with a bit of hope that maybe some clues lay there, waiting for her to discover them.

The walk to Jo's place was quick. Quick, but not quiet. Time with Jo was rarely quiet. But it was fast, which made Kenzi happy. Jo's house didn't look too dissimilar to her new home, like they had been built around the same time. But Jo's house looked a bit more worn. Not messier. No. The yard looked immaculate. The kind of yard that looked like it was mowed and trimmed with a ruler to make sure it was all perfect. And although the paint was starting to flake in spots, it didn't look ignored. Kenzi couldn't really put her finger on it. Something about this house looked a bit more 'lived in' than her home.

Jo swung the front door open and led Kenzi inside. Her house smelled faintly of lemon polish and old wood, the kind of scent that clung to a life well-lived. Jo shrugged off her jacket and tossed it onto a chair with careless ease, her bracelets jangling together as if even her movements carried their own commentary. Not surprisingly, there were piles of books scattered throughout the living room. Again, not messy, just lived-in. Before Kenzi had realised, Jo had disappeared down a hallway, yelling, "Just set it down anywhere, Kenz. I'ma grab us a drink and will be right back."

Kenzi looked around for a good spot to place the box. There wasn't one, so she just popped it on an empty spot on the coffee table. She stretched her back and arms, sore from carrying the large box. She looked around the room. Now she was here, in Jo's house, somewhere that obviously meant something to Tom, she was determined to find something useful. There was a large fireplace in the centre of the living room, and a number of picture frames, all mismatched, rested on the mantle above it. Kenzi walked closer, looking intently at each picture.

There was a picture of Jo and Quinn on their wedding day, which was starting to fade. They both looked so young in it. Jo seemed very similar to how she was now, though her hair was bright blonde rather than the faded grey it had been. Quinn looked quite different, much skinnier than Kenzi would have thought, and with a full head of light-brown hair. They looked happy, which didn't surprise Kenzi. The few times she had seen them together, they were still very clearly in love, always smiling and touching each other.

There was a picture of Kelly and her husband on their wedding day. Standing with the couple was another version of Jo and Quinn. This time, they looked middle-aged. Jo's hair was still quite blonde, and Quinn had started to fill out a little. Kelly seemed pretty similar to how she does now, kind of old-school cool. As Kenzi looked at the picture, Kelly's black hair seemed even darker, especially when compared to her parents' hair.

There was another older picture, this one of five young adults. It was Jo's gang, sometime before Tom had died. They were all so close and happy-looking. Jo and Tom were hugging. Quinn was there, right in the middle of them all, somehow even skinnier than he was in his wedding picture, kinda scrawny looking. A man was standing behind Mac with his arms around her. Kenzi figured it must have been her Grandfather. He reminded her of her dad. Kenzi stared at her grandmother. She had her hair pulled back in a high ponytail, wearing glasses on a strap around her neck. Kenzi caught her own reflection in the picture. She hadn't realised she had her hair in a high pony as well, cementing her acceptance of the resemblance between her and her grandmother. She smiled and felt a warm feeling inside.

Kenzi shook it off. She was not there for her. She was there for Mark.

The last picture of the mantle confused Kenzi a bit. It was obviously a picture of Quinn, sometime between his wedding and his daughter's. He had aged, but not a lot. He was rolling on the grass with a young girl and a boy. The boy was younger than the girl, who herself couldn't have been more than four or five years old. They all had huge smiles on their face, like they had been having the time of their lives. The girl must be Kelly, but Kenzi had no idea who the boy could be. Jo had never mentioned another child. Kenzi was intrigued. Who was this boy? Could he have something to do with Tom?

Before Kenzi could think about it anymore, she was snapped back to reality by Jo, who had returned from wherever she had run off to.

"Beautiful, aren't they? The pictures." Jo was right next to Kenzi now and had thrust a glass of water into her hand.

"All my favourite people in one place."

Jo placed her hand on the mantle, smiling softly.

"I like to keep them here, so I can see 'em every time I come home. These are the big moments that mean the most to me."

Jo took a sip of her water and wiped a small tear from the corner of her eye. These pictures all clearly meant a lot to Jo, something that Kenzi could relate to.

This was Kenzi's chance.

"Can you tell me about them? These moments?"

Jo seemed to perk up immediately.

"You betcha! Well, this one's pretty obvious," gesturing to her wedding picture, "this is me an' Quinn on our wedding day. God, we were so young. Had no idea what we were doing. But after Mark, we had both decided that we were just going to live, no matter what, so that's what we did."

Next, she picked up the picture of Kelly's wedding day.

"This was," she paused a bit, "our daughter, Kelly's wedding day. She looked so pretty. Her husband, Johnny, he's a good man, really loves her. Takes care of her. Quinn and I were so happy that she had found someone who would take care of her."

Jo gently placed the picture back down and picked up the picture of her friends.

'This is all of us, when we were younger. It's the last picture we took before Tom's accident. We were so convinced we knew everything about the world. We had no idea what really lay ahead for us." Jo paused and swallowed, pushing back more tears. "Quinn and I are the only ones left now. The last of a time long-forgotten."

Kenzi placed her hand on Jo's shoulder. She really wanted to ask about the boy in the last photo, but she didn't want to dismiss how Jo was feeling.

"I doubt you could ever be forgotten, Jo."

Jo placed the image down and placed her hand on top of Kenzi's.

"Thanks, Love. That's why these pictures and stories are so important. It's how we keep the memory of those we've lost alive."

Kenzi couldn't help but think back to her fight with her mother. So much of it revolved around the photos of her brother and what they both thought about them. Kenzi realised that she and her mother felt the same way, the same way as Jo. Kenzi wanted Mark's photos out in the open so she could see them and keep him alive in the house. Her mother wanted to keep his photos somewhere safe so nothing bad happened to them or to him. She felt like she was finally starting to understand her mother's grief.

The two of them had been standing there in silence for longer than Kenzi realised. She was lost in thoughts of her mother and brother; she forgot why she was there, Tom.

"And who are these people?" Kenzi asked, gesturing towards the last photo—the mystery photo. As Kenzi waited, she hoped it would reveal something important—something that could help Tom.

"Ah, this one is really special. It's Quinn with Kelly and your dad, when they were much younger."

"Oh…" Kenzi was surprised and disappointed. It hadn't even occurred to her that it could be her Dad. She knew that Jo was close with her Grandmother, but she never really thought about what that meant for her Dad. Regardless, this picture was no help at all. She had failed Tom today.

"Yeah. You already know this, but when your Dad was only little, Trevor, your Grandfather got really sick and passed away, so it was just your Dad and Mac. Life was very different back then, so being a single Mum was not nearly as easy as it is now. Heh, not that it meant that Mac needed help, not that woman. But Quinn and me, we helped her anyway, as much as we could."

Jo had picked up the picture now, wiping a bit of dust off the glass.

"Quinn was always such a good Dad to Kelly. I was so thankful for that. And when Trevor died, he really stepped up for your Dad. Did everything he could to fill the gap left by Trevor. Not replace him, just help out as much as he could. This photo was not taken long after Trevor had passed. Your Dad had been so sad, and Quinn had slowly been working his way into his world. This was the first day your Dad had really started to interact with Quinn, kinda the first day he had started to come back alive. T'was definitely the first time that I had seen him smile after your Grandad passed."

Jo gently placed the photo back on the mantle, adjusting its position slightly. She took a big drink of her water and walked over to the large box of books that Kenzi had placed on the coffee table earlier. Kenzi had never thought about what it must have been like for her Dad to have lost his Father at such a young age.

"Sounds like Dad was lucky to have Quinn and you."

"Yep. That man is one of a kind for sure. He's always taken such good care of us all. Never cause he had to, always because he wanted to."

Kenzi looked up from the photos and saw the clock hanging above them. It was getting late. Although she didn't have anything new to tell Tom, she felt like she needed to see him, if only to let him know that she had tried to find something out for him. She quickly drank the rest of her water, placed the empty glass down next to Jo's, and headed for the door.

"I'd better get going. Wanted to ah, work on the car a little before dinner. Thanks for the drink."

"Anytime, love," Jo responded, her head buried in the box of books.

Kenzi gently closed the door behind her and started down the path. She hadn't learned anything about Tom, but the trip to Jo's hadn't been a complete waste. She had learned a bit more about her Dad today, about what his childhood must have been like. He had always been involved in her, Mark's, and Lucas's lives, a good dad, and now she was starting to see where that must have come from: Quinn. She hadn't had much to do with him at all since coming to Esperance, but he was clearly a good person and had played an important role in her life, if only through the way he cared for her Father. Possibly more important than the improved awareness of her father was Jo's perspective on photos and her Mother. Kenzi was getting closer to forgiveness. Not fully there yet, but definitely something she wanted to get to.

Chapter 21
"I'm Sure You'll Figure It Out."

As soon as Kenzi had gotten home from Jo's, she had changed into some old clothes and headed out to the garage. Although she didn't have anything of real consequence to share with Tom, certainly nothing that she thought could help to figure out why he was still here, she still wanted to see him and work on her car with him. She got the feeling that letting him help fix the car would be a way to soften the blow of her failure that day.

Kenzi slowly opened the garage door, unsure whether she wanted Tom there, and it let out a long, drawn-out creak as she did. She slowly entered and looked around. Although she had been out there a few times since her family moved in, it still looked like no one had been there in a very long time. It seemed like a fitting place for her to talk to a ghost. But she couldn't see Tom. She had been apprehensive about seeing him, but now that he wasn't there, she was disappointed. Since Mark had passed, she hadn't felt close to anyone, but she was starting to feel close to people again. Jo and Tom had both helped Kenzi in their own way, and she hadn't realised how much they both were starting to mean to her. Strangely, the sadness about not seeing Tom felt nice.

"That you, Mac?" came a voice from under the car.

Kenzi kneeled down where she stood, twisting her head to look under the car. There was Tom, lying underneath the car, his head under the engine. A little wave of happiness washed over Kenzi.

"Hey! There you are."

Tom effortlessly slid himself out from under the car, like he had done the exact movement a thousand times before. He jumped up. His dark hair was pushed back, though a few loose strands clung to his forehead. His shirt stretched faintly across his chest as he pushed himself upright, sleeves dusting at his elbows. He patted his jeans automatically, like he still expected oil stains to appear.

"Was just takin' a look at what we had ta work with. You ready to get started?"

Kenzi was a bit surprised. She had expected Tom to ask her if she had found anything out that might help him. She thought that, since they had made their deal to help him move on, it would have been the most important thing to him. Helping Tom was important to Kenzi. Probably the most important thing in her life right now, but Tom seemed more interested in holding up his side of the deal. Kenzi wasn't sure if that meant he didn't really think she could help him, or if it just meant that he was willing to put her needs ahead of his. Based on the way that Jo had spoken about him, she decided it must be the latter. Which actually made her want to help him more.

But she couldn't really help him today. Maybe just giving something to focus on, like fixing the car, might make the whole 'ghost stuck watching his loved ones move on' thing a little easier. That would be enough today.

"Yeah. Let's do this thing!"

That was more enthusiastic than Kenzi had meant it to be. Tom looked at her, a little confused, a little amused.

"Ok…How 'bout you pop tha hood, and I'll grab a few tools?"

"Sounds good," said Kenzi, trying to seem less excited.

Kenzi walked over and opened the car door. The handle was tight, and she had to squeeze it hard to open it. She swung the large door open and sat down on the seat. As she did, little particles of dust leapt off the seat. She really needed to clean the interior. She reached under the steering wheel, feeling around for the knob for the hood. She found it, and a lot of cobwebs. As she pulled back on the know, the hood lifted.

Kenzi got out of the car and walked around to the front. Tom had dragged over a metal tray that sat at the top of a metal rod, connected to a rectangular base on wheels. Kenzi hadn't noticed it before, but it must have been tucked away in a corner of the shed. Tom had placed a few tools on the tray and was searching through the pile on the bench for more. Kenzi couldn't help but notice how at ease Tom looked at the moment. He knew that he had worked as a mechanic before he died, but she had never thought about what that actually looked like, or how much he might have enjoyed it. Tom picked up a long metal tool and flipped it in the air, catching it again with ease before placing it on the tray with the others. Seeing Tom like this, it was easy for Kenzi to forget that he was a ghost and just see him as a friend.

Kenzi caught herself staring at Tom, quickly looked away, unlatched the hood, and raised it as high as she could.

"Here, let me get that," said Tom as he pushed the hood higher and propped it up with a rod from inside the engine bay. As he stood there, arms stretched out, Kenzi noticed the short sleeves on his shirt bunched up over his biceps. She hadn't realised how muscly he was before. She thought about the pictures of Quinn when he was younger that she had seen earlier at Jo's house, and how different the two of them were. She found it a bit strange that Jo had been attracted to both of them. Quinn must have really been sweet and caring when they lost Tom, and that must have been what Jo found so special about him. Now that Kenzi knew how important Quinn had been to her father, she wondered if that was why he was always so caring and kind, too. It was strange. Since coming to Esperance and learning more about her family's past, she was starting to see them in a new light.

"Alright, you're gonna need a new alternator, so we gotta get that old one out." Tom pointed to a part of the engine, as if he assumed Kenzi knew what he was talking about. Kenzi tried to look where he was pointing, but the various parts, valves, and tubes meant absolutely nothing to her.

"Uhh…" was all she could muster in response.

Tom moved around to the side of the car slightly, leaned under the hood and tapped on a small part of the engine, about the size of a lunchbox.

"This is the alternator. It pretty much controls the power for the whole car."

"Oh, ok. Cool."

"Now, grab that socket wrench." Tom pointed to the collection of tools he had assembled and placed on the tray near the front of the car. Kenzi looked at them. They all looked different, and yet the same. She was sure they all had obvious, unmistakable names. She had no idea what any of them were, especially which one was a socket wrench. She slowly reached for the tools, but was afraid to grab the wrong one. Tom must have noticed and could have taken the opportunity to tease Kenzi, which he seemed to really enjoy, but, to her surprise, he did not.

"It's the one all the way on the left."

In situations like this, Kenzi would typically try to make a little joke to play off her lack of knowledge or awareness, but to her surprise, she didn't. She just owned up to it.

"Thanks. I have no idea what any of these are called."

Tom stood up a bit and leaned casually against the car. He crossed his arms, thumb hooking through a belt loop, one boot heel resting against the tyre. A slight tilt of his head and half-smile made it feel like he was just some guy killing time after school, not a ghost decades out of place.

"S'all good, Kenz. We all have our own skills. This stuff always came easy ta me, but I know it's not the same for everyone else. I'm sure there's heapsa stuff that you know tonnes about that I wouldn't have a clue about."

Kenzi smiled at Tom. It'd been a while since she'd had a genuine conversation with anyone even remotely close to her age, ghost years notwithstanding, and she'd forgotten how nice and comforting talking with others could be.

She picked up the socket wrench, which was heavier than it looked, and the handle was worn, likely due to years of use. She walked over to Tom and tried to hand it to him.

"Nu-huh," said Tom as he put his hands up in a *stop* motion, "I said I'd *help* you with the car, but you're gonna do all the work yourself. Only way you'll learn."

Kenzi was actually a bit excited by that notion. She was still feeling like a bit of a failure for not learning anything helpful from Jo that day, so the idea of actually doing the work on the car was appealing.

"Alright. Tell me what to do."

Tom leaned back into the engine bay and touched a bolt on the side of the alternator. Kenzi leaned in alongside him.

"First things first, ya gotta unbolt this sucka, so put the socket wrench on here and twist it. You know what righty-tighty lefty-loosey means, right?"

Kenzi placed the socket wrench over the bolt and grabbed the handle with both hands. Before trying to move it, she paused.

"Ah, that means I need to pull it to the left, right?

"Yep. It's gonna be tight, so put some elbow grease into it."

Sometimes when Tom spoke, it was easy to forget that he was technically as old as her grandparents, and sometimes it wasn't. "Elbow grease" definitely made it obvious.

Kenzi pulled hard on the socket wrench; the veins in her arms strained under the force. She felt the bolt start to move slowly and then loosen. She kept twirling the socket wrench until the bolt came out completely. It looked as old and worn as the socket wrench.

"Nice work, Kenz! Now just do that three more times, and we're in business."

Kenzi repeated the process for the other three bolts on the alternator. Although they were all out now, it didn't fall as she expected, stuck in place with dirt, grime, and a lack of use. She grabbed hold of it and yanked it out, almost falling over from the force, but she steadied herself.

She stood there for a second, holding the heavy piece of engine in both her hands. Hands that were now covered in dirt and grease, not unlike her shirt. She looked at Tom, who had turned around from the car to look at her, no doubt to make sure she was ok. He looked pretty impressed with Kenzi, which felt nice. But then she felt guilty. She hadn't wanted to tell Tom that she hadn't found out anything useful today, and she had hoped that focusing on the car would distract him, and she wouldn't have to tell him, and that had worked. She didn't *have* to tell Tom. But she *wanted* to tell Tom.

"Tom, I uh, I forgot to tell you that I did some digging at Jo's today."

Tom reached forward and took the alternator from Kenzi. He placed it on the bench and started wiping it down a bit.

"Yeah?" he said over his shoulder. He didn't sound extremely interested in what Kenzi was going to say, which surprised her a bit. She thought he would have been desperate to learn something that could help him move on. She walked over to stand next to him at the bench.

"Yeah, I was looking at some photos she had on the fireplace mantle. She said they were all really important to her. There was one of you all when you were younger. She uh, she said it was the last photo you were in before your uh, accident."

Tom kept looking down at the alternator as he cleaned it. He was listening, but also focused on the task in front of him.

"Oh yeah, I remember that one. Anything else interesting?"

Kenzi started to play with the tools on the bench, not really sure what she should be doing.

"Not really. I mean, kind of. There was a picture of my dad when he was really little, just after my grandad died. He was playing in the backyard with Quinn and Kelly. Jo told me how sad my dad was at that time, and how Quinn really stepped in to help out my grandma."

Tom stopped wiping the alternator and looked out the window. There was nothing specific out there, just the side of the house, dimly lit by the setting sun.

"That's nice," he said casually. "Wonder if I'da done the same if things were different."

Kenzi had heard Tom talk about the life he didn't get to have before, and it had always made her feel a bit sad, but tonight was a little different. She wasn't sure what would happen to Tom if she helped him move on. After today, she wasn't even sure if she could actually help him move on. But she had to hope that there was somewhere better for him to be. Somewhere, he didn't have to keep watching the people he cared about moving on. Somewhere, he didn't have to watch his friend live the life he was supposed to have.

"I'm sure you would have, Tom. Heck, I'm sure I'd probably be calling you Uncle Tom if things were different."

"Ha! Sure thing, kiddo!" joked Tom, as he rubbed the top of Kenzi's hair, messing her hair, like she was a little kid. She laughed as she jerked her head away.

"There were some other pictures, too. Ah, one of Jo and Quinn from their wedding day, and..." Kenzi became aware that talking about Jo's wedding to another man may not be the best thing to talk about right now, "and a picture of Kelly on her wedding day, but neither of them was overly important. I mean, ah, I mean they are obviously important to Jo, it's just that, ah." Kenzi paused and stopped playing with the tools. Just turned to look at Tom.

"What I mean is, I didn't find anything that might help us figure out why you're still here. I'm sorry."

Tom looked at Kenzi and smiled a little smile.

"Don't sweat it, Mac. I'm sure you'll figure it out. I've got plenty of time."

Tom's words didn't make Kenzi feel any better. It's not that she wanted to get rid of him. He was the first person that she really thought of as a friend for ages. But she also wanted to help him.

They both looked back out the window, and there was a bit of an awkward silence between them. Kenzi didn't know what to say.

"It really is a good picture of Kelly, the wedding one." Tom had a soft smile on his face.

"Ah, you've seen it?" Kenzi turned to look at Tom again, slightly puzzled.

Tom kept looking out the window.

"Well, yeah. I told ya that sometimes I find myself in Jo's house. Not like I can do anything or talk to anyone when I'm there, so I've looked around tha place. I like looking at the photos, they help me see what's happened while I've been gone."

Kenzi looked back out the window again.

"That makes sense, I guess. I'd probably do the same thing."

"She's a good kid, that Kelly," Tom's voice seemed to lift a bit as he spoke, and his smile grew a bit larger. "It's weird, now that I think about it. I've probably been round her as much as Jo. Maybe even more."

"That is weird," thought Kenzi to herself. She had kind of assumed that Tom was following Jo around, and that anytime he was around someone else, like Kelly or Bobby, Jo must have been there too, and that's why he was there. But now that doesn't seem like the case. So, why would Tom be around Kelly if Jo wasn't there? What was special about her?

Then she thought about what Jo had said about Kelly at the bookstore, about how she was born really early, but there were no complications. At the time, she had thought it was a bit weird, but she hadn't paid it any more attention. And just today, when Jo was talking about Kelly, the way she paused before referring to her as Jo and Quinn's daughter, and even the way she mentioned that Quinn never had to be a good dad, it was strange now that she was thinking about it.

Kenzi's mind flashed back to the picture of Kelly on her wedding day, and she once again thought about how dark her hair was compared to that of both her parents. Black hair. Black hair...like Tom's. She thought about the picture of Jo and Quinn on their wedding day. Jo had said they were so young, and how quickly it had happened after Tom had died. She hadn't noticed it earlier, but Jo actually looked a little chubbier than she expected her to be; she was so thin now, and in the other pictures of her she had seen. Could she have been pregnant with Kelly when she got married? Is that why they got married so quickly? And if she was born so early without any complications, maybe she wasn't born early. Maybe Jo became pregnant earlier than everyone had thought.

What if Jo got pregnant much earlier? Like, what if she got pregnant before Tom died?

What if Kelly was actually Jo and Tom's daughter?

Chapter 22
"Is the Truth More Important Than Someone's Feelings?"

Kenzi was walking through the hallway at school. It was full of other kids, all busily engaged in the normal activities you would expect, as everyone hurried from one class to the next, trying to get in their social interactions before the bell rang. As Kenzi moved her way through the crowd, she could see how busy and loud everyone was, but she couldn't really hear it. She didn't get very much sleep last night and had been in a daze all day, just on auto, moving from one task to the next without much thought or effort.

After her realisation about Kelly, Jo, and Tom, she hadn't been able to do much of anything else. She had ended things with Tom pretty quickly, not wanting to talk to him about it. Not really because she was afraid of how he would react; more because she wasn't sure she was right and wanted to make sure before telling him. If she was right, she was pretty sure that was the thing keeping him here, and she didn't want to give him hope if she wasn't right. It was such a big deal, she knew, not just for Tom but for Jo, Kelly, and Quinn. She had no idea if she

was right, and if she was, did anyone else know? If it was
a secret, who was Jo keeping it from? And if it came out,
what would that mean for them all? They all seem so
happy and obviously love each other, so what right did
Kenzi have to mess that up? Even if it meant that Tom
could move on, was that more important than possibly
destroying a family?

Kenzi's own family had been broken for so long
now, and she knew all too well what that was like. She
couldn't stand putting another family through hell,
especially as she was starting to see a way back for her
and her family. But, also, one thing that was becoming
very clear to Kenzi was how important it was for a family
to talk to each other. To be open and honest with each
other. She and her mother had been keeping so much
from each other for so long, and it had created so much
distance between them. It was only through opening up
to each other that things began to feel like they might
start to get better. So, maybe the truth about Kelly needed
to come out. It would be hard, but perhaps better in the
end.

Kenzi tried to balance the different sides of the
matter, but it was hard- too hard. In the last few weeks,
Kenzi had been learning more and more about life and
herself, and she was starting to feel a bit surer of things,
including herself. But now, she was so unsure about what
to do. She was feeling like she was slipping backwards, to
how she used to be, before she tried to kill herself. She

was so unsure about everything, and it was too much. She didn't want to go back to that place. She wanted to move forward.

Kenzi was so much in her head that she hadn't realised she had made it to Mrs Fox's doorway, and was just standing there, in a daze.

"You ok, Kenzi?"

Mrs Fox's words shook Kenzi out of her daze. She looked up at the counsellor, who was sitting behind her desk, looking curiously at Kenzi. She wasn't wearing her usual cardigan and was wearing a tight-fitting top. Not too tight, but tight enough for Kenzi to notice her slim figure. She actually looked more like a person today, rather than just a counsellor. Her dark hair was clipped neatly behind her ears today, and with the fitted top, Kenzi could see she carried herself more like someone who jogged in the mornings than just a school counsellor. Her expression, though, was as soft as ever, the kind that made you want to sit down, even when you didn't plan to. The sun coming in through the windows hit the back of her head, creating a nice glow around the edges. It was surprising.

"Huh? Ah, yeah, all good."

Kenzi quickly sat down in the chair opposite Mrs Fox, dropping her bag onto the floor beside her. She sat low in the chair, slumping a little, as if the weight of her thoughts were pushing her down. She could feel the difference today. In the last few sessions, which had been better, she had felt better in the chair, but now, it was the same as the first few times she was here. It wasn't Mrs Fox's fault, not at all. In fact, Kenzi was starting to not hate her meetings here. If she didn't have the Kelly stuff going on, she'd probably be happy to jump straight into a conversation about her grandmother. But she didn't. She just sat there, wallowing in self-doubt.

Mrs Fox looked at Kenzi. She could tell something was up. Kenzi was slouched over, looking down at the chair handle, and she was picking at the felt that was starting to peel away. This was not the Kenzi she was expecting. This is not the Kenzi she had seen lately. She had seen a real change in Kenzi in the last few sessions. It was clear that hearing about her Gran was making a difference, and she had seen a spark starting to appear. Today was different. Today, she could see something pulling her down. She knew how easy it was for teenagers to backslide into depression, and that she had to jump on this quickly. Kenzi had tried to hurt herself before, so that was also on her mind, that if things slipped too far, she could try again. She wasn't going to let that happen. She knew she had to do something, but it couldn't be too much, too fast.

So she just sat there, watching and waiting, saying nothing, hoping Kenzi would notice and start talking. She thought that if she could get Kenzi to initiate, that would be good. That would show here that the new Kenzi was still there. So, she waited.

Nothing.

It was quiet.

Quiet enough to hear the click of the clock on the wall. She tapped one finger lightly against the notepad on her desk, not writing anything down, just keeping time with the clock's steady tick, her eyes never leaving Kenzi.

Although it felt like much longer, a minute passed with nothing. Kenzi just sat there, unengaged. She had tried to give Kenzi the space to open up about whatever was on her mind, but it hadn't worked. So, she had to give her a prompt.

"You're quiet today, Kenzi?"

Kenzi was lost in her thoughts again, and she almost didn't hear Mrs Fox. She looked up at her, just with her eyes, keeping her face turned down.

"Yeah..."

Kenzi knew she should say more, but she couldn't really focus right now.

Mrs Fox knew she would have to push a little harder.

"Everything alright?"

"Yeah..."

Nothing. Mrs Fox was starting to get concerned now. She had to try a different approach. She leaned forward a bit, resting her forearms on the table.

"Kenzi, you know a big part of my job is making sure the students are doing ok. That's especially important with students who are considered high-risk for hurting themselves. I know things were terrible the last time you did something like that, but I thought things were getting better for you lately. So much so that I was even considering signing off on you, and stopping our chats altogether."

Mrs Fox leaned further forward, looking Kenzi squarely in the eyes.

"But right now, seeing you like this, I'm genuinely concerned."

That was enough to catch Kenzi's attention. She sat up straight. Kenzi knew that she wasn't in the best of moods today, but didn't Mrs Fox really think things were that bad? The last thing Kenzi wanted was for alarms to be raised and for the school to contact her parents. While things weren't great at home, they were definitely better than they had been, and Kenzi didn't want to do anything to disrupt that. Not only would that add more stress on her parents, which she didn't want, but it would probably jeopardise what she was doing with Tom, and she really didn't want that to happen. She had to fix this. Fast.

"Thank you, but I'm good, I swear." Kenzi was trying to put on a reassuring smile. "I'm not depressed, and definitely not thinking about…that stuff. I promise."

Mrs Fox leaned back a little. She had shaken Kenzi up, and now she was engaging. Kenzi could just be telling her what she thought that she wanted to hear, but her words actually seemed genuine. So, what was troubling her?

"Ok, Kenzi. I believe you." Ms Fox tilted her head a little, trying to put Kenzi at ease a bit more. "But something is clearly troubling you. I'd love to help, if I can?"

Kenzi didn't know what to say. She definitely didn't know what to do about Jo and Kelly. But, she didn't really think she could talk about it so openly with Mrs Fox. That could lead to further questions, and Kenzi did not want to risk that. She would have to be careful.

"Ok, well. I ah, I think I've figured out, ah, a secret about someone I know. And it's a big secret, like, world-changing stuff, and I'm not really sure if I should talk to the person about it."

Mrs Fox didn't reply. Not yet. She wanted to see if Kenzi would keep going. She could see this was important to her, so she tried to give her ample opportunity to talk it through.

Kenzi continued, "See, this secret, it actually affects a number of people and, and they all probably deserve to know. But, it's probably gonna hurt, and could really make things worse."

Mrs Fox was really impressed. This session was the first time that she had seen Kenzi really considering other people's thoughts and feelings. It was an excellent sign that she was getting better. She gave her one more chance to keep going.

"So, so I guess what I want to know is. Is the truth more important than someone's feelings?"

Mrs Fox leaned back in her chair, taking it all in. This was a really mature question. Whatever doubts she had about Kenzi earlier in the session were all but gone now. She was clearly putting a lot of care and thought into this situation, and she could see she really cared about whoever she was talking about. But this was not a question that she could answer for Kenzi, which was pretty common in her role. In fact, that is pretty much the opposite of what she was there to do. This was a problem for Kenzi to solve. Mrs Fox knew Kenzi could figure out what to do herself and that it was very important for her to do that, so she just had to support her in doing that.

"That's an excellent question, Kenzi. And sadly, not one that I can answer for you. No one can."

Kenzi slouched a little, obviously upset by what Mrs Fox was saying.

"A few years ago, back before I started here, I used to work in an HR department for a large company. Nothing major ever happened there, but there was this one lady. She'd always been so perky, but then I started to notice her withdraw a bit from everything, like something had happened. She never said anything, and I didn't hear any gossip around the workplace about her, but I was still a bit concerned."

Kenzi leaned forward a little, listening for something in the story that could help.

"I wasn't sure if I should approach her about it. Situations like that are always tricky, and when confronted, people can become embarrassed and pretend nothing is happening, which usually makes things worse. So, I didn't. A little while later, she got a new job somewhere else and moved on."

Kenzi slouched back again. That was no help at all.

"I still think about her sometimes. I was worried that saying something would make things worse. I don't know if things got better for her when she left. I hope they did, but maybe they didn't. Maybe if I had said something, things could have been different, but I'll never know. No one can, and I think that's just part of life. We each have to make choices every day, most are small, but sometimes, we have to make a big choice, and it's hard, and we might make the wrong choice, but we make it anyway."

Mrs Fox leaned forward again, somehow, with more intent, and it pulled Kenzi in.

So, Kenzi, my answer to your question is another question…what do you think?

Chapter 23
"I'm Not Going to Let That Stop Me Anymore."

"What do you think?"

Mrs Fox's words echoed in Kenzi's mind since she had left her session with the counsellor, and the rest of the school day had been more of the same from the morning. Kenzi was there. She attended her classes, listened to her teachers, and took notes, but she wasn't really there. She was still on autopilot, her mind too focused on other things. Important things. Dangerous things.

Now Mrs Fox's words followed her like a shadow, stretching long under the late afternoon sun. She kicked a gum wrapper off the footpath, letting the silence of the suburban street wrap around her. The houses looked the same as always—too bright, too clean, like they didn't know what it meant to break. The air was muggy in that way that made everything feel slower. Kenzi's school bag thumped softly against her hip as she walked, each step more about motion than direction.

Kenzi still had no idea what to do about Kelly. She wasn't really confident that talking about it, at least *kind of* about it, with Mrs Fox would help, and it hadn't. Not really. Even the story that the counsellor shared hadn't helped. If anything, it made things worse. This was the hardest choice that Kenzi had ever had to make in her life. One that she didn't want to make. It would have been so much easier if Mrs Fox had simply told Kenzi which option was the right one. Then she would know what to do. Then it wouldn't all be on her. Whatever fallout there was, it wouldn't be entirely her fault. But no. That's not what Mrs Fox did. It *was* all on Kenzi.

Kenzi hadn't been paying attention to where she was, and before she knew it, she was outside her home. When she reached the front gate, her fingers hovered above the latch longer than usual. The metal was warm. Familiar. The front gate creaked as she pushed it open. The noise it made seemed fitting, given how Kenzi's thoughts had been so slow and drawn today. As she walked up the path towards the front door, she took comfort in how everything looked the same. There was a little playset of Lucas fading in the sun. The shoe rack on the landing still had an odd number of shoes. The front door still had small flakes of paint peeling, showing its age.

Kenzi prepared herself for the Lucas-fuelled chaos that was no doubt occurring on the other side of the door. She actually kind of hoped for it. Maybe that would be a distraction from the choice she didn't want to make. She opened the door, entering slowly, bracing for the noise. As soon as she stepped inside, the house felt different.

Warmer. Like home. She gently closed the door behind her, kicked off her shoes, and looked around for Lucas or her mother. But they weren't there. As she looked around the room, her eyes, like a searchlight in the night, homed in on a missing person.

There was a new picture on the mantle.

It was Mark.

It had been years since there was a picture of Mark anywhere in the house. Kenzi's chest tightened, and her breath all but stopped. She didn't move. She couldn't move. It was too much for her. Mark was so important to her, and when his pictures went down, it broke her. The idea that he wouldn't still be visible in their home felt like her parents were trying to pretend that he never even existed. It had been the thing that had tipped her over the edge. It had been the thing that her fight with her mother was all about. Maybe that's why it was out now? Maybe her fight with her mother had helped her to understand how Kenzi felt about Mark's photos? The fight certainly made Kenzi understand how her mother felt about it.

Kenzi walked towards the mantle, slowly and effortlessly, manoeuvring around the furniture and toys left on the ground. She stood in front of the mantle, slowly reached out towards the picture. She touched it, and a warmth washed over her body. Over her soul. It was a picture of Mark from his seventeenth birthday. He was sitting in their old dining room, a large chocolate cake on the table in front of him, candles still slightly smoking. He was wearing a dorky party hat and a big smile. There was a little smear of chocolate on his face. It never mattered how careful he was, he ALWAYS got chocolate on his face when eating cake. Kenzi remembered the events so vividly. Her whole family was there. They always celebrated birthdays like that- just the four of them. She remembered being so happy. Seeing her brother like that always made her feel happy. He had that effect on everyone.

Tears started to roll down Kenzi's cheeks, but she didn't wipe them away. She just stood there, lightly touching the picture and her brother. Warm. Content. Happy. She was so caught up in the moment that she didn't hear her mother enter the room.

"It's a great picture, isn't it?"

Kenzi turned, still touching the picture, to see her mother standing in the doorway between the living room and the dining room. There was something different about her mother. Not her clothes or hair. She was dressed as usual. Loose-fitting jeans, with a nice blouse. Her hair was out, hanging neatly around her face. But still, she looked different. Kenzi couldn't put her finger on it. Fuller maybe? Not fatter. Like a missing piece inside her was back.

As soon as their eyes locked, Olivia, noticing that Kenzi was crying, started crying herself. She had been crying most of the day, so it wasn't going to take much to set her off again.

"Yeah, it is. But I thought you said-" before Kenzi could finish, Olivia, moving closer to Kenzi, cut her off.

"Kenz. I'm sorry. When I put all of Mark's photos away, I thought I was doing it to protect him from Lucas, but I didn't think about what that meant for you, and I'm so, so sorry. I never wanted you, or anyone else, to think that I was trying to hide or forget Mark. I should have spoken with you about it, about so much more, but I just couldn't, I couldn't talk to anyone, it was just too hard."

Olivia was standing right in front of Kenzi now, both of them in front of the mantle. Kenzi still had her left hand on the photo of Mark. Tears were freely flowing down both of their faces now.

"It's still hard, so hard, but I'm not going to let that stop me anymore. I want you to feel like you can talk about Mark, and anything else, whenever you want to. That's why I put his photos back up. So that we could all see him. Remember him. Talk about him."

"But, what about Lucas?"

Olivia placed her right hand on the edge of the mantle, near the picture of Mark. Her fingers hovered just above the photo frame before she touched it, the same way she sometimes paused before touching Kenzi — cautious, as though afraid the connection might be too much. The picture had brought her and Kenzi physically closer. Probably closer than Kenzi had allowed her to get in a long time. There was an energy between them, trying to pull them closer, but there was still a lot keeping them apart.

"Lucas is older now. Sure, he's still possibly, probably, going to get his hands on these pictures, but he's got to learn how to treat important things."

For some reason, the word *important* hit Kenzi right in the chest. Mark was important. So important to her. It was so good to hear her mother talk about him the same way.

They both just looked at each other for a moment. Neither is sure what to say next. It was different from when their fight ended. Their fight had ended with a release, but this, it felt more like a return. Like a road that had been blocked for construction reopening, allowing a routine to recommence.

Olivia turned to face the mantle. The tears had stopped flowing, but the stains of their path remained.

"He really loved chocolate cake, didn't he? Olivia's voice was softer. Calming. Warm.

Kenzi turned to face the picture, too. She was standing side by side with Olivia now. Her free hand fell between them, almost touching her mother's hand.

"He really did."

"Maybe I'll grab some next time I'm at the shops." Olivia's tone was the most casual that she had felt comfortable using with Kenzi in a while. It was just a conversation, not a guarded interrogation.

"That'd be nice."

Olivia's hand slowly moved closer to Kenzi's. She so badly wanted to hug her daughter, but she knew that was too much, too soon. She thought about holding her hand, but that also felt a bit too far.

Her hand moved closer.

The backs of their fingers gently touched.

Olivia prepared herself for Kenzi to pull away. That had been how most of her attempts to connect with her daughter had gone over the last few years.

But she didn't.

She let the connection linger.

Kenzi could feel her mother's touch. The first time in a long time that it felt truly *motherly*. She hadn't realised how much she had missed it. She could feel a warmth growing inside her, making its way up, threatening to force more tears out. She held them back, though. She just wanted to bask in this moment.

Right here. Right now. It was just Kenzi, her mother and Mark.

Everything else just slipped away.

Whatever struggles Kenzi was dealing with earlier. Tom. Kelly. Jo. They didn't matter right now. Kenzi still wanted to help them. But here, she was helping herself.

And that was ok.

That was good.

Mrs Fox's question flicked through Kenzi's mind again. "What do you think?" She still didn't know the answer, but right now, she felt like she might be able to find one.

She was starting to let go of her pain, so maybe she would be able to help others with theirs.

Mark was still gone.

But he was still here.

The loss was still there. It would always be there.

But right here, it felt like she didn't have to carry it alone anymore.

And that was good.

Chapter 24
"Aha!"

The rest of the afternoon had been one of the nicest that Kenzi had had with her family for a long time. There was nothing really different about it. Dinner. Homework. The events were all the same. But the feeling, that was different. Lighter. Easier. Kenzi knew that she would have to return to the mission to help Tom and regretted not going out to the garage to see him, but she just wanted to enjoy her own family for a bit longer.

It was the next day now, and Kenzi was back to reality, back to worrying about Tom and Kelly and Jo. And that was even harder now that she was in the bookstore with Jo.

As Kenzi stacked books onto the shelves, she peered through the gaps above them at Jo, who was sitting behind the counter. Her arms were waving about as she spoke vividly about some misadventure with Mac, which normally would have captivated Kenzi, but today, she was having trouble paying attention. She really wanted to help Tom, but she also didn't want to cause any trouble for Jo's family. Jo had been so good to her, and she felt like she could probably talk to Jo about anything, including this, but she didn't know how to do it.

Kenzi placed the last book back on the shelf and started to push the old, banged-up trolley back towards the storeroom. It was stiff to move, and one of the wheels twirled round and round, not touching the ground properly. The bookstore was old in a good way — like it had lived a hundred lives and remembered every one. Just as Kenzi walked into the storeroom, the front bell rang, so someone must have come into the shop. Kenzi pushed the trolley into its resting place in the corner and headed back out to see who was there.

It was Kelly.

Of course, it was Kelly.

She was standing on the other side of the counter from Jo, and actually looked a little frazzled today, which was strange, cause she always seemed so put-together. Her hair, which was normally out, allowed to hang down around her face, was up, but not neat, almost rushed. She had a scarf looped hastily around her neck, one end longer than the other, and her cheeks were still pink from the cold air outside. Even frazzled, there was a brightness to her that reminded Kenzi of Jo's warmth, but sharper, quicker, like her energy could fill a room if she wanted it to. Either way, seeing her here, looking more and more like Tom, was making Kenzi feel surer about her suspicions. Which made Kenzi more upset about it. Kenzi hovered near the back — not hiding, exactly, but not joining in either.

Jo was leaning down behind the counter, shuffling around in the boxes on the shelves. Kelly was now leaning on the counter, looking over at what her mother was doing. Her hair, which was in a messy bun, slid forward a little, and she quickly jerked her head back, not wanting it to fall loose.

"Aha!" Exclaimed Jo, as she grabbed hold of a small wooden box. She stood back up and wiped the dust off the top of the box. She gently placed the box on the countertop as Kelly jumped back off it.

"I knew they were in here somewhere, Kell."

"Yeah, but is behind the counter in the shop really the best place to keep them? Teased Kelly as she turned the box around to face her and opened it. It was full of Polaroid pictures. The way the sunlight outside shines onto them and is reflected as a rainbow of colours makes them seem magical. They were clearly old, from when Jo was much younger. Kelly flicked through a couple of the photos. There was one of Jo and Quinn dancing. And one of Trevor working on a car. And another one of Mac, sitting behind the wheel of her car.

"I knew where they were, so that's the best place for them, thank you very much." Jo's voice was a little stern, like a mother scolding her child, which made sense, but also seemed weird. Kenzi had pictured their relationship as perfect, but that was silly, because, of course, they weren't perfect; they had the same little give-and-take that all mother-daughter relationships had.

"These are great! They'll be perfect for the slideshow." Kelly closed the box and picked it up. She leaned over the counter and gave her mother a soft kiss on her cheek. Kenzi was reminded of her mother's gentle touch yesterday. It was so clear how these two felt about each other, regardless of any secret that Kenzi might think she knows.

Kelly leaned back and caught a glimpse of a figure in the corner of her eye. She turned and spotted Kenzi, hiding in the back.

"Hey, Kenz! I gotta jet, but you're coming to the party, right?"

Kenzi started walking closer, giving a little hello wave as she did.

"Oh, ah, hi, Kelly. What party?"

Before Kelly could respond, Jo did. Seemed she was the same bossy person with everyone.

"Quinn's 75th is in a few weeks. This one's planning a big event for it. Always been a bit of a daddy's girl, she has."

Kelly rolled her eyes, only allowing Kenzi to see. She poked her tongue out a little, making fun of her mother. Kenzi snickered a little.

"Don't be jealous, Mum. I promise to make your 75th a big deal, too." Anyway, I've told your Mum and Dad all about it, Kenz, and they're coming with Lucas.

You HAVE to come, too. We haven't had a good chance to catch up, and I'd love to hear about how everything's going right now."

Kelly's words felt so genuine, like she really wanted to talk to Kenzi. It was nice. She was just like her mother; she seemed to really care about people. Kenzi was a bit sad that she hadn't been able to spend more time with these people when she was younger. They both were so important to her Grandmother and her Father, but until recently, she didn't really know they existed. That was the past, and Kenzi was determined to move forward. She wanted to get to know Kelly better. Not because of Tom, but because she was a good person, and Kenzi wanted more of that in her life.

"Yeah, that'd be great. I'll be there."

"Great! You can meet Bobby, I mean, re-meet him."

Kenzi had heard Jo and Tom both talk about Bobby before. He was Kelly's son and was studying at Curtain University. Kenzi must have met him when she was younger, but he was yet another person from her family's past that she didn't remember. She wondered what he looked like, and what he was like. Would he have the same black hair as Kelly? She guessed she would find out in a few weeks.

Jo perked up at the mention of her grandon, almost jumping up in excitement.

"He's gonna make it back for it?"

Kelly turned to face her mother, tucking the box up under her arm.

"Yep, booked the flights this morning. But keep it a secret from Dad, please. It'll be a nice surprise for him."

"Of course, sweetie. He'll love that."

Kelly turned and darted out the door, yelling "See ya" over her shoulder as she did. She really was a whirlwind.

Jo sat back on her crate, seemingly exhausted from the whole interaction. She let out a big breath. Her shoulders sagged forward, cardigan sliding down one arm, and the little lines at the corners of her eyes deepened. She looked both exhausted and amused, like every part of her had been used up just keeping pace with her daughter.

"That girl! Kept Quinn an' me busy when she was younger. That's for sure!"

Kenzi leaned against the corner, using her elbow to brace herself. She looked out the front windows as Kelly disappeared from view. Seeing Kelly today hadn't made things any easier for Kenzi. In fact, it made them harder.

"It's nice that she's making a big deal out of Quinn's birthday." Said Kenzi, trying to keep the conversation about Kelly while she tried to figure out what to do.

"Yeah, she always does." Jo was looking out the window now, too, almost daydreaming.

"They've always been close, she and Quinn. He doted on her when she was younger, really spoiled her. I know that man loves me, but if there's one person in the world who he loves more, it's that woman."

Kenzi turned her head to look at Jo. She looked so happy. She always looked happy when she was talking about her family, but she looked especially happy right now. The relationship between Quinn and Kelly was really important to her. Kenzi thought for a moment that maybe Jo didn't even know the truth, and that all that happiness might be built on a lie. Kenzi didn't want to spoil that. At least not today. She would let Jo bask in that happiness for now, just as she had done herself the night before. It was ok to enjoy the nice stuff and leave the bad stuff for another day.

"Well, I, I better get back to it." Kenzi stood up from the counter and headed back to the shelves. Jo just nodded, still looking out the window.

Kenzi set about checking the books on the shelves, making sure they had been put back properly. As she shuffled a few around, she thought about Tom. He had never said anything specific about Kelly beyond casual comments. If he had been floating in and out of their lives, maybe he had seen or heard something that shed some light on Kenzi's suspicions. She wasn't ready to talk to Jo about it, not yet, but she was ready to talk to Tom about it. She had promised to help him figure out what was keeping him here, and if Kenzi was right, and it was the secret about Kelly, he deserved to know the truth. She owed him that much.

Chapter 25
"What Do We Do Now?"

Kenzi was standing outside the garage. It was dark and cold in the night air. The light above the garage door was on, casting a glow into the yard, and insects circled it. Kenzi was taking a moment before talking with Tom. Her afternoon at home after her shift at the bookstore had been nice, like the previous day's. Things with her family, at least with her parents, were starting to feel better, and she was really enjoying that. But she still had to help Tom, and she was committed to talking to him about Kelly. Tonight.

She held her hand above the doorknob, hovering in the air for a moment. She took a deep breath and opened the door. As she walked inside, the door creaked, like it always did, and it sent a little shudder down Kenzi's spine. The still, musty air of the garage hit Kenzi in the face, the smell of oil and grease flooding her senses. It was warm in the garage, much warmer than outside, and that put Kenzi a little at ease. Nothing had changed in the garage since she was there last; it was still a mix of organisation and chaos, with some things clearly in their place and others left on the floor or on benches from where they were last used. Kenzi took comfort in that. That this place was safe from the outside, she would be free to talk to Tom without fear of anyone overhearing it.

And there he was. Standing in front of one of the workbenches, cleaning a tool with an old rag. The rag twisted in his hands, his fingers moving with practised rhythm, like the cloth itself might remember the grease and grit of years gone by. The light from the window caught the line of his jaw, sharper than Kenzi had noticed before. He looked so at home right now. Like it was something that he had done a thousand times, but he still found joy in it. The light from the moon outside was shining in through the window in front of him, and if it weren't for the lack of any shadow coming from him, it would be so easy to forget that he was a ghost.

Kenzi closed the door behind her, another creak, and walked over towards Tom.

"Hey, Tom. How's, ah, how's it going?" It seemed like such a stupid question to ask a ghost, but Kenzi didn't really know how to start a conversation with a ghost in a way that made sense.

"Heya, Mac," replied Tom, not looking up from what he was doing, but not ignoring Kenzi. "Missed ya last night."

Kenzi was standing next to Tom now, facing him, not the window. She placed a hand on the bench and leaned on it a little. While she and Tom had agreed to help each other, they never said that they would meet in the garage every night, especially as Tom wasn't always in control of where he would be. Kenzi had told herself that he might have been somewhere else last night, so it wasn't a huge deal that she had chosen to stay with her family instead of seeing him. But he must have been here, waiting for her.

"Yeah, I ah-" Kenzi thought about telling Tom about what had happened with her mother yesterday, about the photos of Mark, and how things were feeling better. But she didn't want to make this conversation about her. She was there for Tom, and only Tom tonight.

"Tom. I've been thinking about you."

Tom turned his head to look at Kenzi, a cheeky smile on his face.

"Oh, really?"

Kenzi realised what she said, and blushed a little. She quickly tried to recover.

"No! Ah, not like that, I mean, I've been thinking about your, situation. About how maybe there was something keeping you here. Stopping you from, moving on."

Tom turned back to the tool he was cleaning.

"Yeah?"

"Yeah. I was thinking about something you've said, like, about where you go sometimes, and I was thinking about some things that Jo had said, and, and there were these pictures at her house, and, ah, some things didn't really make sense, and ah-"

Kenzi could tell that she was rambling. There were so many thoughts flying around her head, and she had so much doubt about it all, but she wanted to get it out. Needed to get it out. Tom just kept cleaning the tool. He was obviously listening, but his lack of attention was distracting Kenzi.

"Tom!" She didn't yell, but her tone was clear.

Tom stopped cleaning, put down the tool and rag, and turned to look at Kenzi. He was staring right at her now. His face was serious, but still had the usual charm to it. A little smile was creeping out of the corner of his mouth. His black hair always looked as though it had just been slicked back. His brown eyes were soulful but seemed to hide deep pain. It was the first time that Kenzi had really looked at him like this. It put her at ease. She could tell him.

"I think Kelly is your daughter!" It blurted out with far less tact than Kenzi had hoped.

It hung in the air between them for a moment.

Then it sank in, and Tom looked surprised, confused, and shocked all at once.

"What?" He said. Not because he didn't hear what she said, just that it didn't make sense.

"I know it sounds crazy, but, but, after you died, Jo said that she and Quinn got together really quickly, and she also said that Kelly was born early, like *really* early, and her hair, Kelly's hair is jet black, just like yours and, ah-"

Kenzi was rambling again, but there was no other way to get all her thoughts out. To help Tom understand why she thought what she thought.

Tom stepped back a little. His arms dropped down beside him, and he looked down, away from Kenzi's gaze. He stood there, silent. He seemed to be trying to process what Kenzi had said. She didn't know what to do. She knew that it would be hard to talk to Tom about this, but she hadn't really thought about how he would react.

He kept standing there, silent.

Kenzi started to think that maybe this was a ghost thing. Like that, hearing the truth had some physical effect on him.

"Yeah..." he said softly. Softer than he had spoken before.

"I think you're right. I mean, I know you're right. I've, I've always known, I just, ah, forgot, I think."

Kenzi slowly reached forward, intending to gently touch his arm. She wanted to say something to help, but she could see that Tom was working it through in his mind, so she stayed quiet, letting him process, just as Mrs Fox had with her at their last session. She could tell this was a big deal, and Tom needed to feel this in his own way.

Tom shook his head a little, like trying to wake up when you're tired. He looked up at Kenzi. He wasn't smiling, but he wasn't sad, or angry, just plain.

"She is. She is my daughter. Jo never said anything ta me, before I died, but I know it. I can feel it. It makes sense. That's why I'm still here. That's why I visit her sometimes. She's my daughter."

Kenzi could see the reality of it all crashing on Tom. It was like when she put the pieces together, only worse. When they first started talking weeks ago, he had said he felt he was watching a life he never got to live, passing him by. That felt so true now. So painful. She didn't say anything. There was nothing she could say now.

"Does Jo know?"

Tom's voice changed a little. It was deeper now. He put a hand down on the bench. The tendons in his arms were tense under the pressure.

"I ah, I'm not sure. She's never said anything about it directly, and I haven't asked her about it. I ah, I wanted to talk to you about it first."

"I bet she does." His words were sharp, slightly venomous now. "I bet Quinn does, too." His face was definitely showing some emotion now. It was anger. It started to scare Kenzi a little. She suddenly realised she had just angered a ghost, and she had no idea what he could really do.

"It wasn't enough that he stole my girl, he had ta steal my kid, too!"

Kenzi took a small step back, away from Tom. She wanted to try to calm him down, but also wanted a little space between them.

"Tom, I'm sure it's not like that. I'm sure-"

"HE TOOK EVERYTHING FROM ME!" Shouted Tom as he grabbed the tool that he had cleaned and threw it across the room. Tom's body stuttered in and out of vision, like bad reception on a television set, as he moved, and there was a blast of coldness coming off him. His eyes seemed darker now, deeper, like shadows were spilling out of them. The veins in his neck stood out, and though he still looked like the boy in Jo's photos, there was an older, harsher edge to him in that moment. A gust of wind flew out, shaking the car a little and ruffling the tarps and curtains in the room. It caught Kenzi off guard, and she jumped back out of fear and instinct.

Tom noticed Kenzi shudder, and he quickly turned to face her. He looked shocked. He slowly put his hands out towards her; they were shaking, but it didn't look like they were shaking in anger anymore. It looked more like fear.

"Mac, er, Kenzi, I'm sorry. I didn't mean to get so upset. I'm ok now. I promise"

Kenzi had never really experienced anything like this before. Someone getting physically angry like that, but she had seen enough movies. She heard enough stories about domestic violence that she knew how the men would always apologise, and that it was never genuine, and they always did it again. But that didn't seem true right now. Kenzi could tell that Tom was being honest. He was just as upset by his actions as Kenzi was. The coldness that had come off him had gone now. It was just the warmth of the garage air that Kenzi could feel. His form had settled as well. Whatever had changed before had changed back now.

"It's ok, Tom. I understand. This must be a lot for you."

Although Tom had calmed down, Kenzi could still see that he was struggling with it all. The idea that Jo and Quinn had done this to him was obviously quite painful to him. But they didn't know if that was true. All they knew was that Tom was Kelly's father, nothing else. It would be easy to assume the worst right now, but that wasn't fair. Kenzi thought back to her fight with her mother, about how she had believed the wrong thing about her actions, and it had caused such a rift between them. If she had been open and just spoken to her mother about it in the beginning, who knows how differently things could have been? For all of them. That's what they had to do now.

"But we don't know anything more than what we know. We don't know who knows what, or who's keeping what from whom. Maybe all of them know, maybe none of them know. We don't know."

Tom had calmed down entirely now and looked much more relaxed. He turned to look back out the window again. He still wasn't smiling again, but he wasn't looking angry anymore. Serious.

"You're right. So, what do we do now?"

That was a good question. Even if it were true, it could still potentially cause a lot of harm to many good people. People Kenzi cared about. People who had really helped Kenzi. But she could see how much it was hurting Tom now, and she wanted to help him. Kenzi had to see this through.

"I'll talk to Jo. Next time I'm at the bookstore. I'll tell what I know, and find out who else knows, and we'll go from there. I'm sure this is what's keeping you here, and maybe if it all comes out, it'll be hard, but, but maybe then you can move on, Tom."

Tom turned to look back at Kenzi, his expression slowly changing from serious to relieved.

"Maybe."

There was a long silence between them. They both basked in the sense of relief. Kenzi had gotten through the conversation with Tom and learned that she was right about Kelly. And Tom had remembered that he had a daughter, and that maybe soon, he would be free from this half-life he had been stuck in for decades now.

"Kenzi?" Tom began, a little shaky. "Can I be there, at the bookstore, when you talk to Jo? I think I need to see her when she tells you the truth. I'll ah, I'll stay out of the way, and just watch. Please?"

Kenzi could see how important it was for Tom to be there when she spoke to Jo about it. It made sense. It was a big deal, and her doing it alone and then reporting back to him didn't seem like the best approach. Tom had a right to be there. If everything that he feared was true, it would be better if he heard it from Jo. To see her face. To know for sure.

"Yeah, Tom. That'll be ok."

Chapter 26
"Just Trust Yourself, Kenzi."

The house was quiet. Lucas had gone to bed some time ago, and her parents were in their room. Kenzi had gone to bed, too, but she was still awake. Kenzi lay there, on top of her sheets, still fully dressed, lying flat on her back, staring at the ceiling. Her window was open, and a gentle breeze was flowing in, cooling the room. The distant sound of crickets outside wasn't distracting, but a calming white noise. The light from the glowing moon shone in, dimly lighting the room just enough to make out all the furniture in her room clearly, as well as the various spiderwebs in the corners of the ceiling. Although the moon was bright, it wasn't so bright that it was keeping Kenzi awake. No, it was Kenzi's own mind that was keeping her awake.

The past few days had been filled with uncertainty. Uncertain if her suspicions about Kelly were true, and uncertain if she should do something about it. But now, after talking with Tom, those doubts were gone. She knew the truth and that she had to speak to Jo about it. But knowing those two things wasn't making things any easier for Kenzi. Now she was wrestling with how to do it, how Jo might react, and what Kenzi could do to make it ok. She cared a lot about Jo, probably more than she would have thought she could a few months ago, and she didn't like the idea of hurting her. Her mind was racing through all the ways that the conversation could go. What if Jo denied it? What if Jo confirmed it, but refused to come clean? What if Jo got so upset that she didn't want Kenzi to work at the bookstore anymore? What if it all came out and destroyed Jo's family?

Kenzi tried to come up with plans for all the different scenarios, but no matter what, it was going to be hard, and someone would get hurt. Kenzi clenched her fists, banging them down on the mattress and kicking her feet in frustration. She almost wished she had never met Tom and hadn't learned this secret. But that wasn't true. She liked Tom. He had been there for her when she needed a different perspective, and was a good friend— something she hadn't had for a while. She would do this for him. She would be strong. She was done thinking about it for the night. She sharply rolled onto her side, trying to will herself to sleep.

No luck.

As she lay there, closing her eyes tightly, she could hear the sound of footsteps coming down the hallway. It must have been her father, doing his last rounds of the house before he and her mother went to sleep. His footsteps were light, lighter than they would be during the day, obviously trying hard not to make too much sound. He stopped outside her door. Could he tell that she was still awake?

He gently tapped on her door and almost whispered, "Kenz? You still up in there?"

She didn't respond right away.

She probably would have pretended to be asleep a few weeks ago, but not anymore.

"Yeah," she said in a low, frustrated tone.

There was a pause, and Kenzi thought for a moment that maybe her father hadn't heard her and was moving on. But then the doorknob slowly turned, and her door edged open. Peter tentatively stuck his head in through the gap, not coming all the way in.

"Everything alright?"

Kenzi almost blurted out a quick 'yeah' out of habit, but she was able to hold in. Instead, she opened her eyes, took a deep breath, and was honest.

"Not really."

Peter walked in a bit further, half-closing the door behind him, but keeping it open a little. He didn't walk too far into the room, giving Kenzi her space. His shirt was half-untucked, sleeves rolled clumsily to the elbows, like he'd been too tired to do it properly. The hallway light cast a halo against the greying hair at his temples, making him look both softer and older at once.

"You, you wanna talk about it?" His voice was soft and calm, almost nervous.

Kenzi paused, again.

Then she sat up, turned to face her father, letting her legs drop over the edge of the bed. She slouched a little, showing the weight of what was on her mind. She didn't want to tell her Dad everything, but she wanted to tell him something. Maybe just by talking it out with someone other than Tom, Kenzi might feel a little better about what she had to do. It definitely couldn't hurt.

"So, I've figured something out about someone, something big, and er," she was picking her words very carefully. Her Dad was obviously pretty close with Jo and Kelly when he was younger. She was just realising now how this all might affect him, if only to a small extent, "I'm going to talk to them about it. It's a pretty big secret, and they're probably going to get upset talking about it. It could make things really bad for them, but I think it's important, I know it's important that it comes out."

Peter didn't respond right away. He stood there for a second. He could tell whatever Kenzi was talking about was obviously important to her. More importantly, he knew what a big deal it was that he was just sharing it with him. She had kept so much to herself over the last few years, too much, and the fact that she was finally starting to open up again was not lost on him. He slowly walked over and sat on her bed. Not right next to her, there was still enough room between them that it didn't feel overbearing. He leaned forward slightly, elbows resting on his knees, his hands loose, almost uncertain. It was the same way he used to sit with her when she was little and afraid of thunderstorms. They were both looking forward, not at each other.

"Yeah, that's a tough one, Kenz. When the truth hurts. This person, the one with the secret, they're important to you?"

"Yeah."

"And you don't want to hurt them?"

"Yeah."

"But you have to?"

"Yeah."

"That sucks. Believe me."

Kenzi turned her head to look at her Father, who was still looking forward. The light from the moon outside was shining on the back of his head, making the few grey hairs seem more prominent. Parts of his face were in shadow, but he still looked so soft. The lack of distinct details on his face made him look a bit younger, and Kenzi could really see how much Mark used to look like him, making him seem even softer.

"So, how do I do it? Without hurting them?"

Peter turned to face his daughter. There was a real sense of worry and concern on her face. Seeing her like this, it was hard not to see her as a little child, needing his protection. But she wasn't. She was growing up. Whatever worry he had about her, he had to let some of it go. She had to go through this.

"You probably can't."

Kenzi looked away from her Father, looking forward again, at nothing. She didn't know what to say.

"But that's not always a bad thing. Sometimes people need to hear the truth, even if it hurts them. As long as you're telling them for the right reason, which I can tell you are, give them the benefit of the doubt, and accept what they say, without judgment, then I'm sure it will be ok."

Kenzi turned back to look at her Father, her face a little more hopeful than before.

"You sure?"

"No. But you've gotta do it anyway. Just trust yourself, Kenzi. I know I do."

That one hit hard. In a good way. Through everything, Kenzi never really lost faith in her dad. She loved him, obviously, but she also respected him. He always seemed to do the right thing. Hearing that he trusted her judgment meant a lot. She let out a breath, bigger than she realised she needed, and her whole body seemed to relax. Her fingers, which were tightly gripping the bed, let go, and tingling, the blood rushed back to them.

"Thanks, Dad. That really helps."

That one hit hard. In a good way. Peter loved his daughter so much, and finally being able to help her again, it really meant a lot. He wanted to hug her, but that was probably too much.

"You betcha, Kenz." He leaned over and nudged her shoulder with his, pushing her a little. "I've gotta be good for something other than cooking half-decent dinners."

Kenzi chuckled a little as she pushed back against her Dad. They both set themselves upright and looked forward again.

There was a moment of silence that the two enjoyed.

But then it dragged on a bit too long, and started to become awkward.

Peter jumped up and headed for the door. He could tell that the moment had passed, and it was time to leave his daughter alone.

"Well, I ah, better go. Your Mother's feet aren't gonna warm themselves."

Kenzi scoffed as she watched her Father quickly head towards the door. He opened it and walked out. He turned back to see her before he closed it. He was fully lit by the hallway light above him, giving him a somewhat eerie, almost angelic glow.

"Night, Kenz. I love you."

"Night, Dad." Kenzi paused a little, but it felt right to continue, "Love you, too."

She could see her Dad trying hard to contain a big smile as he closed the door.

Kenzi lay back down, this time getting under her sheets. She was still in her clothes from the day, but it didn't matter. She was feeling much better about what she had to do. Talking it out with her Dad had helped, probably more than she thought it would. She turned her head to look out the window, gazing up at the stars. Kenzi couldn't help but think back to the last thing that Mrs Fox had said to her. She had her answer now. The truth wasn't more important than someone's feelings. It was equally as important. And she would do her best to make sure both were taken care of.

Tomorrow was going to be tough, but she would get through it.

Chapter 27
"Just as Sharp as Your Bloody Gran You Are."

Kenzi was standing on the sidewalk, just down from the bookstore. It was mid-afternoon, and the sun was starting to drop behind the building skyline ahead of her, making elongated shadows of people as they walked by. There was a little chill in the air, nothing to do with Tom or anything supernatural, just normal mid-afternoon cool. Kenzi was on her way to start her shift at the bookstore and had paused, just out of view from inside, to compose herself. She was going to talk to Jo about Kelly today. She was done with running through all the possibilities; she was ready to do it. It had to come out, not just for Tom's sake, but for Kenzi's. She cared deeply about Jo and respected her, so she needed to know why Jo did what she did. She needed to understand her motives. She didn't think it would change how she felt about Jo. Not really. But it still mattered to her.

As she stood there, on the sidewalk, she took a couple of deep breaths, composing herself for what was about to happen. She was just about to start walking when a big gust of wind came from behind her, ruffling her clothes and blowing hair into her face. She held tight to her backpack to keep it from falling off her shoulder. Some leaves on the ground flew past her. She thought for a second that maybe it was Tom, using some ghostly powers to urge her on, but that felt silly. It was just the wind. She walked on, towards the bookstore. Towards Jo. Towards the truth.

Kenzi opened the door, and the little bell above the door chimed a little "ding," announcing her arrival. It was warmer in the bookstore, safe from the cool breeze outside. The usual scent of old books and lavender greeted Kenzi, wrapping her in a sense of safety. Kenzi looked around the shop quickly. From the door, you could see every part of the store, from the mismatched chairs in the 'reading area' to her right, across all the shelves filled with books in the centre of the shop, to the front counter. There was no one else in the store, which wasn't a surprise. It was never anything close to busy in the store, with only a few people popping in from time to time. Maybe it was busier during the day, when Kenzi was at school. Either way, Kenzi was relieved that she and Jo would be alone. Jo was in her usual spot, behind the counter. He head was buried deep in a book, like it always was, her hair falling forward a little as she leaned over, enthralled in what she was reading. Her glasses were slipping down her nose, and she pushed them up absently with one finger, eyes crinkling in that familiar way when she smiled. She looked so ordinary, so gentle, it almost hurt to think about the secret she'd been carrying. She looked so sweet, sitting there. Far too sweet to be hiding such a huge secret for the wrong reason.

Jo, alerted to Kenzi's presence by the sound of the bell, looked up from the book.

'Heya, hun," she casually said. Jo folded the corner of the page over, closed the book, and placed it on the counter. There were a few other books there, too, probably lying where they were left after Jo had read them. It wasn't messy, but it definitely wasn't organised. Jo looked happy to see Kenzi today. She always looked happy to see Kenzi. Usually, that would be cause for comfort, but it made Kenzi feel a little awkward. Her stomach started to churn a little. This was going to be hard.

"Hey, Jo," was all that Kenzi could muster right now.

"I'm glad you're here. Lookin' through those pictures with Kelly yesterday reminded me of this time that Mac got into a fight with a pelican. Pop your bag away an' I'll tell ya all about it." Jo gestured towards the back room, where Kenzi usually put her school bag. The idea of hearing about Mac fighting with a pelican sounded appealing. Normally, she would love to just sit and listen to Jo's stories, but if she wasn't going to talk to Jo about Kelly, it had to be now.

Kenzi moved closer to the counter, placing one hand on it.

"Actually, Jo. There's, ah, there's something that I wanted to talk to you about."

Jo's demeanour changed. She didn't look upset by the idea of not telling her story. She looked concerned. Kenzi was feeling nervous, and Jo must have picked up on that. Of course, she picked up on it. That was one of the things that Kenzi liked about Jo. She was fun, but she also knew when and how to be serious.

Jo stood up from her crate and started to walk around the counter towards Kenzi. Kenzi felt her chest tighten, and without thinking, she started holding her breath.

"Of course, hun. Come, let's sit down."

Jo waved Kenzi over towards the reading area. As Kenzi followed, she let her bag slip off her shoulder, and it dropped to the ground against the front wall. She took a couple of deep breaths, trying to calm herself. As Kenzi walked over, she saw a figure out of the corner of her eye. She looked over at the shelves against the far wall. It was Tom. He was leaning against the shelves, watching. He wasn't staring; it was softer than that. He locked eyes with Kenzi and gave a reassuring nod. It made Kenzi feel better, having him there. Even though he couldn't be an active part of the conversation, his presence was enough to support Kenzi. She was a little worried about what might happen when he heard Jo's answer, considering what had happened in the garage. But seeing him here, he looked so calm. It would be ok.

Jo sat down on the large red-cushioned chair. It was a large chair, and she looked a little silly, being so small-framed, almost like a little kid. Kenzi sat in the other chair, a faded grey vinyl-covered chair. As she sat on it, she could feel the air escaping from the cushion, and she sank into it. The jagged edges of wear, some of the vinyl had peeled away, jabbed into the bag of her legs. The chairs were both angled in, towards each other, and Kenzi looked straight ahead for a moment, not at Jo. Pausing to prepare herself.

"Everything alright, Kenzi?" Jo's voice was soft and nurturing, like Kenzi could say anything, and it wouldn't matter. It was so maternal. Kenzi wondered if her own grandmother was the same way, before she died. She wondered for a second if Mac knew the truth about Kelly. Was she also part of the secret? All of her feelings about her grandmother had come to be based on the stories Jo told. She really liked the person Jo was, and she didn't like the idea of that image being tainted by involvement in something like this. Kenzi shook it off. That wasn't important right now.

"Jo, I ah, I have to ask you something." Kenzi turned her head to look at Jo. Her face was so calm-looking.

"You can ask me anything, Kenzi," said Jo as she reached out and placed a hand gently on Kenzi's arm. Her touch was soft, and warm. The warmth moved up Kenzi's arm to her chest. She took a deep breath. It was time.

"Jo. Ah, Kel-I ah, " Kenzi started to stumble. She looked over at Tom, who looked back at her. "Quinn isn't Kelly's real father, is he?"

It was out there now. There was no taking it back. As much as Kenzi might want to stuff the words back into her mouth now and forget the whole thing, it was too late. This was happening.

Jo didn't say anything. She was in shock. It was like the first time they met, when Kenzi crashed into her on the street, and she kept staring at her, in shock at how much she looked like her grandmother. Her face dropped a little as the realisation of what Kenzi said washed over her.

"Wha- ah," she looked away, "What are you-" she turned back to face Kenzi. "Ah," She paused again. She was staring blankly at Kenzi. Kenzi considered saying more, but she could see that Jo was still processing it. Kenzi knew that if it was true and a secret, this would be a huge deal to have someone talk about it. She waited for Jo to speak.

"No," she said quietly, almost too quietly for Kenzi to hear. A tear started to fall down the side of her face. "No, he's not."

Jo's eyes looked away from Kenzi, possibly not wanting to see a look of judgment. Kenzi could see how hard it was for Jo to admit it. Like saying the words was hard, but also a release. Like when you open a bottle of soda that's been shaken, carefully letting the pressure out slowly so it doesn't all spill over the place. Kenzi felt the temperature in the bookstore change slightly, cooling. She looked over at Tom. He didn't look upset or angry. He looked sad. He wanted to know the truth, to hear it from Jo. He cared a lot for her, and it must have hurt him to see her this way.

Kenzi looked back at Jo, who was still looking away, almost in shame. So many questions rushed through Kenzi's head. She wanted to know why, and who else knew; she wanted to understand. But right now, this was about Jo, not her. So she didn't say anything, she just placed her hand on top of Jo's and squeezed it gently.

They both sat there, quiet for a moment.

Jo sniffed, pulling back more tears, and turned her attention back to Kenzi.

"How, ah, how did you know?" Jo seemed a little worried. Like maybe someone else knew, and they had told Kenzi. Like her secret wasn't safe anymore.

Kenzi considered telling her all about Tom, but that was too much. That wouldn't be fair to Jo. This moment had to be about her and her truth, not some big revelation about the existence of ghosts.

"It, it was a few things, really. Ah, her hair, for one thing, it's so black, and neither you nor Quinn has hair anything like that, but Tom did. And then there's the picture of your wedding day, I'm sure you're pregnant in it, and, and you said that you and Quinn got together so quickly after Tom died, and the way you talk about how good a father Quinn is to Kelly, and how you were really thankful for that, and ah-"

Kenzi was rambling now, like the top had come off her soda bottle, too.

"Oh," interrupted Jo, "that's ah, that's a lot." She snickered a little, "Just as sharp as your bloody gran you are."

Hearing Jo talk about her grandmother, saying how alike they were, it made Kenzi feel better, like she was doing the right thing. Kenzi wanted to know more, but she couldn't be pushy. She thought about what Mrs Fox would do right now.

"Do, do you want to talk about it?"

It was up to Jo now. Kenzi wanted to know more, and she knew Tom did too, but Jo was more important now.

"Yeah," she took a big breath, sitting up a bit straighter, "Yeah, I think that would be good."

Kenzi didn't move; she just kept holding Jo's hand, not squeezing it, just holding it.

"You're right, I was pregnant at my wedding. Quinn knew, not about Tom, just that I was pregnant, pretty sure that's why he married me." Jo looked away from Kenzi, out the front window, like she did whenever she told one of her stories. Like she was watching it all play out on a large screen projector.

"Tom and I were pretty serious, before he died, probably too serious, but we were so caught up in each other that it didn't matter. And then when he was gone, we were all so broken, and Quinn and I were there for each other, and then it became something more. It wasn't anything either of us planned; it just happened. By the time I figured out I was pregnant, Quinn and I were really together. I was sure it was Tom's, but I didn't know how to tell Quinn."

Kenzi looked over at Tom, who looked much calmer than Kenzi expected him to be. He was still leaning against the shelf, but not in his usual, arms-folded, pin-up-cool way. His arms hung down beside him, focused on what Jo was saying. She looked back at Jo, still staring off into nothing. She looked a little more content now.

"Tom was gone, and Quinn was so happy at the thought of being a dad, it, it was just easier to pretend. I didn't think I was hurting anyone, like, Tom didn't have any family, he never knew 'em, so I wasn't keeping Kelly from anyone, and Quinn was so good to her, so I, I didn't think she was missing out on anything. After a while, I just kind of," Jo turned to look at Kenzi, looking for reassurance.

"I put it away, the truth. It wouldn't help anyone to know, and, I thought it wasn't hurting anyone. You have to believe me, Kenz, I would never have-"

'I know, Jo. I know. It's ok." Kenzi squeezed Jo's hand, trying to reassure her.

Kenzi had her answers. She knew the truth, and more importantly, she understood why Jo did what she did. It made her like her even more. She'd carried that burden alone for so long. It must have been so hard to live like that every day. She wanted to help her, but she didn't really know how. There was nothing she could *do* for Jo, except to just be here now. Kenzi looked past Jo. Tom had moved closer to them and was crouching down next to Jo. He looked happy, and sad, but mostly relieved. The temperature in the bookstore shifted again; this time, it warmed back up and comforted Kenzi, like a heater kicking in on a winter's day.

Jo must have felt it, too, as she perked up a little and looked over towards where Tom was. Kenzi thought for a second that maybe Jo could see him now, but she was still so calm; she must have just been reacting to the warmth. Still, it was nice to think that Tom was able to do something in that moment to make Jo feel better.

"Thank you for trusting me with this, Jo," said Kenzi, pulling her attention back to her.

Jo looked at Kenzi, the trail marks of tears still visible on her cheeks. She wiped one away and then placed her hand on top of Kenzi's, which was still squeezing her other hand. Their hands now formed a warm pile.

"Thank you, Kenzi. It ah, it actually feels really good to say it out loud. I've been holding it in for so long now, I hadn't realised what it was doing to me. I feel lighter."

"What, ah, what will you do now?" Kenzi released her grip on Jo's hand, and she did the same, and they both pulled their hands away from each other.

"I've got to tell Quinn, and Kelly, of course, but Quinn deserves to hear it first; it's only fair."

Jo stood up. Kenzi followed her lead.

"I'm sure he'll understand, Jo. It'll be ok."

"I hope so, Hun."

There was a pause, neither of them really sure what to do now.

"Can ah, can you hold down the fort here. I need to do this now, while I still have my courage."

"Yeah, of course, Jo. Whatever you need."

Kenzi couldn't do much to help Jo with what she had to do next, but she could do this little thing. Kenzi thought Jo was about to leave, but she turned back and grabbed Kenzi in a big hug. Kenzi hugged her back, and they stood there for a few moments in each other's arms.

Jo broke free, gently, still holding onto Kenzi's upper arms, gave them a squeeze, and then walked out of the shop, grabbing her bag on the way out. When she disappeared out of view, Kenzi looked back at Tom, who was also standing now.

"I ah, I think I need to go with her, to be there, when she tells Quinn. I mean, I'm not-" Tom actually looked a bit unsure as he spoke, which was a look Kenzi hadn't seen on him before.

"It's ok, Tom, I understand. Go, I'll be fine here."

"Thanks, Kenzi," said Tom with a calming smile, and then disappeared.

Kenzi was alone in the bookstore now, and the temperature dropped again. Not as cold as it was before, but not as warm as it was with Tom there. Kenzi realised she had a few tearstains on her face, too, and wiped them away.

Kenzi felt good.

She felt like she had helped. Not just Tom, but Jo, too. Kenzi knew what it was like to let out feelings that had been kept secret for so long, and how that could lead to change.

Kenzi took a big breath in and let it out, resetting herself.

That had gone a lot better than she thought it would. She didn't know what would happen now. Would Quinn understand? Would Kelly? Would Tom move on now? Kenzi definitely hoped that Jo's family would be ok, but she wasn't sure about Tom. She wanted to help him, but now that she had, and with the possibility that he might leave, she was conflicted. She had grown close to Tom, and she wasn't sure if she was ready to lose him.

Kenzi took another big breath and let it out.

There was nothing more she could do now. She would have to wait till she got home to see if Tom would be waiting in the garage for her.

Chapter 28
"It Never Mattered."

Jo's footsteps echoed down the quiet street as she made her way home. She'd left the bookstore in a hurry, but now that she was here, outside the small weatherboard house she and Quinn had shared for decades, her courage wavered. The late-afternoon light spilled across the front steps, turning the peeling white paint to gold. She stood still for a moment, clutching her bag strap like it might hold her together.

As she walked up the stone path to the front door, she couldn't help but think back to when she first told Quinn that she was pregnant. She was pretty sure that it was Tom's, and she had thought about telling Quinn that it might not be his, but when she saw how happy he was at the thought of being a father, she couldn't go through with it. She had told herself she was doing it to protect Quinn and the child, and that was true, more or less, but she knew she was protecting herself more than anyone.

Jo stood in front of her front door. A door she had opened over a thousand times in her life, each time effortlessly. But today, the door seemed like a giant bank vault, heavy with secrets. Secrets Jo had been keeping for too long. Secrets that were out now. She had to come clean, no matter what might happen. She opened the door and walked in; the faint smell of eucalyptus, no doubt from a candle Kelly had recently gifted her, filled the air.

Jo could see Quinn sitting in his usual chair, next to hers. The chairs were mismatched, but most of the furniture in the house was mismatched, which actually made it look like it matched. Quinn was wearing the light blue shirt she had asked him so many times to throw out because of the large coffee stain on the front. He never liked to throw things away, not until he absolutely had to. One of his suspenders had slipped off his shoulder and hung loosely around his upper arm. He was concentrating on the puzzle book, which he held tightly in his hand. The crossword pencil was clutched like a soldier's weapon, his knuckles pale, though his posture was loose, comfortable in the sag of his chair. His suspenders always made him look older than he acted, and tonight, with his shirt stained and one strap slipping, he seemed almost endearing in his stubbornness. He always did his crosswords in the afternoon while she was at work, mostly so he could do them without interruptions.

As Jo closed the door behind her, the sound of the latch snapping shut caught Quinn's attention, and he looked up at his wife.

"You're home early, Jo," he said with a bit of surprise.

"Ah, yeah, I ah," Jo had planned on jumping straight into, but now, seeing him look so peaceful, she hesitated; she needed a little more time. "I'm just gonna make a tea, and then I'll be right out. You, ah, you want one?"

Jo quickly darted towards the kitchen, out of view.

"Nah, I'm all good, thanks," Quinn shouted from the loungeroom.

Tom was standing in the kitchen. He had been there since leaving the bookstore. He felt a bit weird being there while Quinn was in the living room, but he wanted to wait till Jo got home. Jo walked into the kitchen, utterly unaware that Tom was there, and set about making a cup of tea. She looked scared. Tom wasn't sure how Quinn would react to the truth. Any time Tom had seen Quinn and Kelly together, it was clear that he loved her very much, so it might really hurt him to find out that she wasn't really his. But he always treated Jo well, and he and Tom were good friends, so he might be ok with it.

As Jo made her tea, her hands were shaking, spilling a little sugar as she tipped it into the cup. She picked the cup up with both hands. She slowly brought it up to her mouth, taking a small sip, the smell of jasmine helping to calm her. As she swallowed, she felt the warm fluid travel all the way down to her belly and then radiate out. She had stalled as much as she could. She had to do this now. He was a good man. A kind man. An understanding man. It would be ok.

It had to be ok.

Jo walked into the living room and sat down next to her husband, who was still engrossed in his crossword. Tom followed, but kept his distance from both of them. Even though they didn't know he was there, he wanted to give them some space. Jo took another sip of her tea and then shakily placed it on the side table between her and Quinn. She took a deep breath. It was time.

"Quinn," she said, her voice almost cracking.

"Hmmm," he responded, not looking up from his work.

"I ah, I have to tell you something."

Quinn, aware that this was a serious conversation, closed up the crossword book, placed it on his lap, and looked at his wife. She looked different today, almost worried, which worried him a little. A cup of tea would actually have been nice now.

"What's wrong, Jo?"

Jo looked at her husband. Although his face had changed over the decades, his eyes were still the same. Brown. Soft. Caring. Looking into them had always made her feel safe, and while they helped today, Jo was still worried about how he would react. But that didn't matter. The truth mattered now.

"There's something I should have told you, a long time ago, and I'm, I'm scared, scared about what you'll think of me."

Tears were starting to form in the corner of Jo's eyes now, and her voice was still shaking. Quinn reached over and placed his hand on Jo's arm, gently squeezing it, giving a reassuring smile at the same time.

"You can tell me anything, Jo. You know that."

Jo looked at Quinn. Her heart was racing in her chest. This was the hardest thing she had ever had to do. When Kenzi had asked her about it earlier, it had just flowed out, almost without control. But it felt like every fibre of Jo's being was fighting her now, desperate to keep the secret safe.

She took another deep breath and pushed through.

"It's Kelly, she's," another deep breath, "she's ah, not really yours."

It felt like time froze for Jo. Any noise that was coming from outside seemed to just stop, as if the whole world was in shock from what she just said. Her heart, which had been racing, also stopped. Even Quinn seemed to stop moving. Strangely, he didn't look shocked, or upset, or angry; he was just looking at her, taking it in. Jo knew how Kelly meant to Quinn, and could only guess how much of a betrayal this must feel like to him. She was worried about what he would say, and she wanted him to understand why she did it.

"It's just that, Tom died so suddenly, and then ah, then we got together so quickly, and, and then when I found out I was pregnant, I ah, I was so scared about what it meant, I w-was pretty sure it was Tom's and I didn't know w-what to do, and then w-when I told you, you were just so-"

Quinn quickly slid off his chair and knelt on the ground in front of Jo, tears flowing freely down her cheeks, and tried to take her hands in his. She pulled away out of instinct, slightly, but he grabbed them and held them tightly. It wasn't aggressive, though; it was calming.

"Jo, stop, Jo. It's ok."

Jo stopped rambling, but that was hard. She was so desperate for Quinn not to hate her or think badly of her that the words were just spilling out. His touch helped her to gain control and stop. Her heart, which had started racing as she spoke, had slowed now. She took a few deep breaths, forcing her body to relax. Through her tears, she could see Quinn's face. So calm. So caring.

" I know," he said. His face said it, too.

Jo was in shock.

"Wha-what?"

She needed to hear it again.

"I mean, I've always suspected."

A massive weight was lifted from Jo's chest. More so than when she came clean to Kenzi earlier. She took a few breaths, which seemed to allow more air into her chest than they had in a long time.

"But ah, y-you never said anything."

"'Cause it never mattered. Not to me." Quinn squeezed Jo's hands. "I loved you so much. Tommy was gone, and if the baby was his, then the least I could do for him, and you, was to take care of it, and you, so that's what I did."

It was strange hearing Quinn call him Tommy. He always did, all the boys did, but he was always Tom to Jo. Even though Jo had told Kenzi many stories about that time in her life, most of them focused on Mac, and she had all but forgotten about how close Quinn and Tom were.

"And it's been the most wonderful thing that I've gotten to do, taking care of you and Kelly. *Loving* you and Kelly."

Jo gently pulled one of her hands away from Quinn's and wiped away some tears.

"You're, you're not mad?"

Quinn leaned forward; he was much closer to Jo now.

"How could I be mad? It was such a gift that you gave me. I'm just sorry that you felt that you had to keep it from me. For so long. That must have been so hard."

Jo fell forward into Quinn, her head resting against his chest, the smell of his deodorant pushing

through the tears and snot resting in her nostrils. He
wrapped his arms around her, holding her tightly.

"It was, it was so hard. I'm so, so sorry."

They both stayed there. Together. Quiet. Lighter.
But stronger.

Tom watched on. It was so comforting to know
what his friend had done for him. To take on that
responsibility. It gave Tom a sense of relief. He didn't feel
like he had been watching someone else's life anymore.
He felt lucky to have seen the wonderful life that Quinn
had given his daughter. It was a gift.

"Jo," said Quinn, as he pulled back slowly from
his wife. She looked up at him.

"Yeah?"

"We need to tell Kelly."

Jo took a breath and sniffed, trying to stop the
tears and snot from running.

"I know, but, I'm scared about what she'll think of
me."

Quinn raised a hand to his wife's face, and she
closed her eyes and leaned into his palm.

"She loves you. We raised a kind and caring
woman. She'll understand. Whatever happens, we'll deal
with it. Together. As a family."

Those words really meant a lot to Tom to hear. He
looked over at the mantlepiece above the fire, and all the
photos of their lives throughout the years. There was so

much love in all the photos. He knew they were going to be ok.

He took one last look at Quinn and Jo, still holding each other. He didn't need to worry about them anymore. He smiled and then left.

Chapter 29
"If You Have Any Ideas, We Would Love to Hear Them."

The rest of Kenzi's shift at the bookstore was utterly uneventful. After Jo and Tom had left, she had been alone for the rest of the afternoon. It was equal parts peaceful and lonely. There weren't usually many customers, so most of her shifts were filled with Jo's stories about her Grandmother. Jo had other stories to tell today, so it was just Kenzi. She kept herself busy, rearranging books on their shelves, wiping down benches, and emptying bins. She had tried to stay busy, if only to stop her mind from worrying about Jo. Although she was happy she had helped Jo unburden herself of keeping the secret about Kelly, and that she knew telling Quinn was the right thing to do, she still worried about how he and Kelly would react. When Kenzi and her mother's secrets had come out, it was hard and painful, but it led to things getting better, so she hoped the same would be true for Jo.

As Kenzi walked down the sidewalk to her house, the streetlights started to come on, creating circles of light on the ground ahead of her. It wasn't that late, but the days were getting shorter, so the lights were coming on earlier. As she walked under each light, she looked down as her shadow split, each a different shade and shape, spinning around her and then reforming. She couldn't help but think about how fitting that seemed. When Mark died, she felt like she had been broken into smaller, weaker pieces, but lately, she felt like she was starting to come back together again. Meeting Jo, learning about her grandmother, and now, helping Tom, they all made her feel like she was putting the pieces of herself, and her life, back together.

Kenzi's house was in view now, and she could see the sun setting behind it. The glow of the waning sun shimmered around the structure's outline, making it seem like a safe, warm place. For the first time, since moving to this house, that seemed appropriate. The house was starting to feel like a home, something that Kenzi hadn't felt in years. It gave her a warm feeling inside, making it easier to handle the chill that was beginning to creep into the air.

Kenzi opened the gate and headed towards the garage. Most nights, she would go inside the house first, take her bags in, get changed, and then head out to the garage, but she was desperate to hear from Tom how Jo's talk with Quinn went. She quickly snuck down the side of the house, trying to stay out of view of anyone inside the house, and quietly opened the garage door. Luckily, the normally loud creak of the door opening wasn't there, and she could continue her stealth mission to see her friend.

The air in the garage was cold and still tonight, even colder than outside, which was very strange. Usually, it was warmer inside. The stillness pressed against her eardrums, like the whole place was holding its breath. Dust motes floated in the beam of light from the door, barely moving. There was no hint of grease and oil; instead, it just smelled stale. Kenzi looked around the room. Everything was still in its messily arranged state, the car hood still in the air from when they removed the alternator a few nights before. Her gaze caught on the socket wrench they'd used, resting exactly where Tom had left it on the tray. For a second, she could almost see him there, wiping his hands on a rag, ready with a teasing comment. But the space beside the car was empty, and it stayed empty. Kenzi took a few steps further into the garage, towards the car.

"Tom?" she said apprehensively, "You, you there?"

Nothing.

Just silence.

Not even the sound of crickets, or any sort of life, outside.

It was dead quiet.

Kenzi walked to the car, placing a hand on the roof, looking for some sort of grounding from the vehicle.

But it was cold, too.

Her reflection in the dusty car window stared back at her, hair messier than she'd realised, her eyes red-rimmed. She looked less like someone who'd just finished a shift at the bookstore and more like someone who'd said goodbye without meaning to.

She wondered if Jo's conversation with Quinn had gone well, and if Tom had seen that, maybe that was enough for him. Maybe now that the truth about Kelly was out, and Tom had learned why Jo did what she did, and how Quinn felt about it all, it was enough for him to find peace and move on.

Maybe he was gone now.

Tears started to form in the corners of Kenzi's eyes. She wasn't sure if they were happy or sad tears.

She lingered there, one hand resting on the car's frame, letting the cold sink in.

If Tom had moved on, that would have been a good thing. He didn't have to linger here, removed from everything and everyone. He could find peace, whatever that meant. So that had to be a good thing, right?

But if he was gone, then she would never see him again, and she'd be alone again. Well, not completely alone, like when Mark left. She was feeling closer to her Mum and Dad lately, and she had Jo, so it wasn't that bad. But still, Tom was her friend. Kind of her only friend, and the thought of him being gone was hard. She would miss him. A lot.

Kenzi took a deep breath, still only getting the musty smell of old tools and blankets, and wiped the tears away.

It was a good thing, that Tom moved on. And she had done that. She had helped him, and hopefully Jo and her family, too. That felt good. She didn't feel as cold right now. She held onto that and headed into the house. She still had to install the new alternator into the car, but that would have to wait for another day. Tonight, she would just spend more time with her family, and that would be ok. Actually, that sounded better than just ok.

By the time she stepped back into the evening air, the garage door closed behind her, and the warmth of the house seemed to glow against the twilight. She wasn't sure if the change was real or if it was just her, trying to shake the chill from her bones. Either way, the thought of stepping inside felt like a relief.

As Kenzi headed towards the back door of the house, she could see both her parents in the kitchen through the flyscreen. They were both leaning against one of the counters, looking quite casual. As Kenzi opened the back door, she could hear the conversation they were having.

"Pizza?" said Peter, slightly unsure.

'Chinese?" Responded Olivia, continuing the back-and-forth between the two of them. As Kenzi closed the door, they both stopped and looked at her, seemingly excited for her arrival—more than they usually were after her shift at the bookstore.

"Excellent timing, Kenz. There's kind of nothing to cook for dinner, and your Mother and I can't decide on what take-out to get, so-" said Peter, excitedly. Trying to encourage a similarly excited response from Kenzi, but he was cut off before he could finish.

"So, if you have any ideas, we would love to hear them," finished Olivia, in a much more casual tone.

Kenzi snickered a little. It was always amusing watching her Mother try to downplay when her Father got carried away. The idea of Chinese take-out sounded good. She thought about the times that they used to get it, back when Mark was still alive. How they would all sit on the floor in the lounge room, in a circle around the various boxes, and just share it all. Maybe it was time for that tradition to start back up again. Perhaps they were ready. That might be nice.

But then Kenzi had a better idea.

"Actually. Why don't you go out for dinner? Just the two of you."

Peter was about to respond, but Olivia cut him off. They were both looking at Kenzi now. Peter looked excited, but Olivia looked a combination of surprised and confused.

"What do you mean?" She said, cautiously.

Kenzi walked forward a bit and gestured towards the pantry.

"Like, it's been ages since the two of you got to go out together, like on a date. I'm sure there's some packet Mac'n'cheese in the pantry that I can whip up."

Kenzi felt like her parents had put a lot of things on hold since she came home from the hospital. Even though she knew that her parents were still close, she felt like they hadn't really had that much *alone* time lately, and she wanted to try to make things easier for them. Helping Tom and Jo had reminded Kenzi how nice it felt to do something for others, and it had been a long time since she had done something nice for her parents.

Kenzi could see that her Dad was keen to accept her proposal, but knew that his wife wasn't quite sold on it, so he was allowing her to take control of the situation. Olivia placed one hand on the counter, using it to hold herself up as she leaned over slightly. She gestured with her other hand towards the living room.

"You sure, Kenz. You'll watch Lucas for us?"

Oh. Kenzi forgot about that. The idea of being alone with Lucas was not even close to appealing, but she couldn't back out now. She wanted to do this for her Mum and Dad, and Lucas was surely old enough to entertain himself for the most part. She could give him some food, let him watch TV, and then put him to bed early. That couldn't be too hard. Right?

"Yeah, totally. I got this. You guys go have fun," said Kenzi as she tried to usher her parents out of the kitchen.

"What do you think, Peter?" Olivia looked at her husband, already knowing his thoughts on the matter. Peter grabbed Olivia's hand and headed towards the back door.

"You had me at just the two of us," he said with a cheeky smile on his face.

Olivia wanted to organise things a bit more, but she could see that her husband was excited to take her out, which was nice, so she went along with it. She followed Peter out the door and yelled back towards the living room over her shoulder as she left.

"Alright. Bye Lucus! Mum and Dad are going out!"

Kenzi watched her parents through the flyscreen on the back door as they rushed down the sidepath to the car out the front, laughing a little as they went. Kenzi couldn't help but smile. It was nice to see them happy.

She stood silently in the kitchen alone for a moment, enjoying the happy moment she had just shared with her parents. She could get used to this.

The silence was broken by the sound of toys crashing over in the living room.

Oh, that's right.

Lucas.

A toy clattered again, but for half a second, Kenzi thought she heard the faint creak of the garage door hinge. She waited, hoping to hear something else. Some sign that Tom might have been there.

But nothing.

It was just her and Lucas now.

Chapter 30
"Second Only to My Rugged Good Looks?"

It was nice and quiet in the restaurant. Olivia looked around the dimly lit room. It was nice in here. The place had obviously been around for a decade or two, but the owners had kept it looking well. All the tables had clean white tablecloths, the chairs were all reasonably modern-looking, with little to no signs of age, and the various pictures on the walls, all showing different Italian-themed landscapes, were clear and set a pleasant, calming tone. There was some classic Italian-sounding music quietly playing from an out-of-sight speaker, further adding to the restaurant's feel.

Olivia looked at the other people in the room. A few other couples were sharing their own *date nights*, and a larger family was seated in a booth over by the corner, most likely deliberately away from the other guests. A woman at the next table had a deep red dress, her lipstick perfectly matching, while another across the room wore pearls that caught the candlelight. Olivia smoothed down the hem of her blouse automatically, knowing she hadn't dressed for this, but not regretting it either. Olivia noticed the clothes that the other ladies were wearing. They were a lot more formal than what she had on, which were still the clothes she put on when she woke up this morning. The other ladies weren't over-the-top formal, but they had definitely put more effort into their appearance than she had. If she had had more time to plan the evening, she would have gone to the same lengths to look nice for her husband. Not that that sort of thing really mattered to him much, but she did like to look nice when they went out to dinner like this. But it wasn't bothering Olivia too much. She was ok with looking more casual than usual. Kenzi's actions had put her in too good a mood to worry about things like her clothes.

Olivia was feeling a lot better about Kenzi lately. Ever since the fight they had, and everything coming out, she felt like she understood her daughter a bit more, and after she put some photos of Mark up, she was feeling like the space between the two of them wasn't the gaping chasm that it once was- it was getting smaller. Olivia would probably never forgive herself for how much she let her daughter down, but she had hope now that she could start to make it up to her.

As well as the potential to mend the relationship between her and Kenzi, Olivia couldn't help but get excited about the idea of Kenzi and Lucas spending some time alone together. Olivia was very aware of how little Kenzi had wanted to have to do with Lucas in the past. It had always bothered Olivia, but she hadn't pushed it, at least not until the fight. She had been hopeful that things between her two children might start to change after that, but she hadn't wanted to force the issue. She knew it was something that Kenzi had to do on her own. And it seemed like that's what was happening. If only as a side-effect of Kenzi's suggestion for her and Peter to go out, but still, they were going to spend some time together, and that was HUGE. Olivia was obviously worried about how things might go, but she didn't want to stress about that too much.

They would be fine.

She wanted to enjoy this time with her husband. Her sweet, caring husband. Her husband, who carried so much for her over the last few years. Even on top of losing his mother. She couldn't help but feel lucky that he was still excited to spend time alone with her. Olivia looked across the table at Peter, who was still in the same clothes he had worn this morning, except they were much nicer, as he had spent the day at work and always dressed reasonably formally. His button-up shirt was a little creased from the day, but it looked just as good as the other men's in the room. It had been a few days since Peter had shaved, and it was easier for Olivia to notice the ever-increasing amount of grey hairs in her husband's facial hair. It wasn't untidy; he still looked good.

As Olivia looked at her husband, she noticed that he hadn't eaten much of his dinner yet. It was carbonara. Peter always got carbonara when they went to an Italian restaurant. Even though he could make it pretty well himself at home, he still ordered it any chance he could get. Usually, he would be almost halfway done with the dish by the time the wait-staff came back to check if everything was ok, but tonight, he had barely touched it. Peter had been so excited about coming out to dinner with his wife that it surprised Olivia when he seemed a little off. He didn't look sad, just a little, elsewhere.

Peter was always so good at knowing when Olivia wasn't feeling great, and always checked in to see if he could help. She wanted to do the same for him.

"Is the carbonara no good, Peter?" She didn't want to ask outright how he was doing. She tried to wade into those waters gently.

Peter looked up at Olivia, a little startled by her words. He was obviously deep in thought.

"Wha? Oh, no, it's fine."

Peter spun a few strands of pasta around his fork and scoffed it down, trying to reassure his wife that everything was fine.

Olivia didn't buy it.

"Ok, so what's wrong then?"

Peter took a large bite of some garlic bread, and through the chewing, responded, "Nothing. I'm good."

Olivia still wasn't buying it. She could tell there was something on her husband's mind. She had tried to be gentle, but that hadn't worked. She could tell he was trying to be strong, not to burden her with his issues. He had had to do it so much of the last few years, but she was doing better now, and she wanted to be there for him, like he had been there for her.

Olivia leaned forward and placed her hand on Peter's, forcing him to stop eating. He looked up at her, and she could see the weight of something behind his eyes.

"Peter. I'm here. I can help."

Peter looked at her. Olivia could tell that he was thinking hard about something. She knew something was bothering him, and she wanted so badly for him to share it with her. To let her help. She looked back at him with a gentle smile.

Peter paused a bit longer.

He let out a small sigh.

"I was just thinking about Mum. How I wasn't there for her, at the end."

Olivia could see the sadness and regret pouring out of Peter now. He didn't look distracted anymore; he looked sad. Really sad.

"Oh, Peter," she said softly, squeezing his hand a little.

"She did so much for me when I was younger, and after we moved, I couldn't be there for her as much as she needed me to be." Peter looked away from his wife. Not at anything, just at nothing. "When she got sick, I, thought there'd be plenty of time to get back to her, but, but then Kenzi, ah," he paused, not wanting to say the words out loud, "and ah, well, I thought that she needed me more than Mum did, so I stayed."

Peter turned back to look at Olivia. She could see small tears starting to form in the corner of his eyes. It wasn't that unusual for Olivia to see her husband cry. As strong as he was, he was always pretty quick to cry, especially when they were watching something sad together. But she could tell this was different. This was real sadness. She wanted to jump up and hold him, but she could see there was more that he needed to get out, so she stayed firm, holding his hand, and listening.

"I stayed to look after Kenzi, and I wasn't there for Mum. At the end, I wasn't there for her."

A few tears ran down Peter's face, leaving tracks along the grooves in his skin and getting caught in his stubble. Olivia leaned forward a little further, placing her other hand on top of her hand, still holding on to his forearm.

Olivia remembered those months all too clearly — the way Peter had carried the weight of the world on his shoulders while she could barely lift her head. He'd worked, cooked, cleaned, sat with Kenzi through the worst nights, and never once complained, even when she knew it was breaking him. It struck her now that his absence at his mother's side hadn't been a lack of love — it had been an act of love for their daughter, the kind that leaves a mark no one else can see.

"Peter. Your Mum loved you so much, and she understood why you couldn't be there for her. She knew how important Kenzi was, and I don't doubt for a second that she would have told you to stay and take care of your daughter if you had tried to come back."

Olivia could feel tears forming in her eyes now, too.

"She would have done exactly the same thing if she were in your shoes. You are exactly the kind of man that she raised you to be. You are exactly the kind of *parent* she raised you to be. She was proud of you right till the end."

Peter sniffed and blinked his eyes a few times.

"You think?"

"I know so. That woman would talk about how amazing you were every chance she got. If it all weren't so true, it would actually be a little annoying," said Olivia, with a cheeky smile on her face, trying to lighten the mood a little.

Peter snickered a little.

"And Peter, look at Kenzi now, she's better."

Peter's eyes softened as he thought about the changes in Kenzi lately — how she'd started meeting his gaze again, the quiet pride in her voice when she talked about the bookstore, the way she'd been the one to suggest this night out. He wished his mother could have seen her like this, lighter and more herself. Maybe then she would have known that his choice had been worth it.

"You did what you needed to do to help our daughter," continued Olivia, "I can't even imagine what might have happened if you hadn't been with us through that whole thing. You did the right thing. You always do the right thing. It's one of the things I love the most about you."

Peter smiled, closed his eyes, and tilted his head back a little, trying to look cute.

"Second only to my rugged good looks, of course?"

Olivia shook her head and laughed a little.

"Of course."

"Look, I'm sorry that you weren't here for your Mum, but I love that you were there for our daughter. I love you for that."

"Thanks, Olive. I love you, too," Peter leaned forward and kissed his wife, awkwardly, as both tried to stay balanced while leaning over the food and cutlery on the table.

As they both sat down, letting go of each other's hands, Olivia noticed that Peter's shirt had touched his food, and there was a small dollop of pasta sauce on his belly.

She giggled.

But she didn't tell him.

He was smiling again, and she didn't want to ruin the moment.

Chapter 31
"He's My Brother, Too."

Kenzi looked down at her shirt. There was a large glob of cheese sauce on it, spat out by the bubbling pot on the stove. She was cooking mac'n'cheese for dinner, but she wasn't giving the dish her full attention, making sure to keep an eye on Lucas, who was playing on the ground with some toys in the living room. Kenzi wiped up the sauce with her finger and flicked the blob into the sink. There was a little stain on her shirt, but she wasn't too concerned; it would probably wash out alright, and if not, it was a pretty old shirt. She looked into the pot and gave the mixture a gentle stir with the wooden spoon. The rich golden sauce was starting to thicken nicely, clinging to the pasta, and shimmered as she moved it around the pot.

Kenzi could tell it would only be a few more minutes before dinner was ready, so she walked over to the pantry, opened the door, and grabbed two of the round plastic bowls. She closed the pantry door with her foot and walked over to the cutlery drawer, grabbing two spoons. She placed the bowls and spoons down on the kitchen bench near the stove. Kenzi had another quick look in the pot; it still needed to thicken a bit more. She looked over to the living room, but she couldn't see Lucas. His toys were still on the ground, but he was nowhere to be seen.

She wasn't too concerned, as he was old enough to be left alone for the most part, and she didn't think there was anything in the living room that he could hurt himself on, at least not majorly. Still, she really didn't want anything to happen that would make her parents regret going out alone tonight; they both seemed excited at the thought, so Kenzi thought it would be best to quickly check on him before serving dinner up.

Kenzi walked quickly through the dining room, swerving around the table to get through to the living room.

"Lucas?" She called out as she went.

There was no answer.

Kenzi's heart started to race a little. And she quickened her pace. She was now feeling genuine concern for her brother. What if he had choked on one of his toys? What if he had fallen off the couch and hit his head? There was no way her family could deal with anything like that. She really should have been paying more attention.

She entered the living room and quickly looked around. She could see Lucas. Thank goodness. He was standing in front of the fireplace, which was off. She let out a breath, and her heart started to slow down to a normal pace. He was standing on his tiptoes, reaching up to grasp the mantle.

"Lucas!" she said, a little louder and sterner than she meant to. She paused, calming herself, "What are you doing?"

Lucas looked like he was trying to pull himself up, as if he was trying to reach or look at something on the mantle. His little feet moved up and down as he tried to make himself taller.

"Look at the photos," he replied in his direct and straightforward manner. Lucas had been talking more and more the last few months, but a lot of what he said still wasn't grammatically correct. It had bothered Kenzi in the past, but today, it actually seemed a little cute.

As Kenzi walked over towards Lucas, she looked at the mantle, which was still filled with different photo frames, the same ones that had been there when Kenzi's Mum had put up the photo of Mark the week before. Kenzi became a little concerned again as she saw Lucas reach up, trying to grab hold of the picture of Mark. Her Mum had only just felt like Lucas was old enough that he couldn't break any of the photos, and right now, there was every chance that could happen.

Kenzi was about to yell, but she didn't want to spook him, potentially making things worse, so she just quickly darted over to the fireplace and held onto the picture.

It was safe.

Mark was safe.

Lucas was still reaching up at the picture, his little hands opening and closing as he tried to grab it. Lucas bounced on his tiptoes with every reach, his hair flopping into his eyes, but he didn't bother pushing it away. His whole focus was on the photo.

"Let me see, let me see," he said, straining to reach up.

Kenzi was a bit surprised that Lucas was reaching for that picture in particular. There were plenty of other photos of the family on the shelf, even one of Lucas, but he was adamant that he wanted this picture of Mark. Aside from it being a picture of Mark, there was nothing special about it.

Kenzi tilted the photo over a little, just enough for Lucas to see it from his height, still holding onto it tightly.

"Do you know who this is?" she asked curiously.

"That Mark! He my brother!" he said, excitedly.

Kenzi was taken aback. Hearing Lucas say Mark's name hit her right in the chest. More than she thought it would. Her Mum must have told Lucas about Mark when she put the pictures back up.

"He's my brother, too," said Kenzi with a slight smile on her face.

Lucas stopped reaching up, letting his arms fall down beside him as he looked up at Kenzi.

"He in heaven," he said in such an innocent manner.

Kenzi felt a little lump in her throat and the start of a little tear in the corner of her eye. She knew that she would never truly be over losing her brother, but wondered when she might be able to talk about him without feeling like she was going to cry. Especially like this. With Lucas. Who didn't know Mark. Who Kenzi had resented for so long for replacing him in their family. But still, hearing him talk about Mark, it was… nice. Even though their connection with Mark was different, Kenzi realised that they both felt his absence. She had never thought about what they shared before.

Kenzi thought about Jo. About how she felt the loss of Kenzi's grandmother differently from her. And how, through sharing stories of Mac, it seemed to help Jo manage her grief. And how it had helped Kenzi better understand her grief and herself. And how it had brought her and Jo closer together. Kenzi had really enjoyed that experience.

She looked down at Lucas. His light brown hair was scruffy from a full day of playing. A few light freckles on his cheeks. She was sure that she had seen pictures of Mark at that age, but she couldn't picture what he looked like. She remembered that her mother had said how much Lucas reminded her of Mark, so maybe Mark looked like this.

Lucas never got to meet Mark, which made Kenzi sad. Mark was so wonderful, and kind, and funny, and supportive. Lucas was really missing out.

But maybe he didn't have to.

Not really.

Kenzi picked up the picture of Mark and carried it over to the couch. She sat down and patted the space next to her. Lucas' eyes had followed her as she moved, and, understanding what her gesture meant, ran over and jumped up to sit next to his sister. Lucas sat right next to Kenzi, almost on her. Kenzi fought the urge to push him away and let him snuggle in against her arm. It actually felt kind of nice, being that close to someone.

Kenzi thought about all the wonderful memories she had of her older brother, searching for one she could share with Lucas.

"So, this one time, a looong time ago, before you were born, Mark and I were walking home from school," as Kenzii spoke, she looked at the photo of Mark in her hand, with chocolate and a big smile on his face, "and I bet him that I could beat him home, so we started racing."

Lucas giggled a little.

Kenzi continued, "No, Mark was a little sneaky, so he tried to take a shortcut through a few of our neighbours' yards. But it had been raining earlier, so the fences were a bit slippery, and he actually fell over one and landed in a big pile of mud!"

Lucas let out a big laugh, which made Kenzi start to laugh a little. Through her laughter, Kenzi tried to continue with her story, "And, when he got home, he was so dirty that Mum wouldn't let him in the house, so he had to take off his clothes in the back yard, and Mum washed him down with the hose!"

Lucas was laughing hysterically now, and she couldn't help but laugh hard herself.

The two say there, laughing together for a few moments.

Something dawned on Kenzi.

She had only ever thought of Lucas as her little brother. She had never thought of herself as his big sister. Mark had always been such a great older sibling to her, and it was the first time she really understood what that meant.

Not just the responsibility.

But also the joy that could come from that.

The connection.

Maybe it was time to explore that more.

"You know," Kenzi said as she looked down at Lucas, who was looking up at her, with a big smile on his face, "I could tell you some more stories about Mark, some other time, if, if you like?"

"Yeah!" Lucas replied, excitedly.

"Great," Kenzi replied.

Mark had been missing from their lives for so long, and not only would his pictures be up now, but his stories, they'd be around, too.

That was nice.

Kenzi sat there quietly with her brother a little while longer.

But then she remembered the Mac 'n' cheese on the stove. She jumped up, handed the picture of Mark to Lucas, and ran into the kitchen.

Kenzi grabbed the pot and moved it off the heated stove plate. She looked inside. All the sauce had completely dried up, and it was all just one hard pile of yellow tubes now.

Great.

Dinner was ruined.

But then Kenzi had an idea.

Lucas was still sitting on the couch, looking at the picture of Mark.

"Hey, Lucas?" Came Kenzi's voice from the kitchen.

"Yeah?" replied Lucas as he looked up to see his sister standing in the doorway between the living room and the dining room. She had a cheeky smile and was holding a carton of ice cream in one hand and a small bottle of chocolate topping in the other.

"What do you say to ice cream for dinner?"

"Yeah!"

"Great!"

Maybe having a little brother wasn't so bad.

Chapter 32
"I'm Always Here if You Need Me."

Kenzi was seated in Mrs Fox's office. As she looked around the room, everything was the same. The same posters on the wall. The same old and dented filing cabinets. Even Mrs Fox looked like she was wearing the same clothes. Her long cardigan hung a little unevenly on her shoulders, the elbows stretched from years of leaning on her desk. A thin silver chain glinted at her collar, almost hidden against the plain blouse. But somehow, it all felt different.

Brighter.

Like, there was more space in there.

The ticking of the small clock on the wall filled the silence between them. A faint hum from the fluorescent light above buzzed every so often, almost in rhythm with the clock, but softer, like a second heartbeat in the room. The air smelled faintly of lemon polish, the same as always, yet today it seemed fresher, less heavy.

Kenzi had just finished telling Mrs Fox about last night's dinner failure, and how much she and Lucas had had eating ice cream on the floor together. Kenzi and Mrs

Fox had both giggled a little and were sitting there, smiling at each other.

There was a brief moment of silence.

"Well, Kenzi, I think this will be our last session together," said Mrs Fox in a quiet and comforting voice.

"Yeah?" replied Kenzi, in an apprehensive tone. She was surprised by what she had heard. She knew that at some point, the meetings would finish, and that that would only occur when Mrs Fox was happy that Kenzi wouldn't hurt herself again.

Kenzi hadn't given it much thought lately.

After Kenzi got home from the hospital, the idea of trying to kill herself again was at the forefront of her mind. Her attempted suicide hadn't really changed anything, and all her feelings were still there. Even after they moved to Esperance, the sadness was still there, so it was always kind of in the back of her mind. But over the last month or so, she had been feeling better and better, and those thoughts had been slipping further and further back, until they weren't even there anymore. Kenzi hadn't realised it had happened until right now. It struck her how quiet her mind had become. For months, every thought had been crowded, loud, pulling her toward the same dark place. Now, it was like someone had finally opened a window in her head, letting in air and space. She hadn't noticed when it happened, but now, sitting here, she could finally breathe.

Mrs Fox scribbled something on a sheet of paper and folded the front of the file over it, sealing away a small pile of documents.

"Definitely," responded Mrs Fox. She slowly pushed her chair back and walked around her desk towards Kenzi.

"I can see how far you've come, Kenzi. The connections you're making, they're really important, and I can see how much they mean to you."

Mrs Fox was now standing in front of Kenzi, leaning back against her desk.

"Obviously, I'd love to see you making some connections with your peers…"

Kenzi shuffled in her chair a little, looking away from her guidance counsellor's gaze. The idea of making friends with the other kids in her school was still a bit much for her right now. Through the office window, Kenzi could hear the faint squeals and shouts of kids changing classes. The laughter and footsteps seemed far away, as though they belonged to a different world—one she wasn't quite ready to step into, but maybe, one she could imagine herself in again someday.

"…but, I'm confident that the support network you've built is all you need for now."

Kenzi let out a little sigh of relief.

"So, unless you feel like there are more things that you'd like to talk to me about?"

Kenzi thought for a second. When she first started coming to see Mrs Fox, she hated the idea of talking about her feelings and couldn't wait for her sessions to end. But over time, she had enjoyed telling Mrs Fox about her life. Her time at the bookstore with Jo. The stories about Mac. Even the progress she had made at home. Saying it all out loud somehow gave it a sense of validation, reassuring Kenzi that she was doing the right thing. It had been helpful, pushing her forward.

She was a little worried about how she would go without these check-ins. She had worked hard to get to this point, and she really didn't want to backslide at all. She thought about asking Mrs Fox to continue. But then she thought about Jo. And her Mum. And her Dad. And how she felt like she could talk to them now. If she was starting to feel sad again, she could talk to them about it, and she felt like that would help.

That would be enough.

A small, steady warmth spread in her chest. It wasn't excitement, not exactly, but a sense of trust—trust in herself, trust in the people she could turn to. She never thought she'd feel that again, not after everything. But here it was, fragile but real, and she didn't want to let it slip away.

"No. I think I'm good," said Kenzi, with a good level of confidence.

"I think so, too, Kenzi," said Mrs Fox as she stood up, and gestured towards the door, "and remember, I'm always here if you need me."

Kenzi nodded, but in her head she repeated the words like a promise. Always here. For the first time, she believed that someone might actually mean it.

"Yeah, I know," said Kenzi as she got up and walked towards the door. She opened it, and the sound of other kids in the hallway grew louder. Before she walked through the door, Kenzi turned back to look at Mrs Fox, who was still standing in front of her desk, watching Kenzi.

"Thank you," she said. A little tear formed in the corner of her eye. Not out of sadness, but happiness.

Mrs Fox just nodded.

Kenzi turned and paused in the doorway, resting her hand lightly against the frame. For a moment, she thought about all the times she had left this office before—angry, embarrassed, exhausted. This time was different. She was still scared, still unsure, but she wasn't running anymore. She was walking forward.

Ready for what was next.

Chapter 33
"You Really Make This Too Easy Sometimes."

Kenzi was walking towards the garage. She hadn't had a shift at the bookstore today. Although she had shared some afternoon tea with her mother and Lucas, it was still reasonably early in the evening, so she considered looking at the new alternator that her father had picked up for her. He had offered to help her put it in. Kenzi definitely needed help with it, but wasn't quite ready to give up on getting some other-worldly help with it first.

The sun was still high in the sky, casting plenty of light onto the garage. As Kenzi approached, she could see clearly through the window into the garage. There was no sign of Tom, but she continued.

She opened the door, and the familiar creak as she did was back. But it was still pretty stale in there. It wasn't cold, but Kenzi figured that was probably just because the sun was still out. She looked around the room, but it was the same as it was last night, except for the new alternator on the main workbench. Kenzi walked over to the bench, the door creaking again as it closed behind her.

The air was thick and musty, making it almost impossible for Kenzi to walk across the room. She stood in front of the bench and placed a hand on the new alternator. The steel was hard and cold. Kenzi stood there, looking down at the piece of machinery. She had gotten so close to fixing the old car, but now that Tom was gone, it felt like she had stalled.

"You know, I kinda wanna just stand here quietly, watching you try to put that thing by yourself."

Kenzi jumped, surprised by the voice coming from behind her.

She quickly turned around.

It was Tom!

He was standing in front of the car, leaning back on it, one hand resting on the front grill, the other slipped into the front pocket of his jeans. He was wearing his usual white shirt and blue denim jeans, but he looked cleaner today. His sleeves were rolled up neatly, showing forearms dusted with faint smudges of grease, as if the garage itself still clung to him. Even the rays from outside seemed to shimmer on him a little tighter.

The whole room seemed to brighten up a little, and the stale smell was replaced with the faint odour of grease and oil. It immediately made Kenzi feel better. Warmer. Happier.

"Tom! You're back!"

Kenzi started to run over to hug him, but soon realised how useless that would be, and stopped herself.

She also realised what his being here meant. He hadn't moved on. He was still stuck here. The truth about Kelly hadn't helped him at all.

"Er, I mean, what are you doing here? Aren't you ready to move on now? Did things not go well with Jo and Quinn?"

Tom stood up and walked over to Kenzi. He was smiling, which surprised her.

"Nah, that stuff's all good. Jo and Quinn are good. He's a good man. A good friend. He's taken good care of my girl, and I'm so thankful for that. They both told Kelly the truth. It was hard, but they worked through it. She's a strong one."

Tom walked past Kenzi to stand in front of the alternator on the workbench. Kenzi turned and followed him.

"I no longer feel like somethin's keeping me here. They're all gonna be ok."

Tom turned slightly to look at Kenzi. He had a calm look on his face.

"And that's all thanks to you, Mac. What you did for me. For my family. I can't thank you enough. You really helped."

Kenzi felt a warming feeling swelling inside her, and could tell she was starting to blush, so she turned away from Tom a little. She appreciated the sentiment, but she hadn't done any of it for praise. She had done it to help, and she was so happy that she had. She was so relieved that, although her actions had probably caused some pain for Jo, Quinn, and Kelly, it had all worked out and, hopefully, led to some healing. It had been that way for her family.

"I was happy to do it, Tom. You, and Jo, you've been really good to me; it was the least I could do."

Kenzi turned back to look at Tom.

"But, I don't understand. If everything went well, and you're, you're feeling better, why are you still here?"

A sad look crossed Tom's face.

"You really want me gone, dontcha?"

Kenzi's heart dropped. She really knew how to ruin a nice moment.

"What? No, it's-"

Tom turned away from Kenzi.

"I mean, I can go if you like."

Kenzi reached out to grab him out of instinct.

"No, Tom-"

Tom turned back around, a big smile on his face.

"C'mon, Mac. You really make this too easy sometimes."

Kenzi should know by now when Tom was messing with her, but she still fell for it. She turned away from him, hiding her embarrassment.

"Oh, whatever."

Tom reached out, touched the alternator, and pointed over his shoulder with his other hand.

"Seriously, though. I know that I can move on now, if I want to, but I'm not ready. Not yet. We had a deal. You help me with my problem, I help you with yours. My family's all good, so now we gotta get that car of yours up an' runnin'."

Kenzi was so relieved, but now she felt a little selfish.

"You sure? I mean, if you're ready to go, I don't want you to stay because you feel like you owe me, or anything like that?"

Tom was still smiling, but it wasn't his cheeky smile; it was a nice and calming smile.

"Of course, Mac. Whatever is waiting for me when I move on, that'll still be there when we're done here. I said I'd help you, and that's what I want to do."

Kenzi was feeling better about Tom being there now. But it was still a lot to process.

First, she had been sad that Tom had left, but then she was happy that he had found peace. But that had meant that she would have to figure out how to finish the car by herself. She had thought about asking her Dad for help, which he would have loved, but now Tom was here, which had made her sad again, cause that meant that he hadn't been able to move on. But now she knows he is just staying to help her finish the car.

It was a lot.

But it was good.

Things weren't always neat and straightforward, but they usually worked out.

Kenzi turned back to face Tom. The sun had started to set outside, and the light shining in through the window had begun to change colour, from bright white to a warmer yellow. The light was catching flakes of dust in the air, hovering around Tom's face, framing his smile.

"Ok. That would be great, thanks."

Tom nodded and reached across the bench to grab a few tools. He gestured towards the tool tray that they had used to remove the old alternator.

"All right then. Grab that tray and let's get started."

Kenzi started to move towards the try, stopped, and turned back to face Tom.

"Tom?"

Tom turned back to face Kenzi.

"Yeah?"

"Thank you."

"Back atcha, Mac."

Chapter 34
"You're Ready."

It was early morning on Saturday. Kenzi was standing in the driveway, looking at her car. The sun had only been up for an hour or so, and there were still droplets of dew over everything, shimming as the light reflected off them. It was still a little chilly, but the warmth of the sun was starting to overtake the chill from the night, and a few little goosebumps threatened to appear on Kenzi's unusually bare arms. She wasn't wearing her usual hoodie today. She was wearing a nice, fitted button-up shirt. Loosely tucked into denim shorts. The soft blue fabric set off the hazel in her eyes, and she'd buttoned it a little crooked, the way she always did when she was nervous but trying to look like she had it together. Her hair was neatly pulled back into a single ponytail. She wanted her first drive in her car to be special.

Kenzi and Tom had installed the new alternator a few nights ago, and Kenzi's car had started without any other issues. Working on it with Tom had been really nice. She had told him about her babysitting adventure with Lucas and how she was starting to appreciate having a little brother more. When Kenzi started the car for the first time, she couldn't help but feel the same way. Slow. Tight. Almost as if it wasn't going to happen. But then it got there and was ready to go. She had thought about taking it for a drive right away, but opted to just stay in the garage with Tom and talk. It was nice to share that time with someone she cared about.

But now it was time.

Kenzi had gotten up earlier than she would on a Saturday. She had eaten a quick breakfast and went out to the garage. Tom had been there waiting for her and assured her that the car would be fine for her first drive. She backed it out of the garage and parked it in the driveway. As Kenzi walked around the front of the car to close the garage door, Tom walked out and stood next to her, looking towards the road. Somehow, he looked even brighter today. Full of life, which was a strange thing for a ghost.

"Now, just watch the change from second to third. The gears in this old junker are a bit tight, but she's still got plenty of life left in her."

Kenzi closed the garage door and turned to face the car.

"Got it, thanks."

Kenzi started to walk towards the driver's side of the car, but noticed that Tom wasn't moving, so she stopped and turned back to look at him. He was standing with the tips of both his hands tucked into his jeans front pockets. The morning light was shining on him.

"Ah, aren't you coming?"

Tom looked at her, a softer smile on his face.

"Nah. You don't need me for this"

Kenzi was a little surprised. Although they hadn't specifically discussed it, she assumed that Tom would come along for her first drive.

"Oh, ok. I'll see you when I get back, though?"

Tom took a big breath, his shoulders shrugging and then releasing as he did.

"Mac, you don't need for anything now."

The words hung in the air.

Kenzi's chest dropped. Her knees felt like they would give way.

"B-but, I know the car's fixed now, and that was our deal, right. I help you, you help me fix the car. But, but, you don't have to g-go right now." Her words were hard to get out past the lump in her throat. Tears were forming in the corners of her eyes, and her heart was thumping in her chest, threatening to burst out. "I mean, wh-what happens if it breaks down, huh?"

Tom took his hands out of his pockets, letting them fall as he walked closer to Kenzi.

"The car's gonna be fine. And so are you. You're ready."

Even as Kenzi said, "I don't want you to go," she knew it wouldn't change anything. This was going to happen. It had to.

"You know I have to, Mac. It's time."

Tom's words were true, but that didn't make it any easier. Kenzi knew that Tom had to move on, and keeping him here, just because she wasn't ready to let him go, wasn't fair to him. He had been stuck here for too long. He deserved to move on. Kenzi knew that, but Tom had helped her so much. Not just with the car, with everything. She was doing much better now, but she was still worried that things could change again.

"But what am I going to do now... without you?"

It wasn't the first time Kenzi had been left behind, but that did not make it any easier. Not in the slightest.

Tom walked closer to Kenzi, close enough to touch her, if he could. At this distance, the height difference between the two was quite obvious, and Kenzi was looking at Tom's chest. Although the sun's rays were warm on Kenzi's skin, she could feel the warmth coming from Tom now, soothing her.

"You do the same thing I'm doing, the same thing as everyone else..."

Kenzi looked up, meeting Tom's gaze as he looked down at her.

"...you move on."

"Thank you, Tom."

"Thank you, Kenzi."

Tom winked at her and then slowly disappeared; his smile was the last thing to fade completely out of Kenzi's sight.

The warmth from Tom's presence faded, but it wasn't replaced with cold; Kenzi still felt sheltered from the morning chill.

Kenzi stood there, alone, taking in a few deep breaths, allowing the tears to slowly fall freely down the side of her face.

Tom had left.

But he would never be gone.

She was by herself.

But she would never be alone.

Kenzi closed her eyes and took another deep breath. She wiped the tears from her face and shook off her sadness.

She walked back to the driver's side of the car and placed her hand on the door handle, which was warm from the sun. She took a deep breath, preparing herself to go it alone, not just in the drive, but in everything. She pulled the car's handle, but stopped before it unlatched.

She had a better idea.

Chapter 35
"You're Good to Go, Kenz!"

The door to the kitchen flung open, quicker than Kenzi had hoped, and it banged into the wall with a loud crack.

Peter and Olivia were seated at the kitchen nook, both eating their breakfast while scrolling on their phones. They were both dressed in casual clothes, their usual attire for the weekend. They were both startled by Kenzi's entrance and looked up to see what the commotion was.

"Whoops, sorry," said Kenzi as she walked in and gently closed the door behind her.

"What's up, Kenz?" said her father as he placed down his phone.

Kenzi walked into the kitchen, a little more, heading closer to the doorway to the dining room.

"Um, do you think I could take Lucas with me, for the first drive in the truck?"

Kenzi's parents looked at her, a little surprised, and then at each other. Kenzi could see that her dad wanted to say something, but was taking his lead from her mother.

Kenzi knew that her request was a bit out of the blue. But her babysitting of Lucas had gone well, ruined dinner notwithstanding, so she thought that the idea of her taking Lucas out with her wouldn't be too much of a stretch.

Kenzi could see that her mother was about to say something, stopped, thought, and then spoke.

"I'm ok with it if your father is."

Before the words were completely out of Olivia's mouth, Peter jumped out and started to dash out the back door.

"Sounds good to me. I'll go get his booster seat from your car!"

Peter zipped past Kenzi, out the door, and disappeared out of view, Kenzi watching him as he went. Kenzi turned back to look at her mother, who was smiling broadly. Kenzi couldn't help but smile back.

They looked at each other for a few moments.

"He's growing on you," said Olivia, with a sly look on her face.

Kenzi crossed her arms, rolled her eyes, and scoffed, "Pfft, he's ok, I guess."

Olivia just kept smiling goofily at Kenzi.

Kenzi looked back at her mother, still smiling at her. After a few moments, Kenzi unfolded her arms, throwing them up and said, "What?"

Oliva, still smiling, said, "It's just nice, is all."

Just as quickly as Peter had disappeared, he returned, rushing through the back door.

"You're good to go, Kenz!" he said as he sat back down and continued drinking his coffee.

"Lucas!" yelled Kenzi towards the living room.

A few moments later, Lucas appeared. He was wearing denim overalls over a plain red shirt. His hair was scruffy, and he was barefoot.

"Yeah, Kenzi?"

Kenzi pulled the keys out of her pocket and gave them a little jiggle. "Wanna come for a drive in my car?"

Lucas jumped up and down, clearly excited. "Yeah!"

Kenzi laughed a little as she opened the back door. "All right then. Let's go!"

Lucas ran past her and headed out. Kenzi took one last look at her parents, who were both smiling at her. They looked happy. Content. Comfortable. Relaxed. It was really good for Kenzi to see them like that. She had worked hard to feel better. To be better. To do better. It felt good to know that it was making a difference for other people.

Kenzi started to head out the door and said, "We'll be back soon."

"Have fun!" replied Peter as he took a bite of his toast.

Kenzi walked through the door and started to close it behind her. Before it closed completely, she turned back to look at her parents.

"Love you," she said

"Love you more," they replied in unison.

Kenzi let the door close and walked down the side path towards the driveway. The warmth of the sun and her parents' love wrapped around her like a cozy blanket.

Lucas was already standing next to Kenzi's car, his little feet moving up and down in anticipation. Kenzi opened her door, and he jumped up and crawled over the bench seat to the passenger side. The old vinyl on the cushion squeaked as he crawled over it. Kenzi hoped in and pulled the heavy door shut. Lucas shuffled in his booster seat, trying to find a comfortable spot. Kenzi reached over him, grabbed the seat belt, pulled it across him, and snapped it into place. He wriggled a bit more, pulling the belt away from his neck and tried to sit up straight so he could see out the window.

Kenzi slipped the keys into the ignition and slowly turned them. The engine stuttered a little and then kicked into life. The whole car started to vibrate, more than her parents' new cars did, and Lucas laughed as he jostled in his seat. Kenzi put her hands on the steering wheel, warm from the morning sun. She looked at the leather band on her wrist. Worn and peeling in spots, but still very much loved. She thought about rubbing it, for good luck. Touching it often calmed her when she was feeling down.

But she wasn't feeling down, or sad, or scared. She was happy. Calm. Hopefull.

Kenzi looked over at Lucas, smiling as he looked out the window. He seemed so excited to be there with her. She looked back at the leather band and thought about how much she enjoyed doing fun things with her older brother.

"Hey, Lucas," she said.

"Yeah, Kenzi," he replied, turning to face her, still jostling in his seat.

Kenzi took a deep breath and carefully untied the leather band. As it slipped off her wrist, the much paler skin underneath was revealed, a stark contrast to the rest of her arm. She leaned over and slowly tied the band around Lucas' wrist. She had to double it over a few times to make it fit.

"This band used to be Mark's. Then it was mine. And now it's yours."

Lucas looked down at it, his mouth wide open in amazement.

"So, you gotta take good care of it, ok?

Lucas cautiously touched it, running his fingers over the creases.

"I will!"

Kenzi turned back and put her hands back on the steering wheel. She looked at the empty space where the band used to be. She thought she would feel its absence,

Mark's absence, but she didn't. She actually felt it more. Like sharing it with Lucas made it stronger.

Kenzi shuffled a little in her seat, getting comfortable and in the right spot for driving. She checked her mirrors and put the car in reverse. She turned back, resting her arm on the chair's top, and slowly backed out onto the road, the car bouncing as it moved from the driveway to the asphalt. She switched it into gear and started driving.

As Kenzi drove along the streets, she looked out at the buildings and people walking along the sidewalks. Kenzi wasn't sure if it was the morning sun, or the different vantage point in the car, or just how she felt, but the town looked different today. Brighter. Newer. More alive.

She looked over at Lucas, who was leaning against the side window, peering at everything that they passed. His hand was pressed against the window, the leather band sliding down towards his elbow.

Kenzi turned a corner and realised she was on Jo's street. She slowed down a little as she passed her house, trying to look in through the front window. She could see Jo and Quinn inside, sitting in the living room. As she drove past, she noticed Kelly walking into view, carrying what looked like a few coffee cups. They all looked happy. Like a family. Kenzi couldn't help but smile to herself.

As they turned another corner, the car started to shake pretty vigorously. Lucas laughed as it shook him around in his seat. The car sounded like it was going to sputter out, so Kenzi turned off to the side of the road.

"Oh, come on!" she said as she brought the car to a stop, and it turned off.

She turned the keys, and it tried to kick over, but just sputtered more and stopped again.

Kenzi let out a big sigh. Of course, this happened. Now!

She looked over at Lucas, who was a little sad that the ride had stopped. "Wait here a second, ok?"

"Ok, Kenzi."

Kenzi reached under the steering wheel, grabbed a small knob, and pulled it. The bonnet jumped a little, and she got out of the car. She walked around to the front of the car, sighing more, raised the bonnet and rested it on the steel rod. She put her hands on her hips and stared into the engine. Even though she had helped to replace the alternator and changed some fluids over, she still had no idea what she was looking at. Nothing was leaking or smoking, so it wasn't immediately obvious what was wrong.

Kenzi was about to reach into her back pocket for her phone when she heard a voice come from behind her.

"Having trouble with your car?"

The voice sent a buzz right through Kenzi. Her heart started to speed up, and a warmth began to swell inside her.

It sounded like Tom.

Was he back?

She quickly turned around to see.

A man was walking towards her. The rising sun was right behind him, and the light shining around his figure silhouetted him, making it hard for Kenzi to make out his details properly, but he definitely had the same figure as Tom. Kenzi raised her arm to block the sun so she could see the person better. As he got closer, his image became clearer.

It was Tom!

But it wasn't Tom.

He looked so similar. The same kind eyes. The same jet black hair. Even his smile looked the same. But he was dressed in modern clothes. A red and green flannel jacket covered a '90s band tee, both of which weren't tucked into his black jeans. His hair wasn't slicked back; it wasn't styled at all, and a little scruffy. He wasn't Tom, but he was a dead ringer. His jaw was dusted with the start of stubble, uneven like he hadn't cared much that morning, and a tiny scar curved just under his left eyebrow, a flaw that made him look even more like Tom in Kenzi's memory.

Kenzi hadn't realised how long she had been staring at him, but it was obviously starting to make him a little uncomfortable.

"You ok?" he said, cautiously.

Kenzi snapped back into alertness. She turned a little back towards the car, placing a hand on the front grill.

"Ah, yeah. Yeah, I am. Ah, something's wrong, but I have no idea."

The man walked closer to Kenzi. Not too close, though. He deliberately let enough space between them so as not to frighten or intimidate her.

"You ah, you want me to take a look? I know my way around engines a little?"

Kenzi's first instinct was to say no and pretend that she had already called her father and that he was already on his way. She knew enough to be wary of strangers. But she wasn't worried at all. Something about this man, who looked so much like her friend, set her at ease. Just like Tom did.

"Yeah? That would be great, thanks."

The man stepped a little closer, holding out his hand and gesturing for a handshake.

"My name's Bobby."

Kenzi reached forward and shook his hand.

"Kenzi," she replied.

As Kenzi shook his hand, it dawned on her. Bobby. He must be Kelly's son. He was back in town for Quinn's birthday. That's why he looked so much like Tom. He was his grandson. He might have moved on this morning, but it was nice to think that a little piece of him lived on, in Bobby. Just like a little piece of Mac was living on in her.

Kenzi was lost in thought again, and the handshake was going on much longer than it should.

"Ah, should I?" said Bobby, gesturing with his other hand to the car's engine.

Kenzi quickly let go of his hand. She stepped back and tried to brush her fringe behind her ear.

"Oh, ah, yeah. Please."

Bobby rolled up the sleeves on his jacket, cuffing them above his elbow. Kenzi noticed the slight protrusion of his biceps under his sleeve. He placed one hand on the front grill and leaned into the engine bay. As he did, his hair fell forward over his face a little. He peered around for a bit. He frowned as he leaned further in, shifting a few cords aside. For a moment, he looked like he wasn't sure, and Kenzi's chest tightened. Then his hand paused, and he exclaimed, "Ah, that'll be it." He reached in and jiggled a cord, pushing it hard into a plug.

"The ignition coil had come loose."

"Ah, I was just about to check that out before you got here," joked Kenzi.

Bobby stood up straight, dusting his hands off on his jeans.

"Heh, of course," he replied, in a joking tone.

He was standing closer to Kenzi now. Close enough for the height difference between the two of them to become apparent. She realised she was looking at his chest, so she quickly tilted her head up to his face, which had a little smile. Her heart was starting to race again, and her hands were shaking a little. There was a warmth swelling inside her, but this felt different to how Tom made her feel.

'Well, why don't you give it a try?" said Bobby, as he gestured towards the car with his head, his hair waving in front of his face as he did.

"Yeah, thanks," replied Kenzi as she walked around to her door. She opened and jumped inside. Lucas was sitting there, just looking out his window, oblivious to what had just happened. Kenzi placed her hand on her keys, took a breath in, and turned them. The engine sputtered a little, but then burst to life.

"Yay!" squealed Lucas, starting to jostle in his chair again.

The bonnet of the car came down, and Kenzi could see Bobby standing there, looking pretty chuffed with himself. The sun's rays clung to his outline, a warm glow encircling his frame. As he walked casually round to her side of the car, Kenzi wound the window down, it squeaking as it stuttered down. Bobby stood right next to the door, facing Kenzi, and placed his hands gently on the window frame.

"You should be good to go now."

"Thanks. I mean, I was just about to fix it myself, but I guess you helped."

Bobby rolled his eyes a little and pushed himself back off the car, "Well, it was a pleasure either way. Guess I'll see you 'round, Kenzi."

"Guess you will," she said back, trying hard to hide the smile on her face.

Bobby took another step back, giving Kenzi plenty of room to drive off. He waved his hand.

Kenzi looked over at Lucas, who was looking past her at Bobby.

"Who's that?" he said, quietly.

Kenzi leaned over towards him, "Just a friend she said, and put the car in gear and slowly drove off.

She looked into the rearview mirror. She could see Bobby, still standing on the road, watching her drive off.

As he faded out of sight, she was reminded of how Tom had faded from her sight earlier. Her eyes flicked to Lucas, Mark's band sliding down his arm.

One chapter had closed for Kenzi.

Maybe another was starting now.

Thank you for spending time with this story.

By the time you reach the end of a book, you've shared hours, emotions, and headspace with its characters, and that means more to an author than I can easily put into words. I hope this story stayed with you, challenged you, or helped you feel a little less alone.

If you enjoyed the book, one of the most powerful ways to support it is to leave a short review wherever you purchased it. Reviews help other readers discover the story and make a huge difference for authors, especially independent ones.

If you'd like to stay connected, hear about future books, or see behind-the-scenes updates, you can find me on social media:

Instagram: joshvanreyk
Facebook: itsjoshvanreyk

Thank you again for reading, and for being part of this story.

Josh